THE
LETTER
OF THE
LAW

Also by Tim Green

Fiction

Ruffians
Titans
Outlaws
The Red Zone
Double Reverse

Nonfiction

The Dark Side of the Game
A Man and His Mother: An Adopted Son's Search

TIM
GREEN

THE
LETTER
OF THE
LAW

WARNER BOOKS

An AOL Time Warner Company

WARNER BOOKS EDITION

Copyright © 2000 by Tim Green
All rights reserved. No part of this book may be reproduced in any form or by any electronic or mechanical means, including information storage and retrieval systems, without permission in writing from the publisher, except by a reviewer who may quote brief passages in a review.

Cover design and art by Tony Greco & Associates

Warner Books, Inc.
1271 Avenue of the Americas
New York, NY 10020

Visit our Web site at
www.twbookmark.com.

For information on Time Warner Trade Publishing's online publishing program, visit www.ipublish.com.

An AOL Time Warner Company

Printed in the United States of America

Originally published in hardcover by Warner Books
First Paperback Printing: November 2001

10 9 8 7 6 5 4 3 2 1

For Illyssa, my friend, my partner, and my love.

SPECIAL THANKS TO:

RICHARD AND JUDY GREEN

PETE PATNODE

MIKE KERWIN

GEORGE RAUS

TRAVIS LEWIN

DR. MARY JUMBELIC, ME

MARK BERRYHILL

THE
LETTER
OF THE
LAW

CHAPTER 1

While he knew the Internet opened a doorway to the world, Walt Tanner had no idea that it would also allow evil to slip in through the back... The raw night was typical of the Texas panhandle in late fall. Swirling leaves and grit chafed the curbside. Tanner, a tall, almost handsome salesman in a powder blue suit, sniffed at the smell of the coming weather and wiped a protective tear from his eye. His hotel, a Ramada Inn, was run-down and seedy, but there was a comforting familiarity in the lobby's musty smell. He'd been making calls on a plastics manufacturer in Stratford for the past seven years, and after a marketing dinner at Calvin's Steak House, this was where he always spent the night.

But tonight wasn't going to be the same as every other. The false promises of the plastics man still ringing in his ears didn't make his stomach churn the way they normally did. Tonight he had a date with destiny. For weeks, he had courted over the Internet, hurrying back to his hotel rooms throughout the Southwest to get on-line and link up. After a time, he was able to convince her to send him a picture, and what a picture it was. There were flaws, yes. At the age of fifty-three, Tanner no longer expected perfection. But she was fine, much younger than he was, and she had a nasty way of talking about sex that thrilled him beyond description.

And now, finally, tonight was the night. It had all been so simple, so beautifully simple. It started with posting a picture of himself along with a description that included his height, weight, education, and occupation on a singles bulletin board on the Web. His few friends had scorned his notion of finding love on the Internet. But he hadn't found it any other way, and now this . . .

His only reservation was with her mysterious idiosyncrasies. She wanted to meet him late at night in a rural location. She didn't want dinner or a movie, or even casual conversation. She wanted sex, raw and hard, or so she said. It stirred him. He had to admit that. But at the same time, something didn't seem quite right about it. It rang false, her insisting that he get a ground-floor room at the end of the building near the exit. He wouldn't have minded as much if his room at the Ramada didn't face a set of Dumpsters that needed emptying. It was as if she were embarrassed about something. But his latent libido had cast caution aside. What did it matter, really? In the worst case, she would turn out to be a man with hopes of committing an illegal act of fellatio, and he would send her, or him, on his pitiful way. But if the whole thing were for real? It would be the beginning of something special.

Tanner unlocked his room and settled in to wait. There was a six-pack of Coors mixed with some melted ice waiting in the sink. With a cold, wet can in hand, he propped himself up against the bedstead with some pillows, picked up the remote, and began channel surfing.

Normally he would get on-line, but he felt funny about that with her coming, like he was cheating on her or something.

In the end, it wouldn't have mattered. Tanner awoke to the snow of an empty channel and three empty Silver Bullets on the night table. He loosened his tie and slouched down into the bed. Before drifting off to an even deeper sleep, he thought fleetingly of the unlocked sliding glass door. The effort to get up and lock it, however, would leave him wide-awake, and he wanted nothing more than for the brutally disappointing night to be over, so he shut down his mind and turned on his side.

He still lay there that way, with his mouth open wide, faintly snoring, when the glass door slid open quietly at three-thirty in the morning. A tall, hooded figure in black peered around the edge of the curtain and looked from Tanner to the hissing television, then back to Tanner. With gloves on his hands and dark wool socks stretched over the outside of his shoes, the man silently crossed the room.

He stood beside Tanner's bed, looking him over carefully, making sure that he, too, hadn't lied about his physical description. He was about six feet five, sadly out of shape, but his frame was large and square-shouldered all the same. His hair, dyed a rusty brown, was drastically thin, but that wouldn't matter, either. From the waist of his pants, the man in black extracted an automatic pistol made unusually long by its silencer.

He could have killed Tanner without his ever knowing what happened, but that wouldn't be cruel. It was nothing personal against the salesman, but a greater need to show his lethal power, the way a gun trader would show off an exotic weapon. Moving close in order to look him in the eye, the killer jammed the pistol's barrel roughly to the roof of Tanner's mouth. Tanner's eyes shot open, alive with shock, but only for a moment. The heavy metal clank of the gun's action erupted, and feathers from the pillow shot up into the air like the small flurry inside a snow globe. A crimson stain quickly appeared on the white pillow beneath Tanner's head and spread rapidly to the sheets.

The killer unfolded an enormous nylon duffel bag from his pack and folded Tanner's long frame in the bedding so that he could roll it inside. Before zipping the bag, the killer took Tanner's laptop from his briefcase and tossed it in beside the body. With both hands, the dark figure dragged Tanner's lifeless form out through the sliding door and into the night.

CHAPTER 2

The spring rain was light and fresh. The air was warm. A sliver of sun had torn through the hem of the western clouds with the promise of better weather. Bright sprouts of grass had recovered from a chilly Texas winter and blanketed the lawns in a shimmering lime green. The trees lining either side of the busy street were exploding with new buds. But Bob Bolinger didn't notice any of that. The heat was getting to him. The air pumping out of his car vents was tepid at best. He needed Freon, among other things. He also needed a date. He knew that. It was almost five years since he had found his wife in bed with his ex–best friend.

Bolinger looked at his watch. Quitting time. He loosened his tie, slid down in the driver's seat, and relaxed for the first time that day. Like Houdini, he squirmed out of his old gray blazer while keeping one hand on the wheel, noticing for the first time a week-old mustard stain on the jacket's sleeve. Maybe he'd get in a quick nine holes before dark. Then he could shoot on over to the Romper Room, have a couple of scotch and sodas and a burger at the bar, and who knew? He might get lucky. What was the lottery slogan? You gotta be in it to win it.

Then the call came in. Bolinger cursed out loud but gladly took the call. The last thing the Romper Room needed was a mangy old cop on the prowl for some love. Anyway, this call was important. Apparently, a young woman, a law student, needed a body bag. He wondered fleetingly if his ex-wife would ever end up in a body bag. He cast that whimsical notion aside and ran a hand up over the top of his bristly gray crew cut, scratching the back of his leathery neck.

From the tone of the call, it sounded like a messy scene. Bolinger spun the wheel and turned back his unmarked cruiser against the grain of the traffic. He shot up Guadalupe and into the old homes near the university. The University of Texas was as big a part of Austin as the state capitol itself. So when a body turned up anywhere near the campus, all kinds of noses got out of joint. No one liked the idea of anyone dying young.

There were already six squad cars and an unmarked at the scene, as well as an ambulance with its lights still flashing. The patrolmen were well into the process of sealing off the area. Bolinger didn't have to show his badge as he dipped under the yellow tape. They knew who he was. The crime lab techs arrived at the same time, jumping out of their van and invading the scene like paratroopers. They spilled around Bolinger and he let them. He was in no hurry to get inside. He wanted to take in the scene. The house was an old two-story surrounded by towering oaks. The number of mailboxes told him the place had been split up into three apartments. A cracked driveway led to the detached garage in the back of the house. The girl's apartment was back there on the ground floor. Bolinger met his best friend on the force, a detective named Farnhorst, on the back steps. He was the first suit on the scene, and his honey-colored skin had a green cast.

"I heard it's ugly," Bolinger said.

Farnhorst looked down at his boss. Bolinger was only five feet six. Tears welled in the bigger man's sad-looking eyes, and this puzzled Bolinger.

"Goddamn, Sergeant." Farnhorst choked. "Goddamn."

"Anyone see anything?" Bolinger asked. His square-cut chin was protruding, and his dark brown eyes bore into his friend like deadly weevils. Bob Bolinger did his job without emotion.

"Nothing yet. No one home in either of the other places. The paperboy found her and called nine-one-one, out of his mind. I guess she'd leave the money on the kitchen table, and he'd just walk in to get it if she wasn't home." Farnhorst let Bolinger pass and said quietly, "Her name was Marcia Sales . . ."

Bolinger could smell the gore the second he walked through the door. When he saw the body, he took a deep breath.

"Holy shit," he uttered.

A tech snapped off a shot and stepped to the side. The girl lay on her back in the middle of the floor, naked. A thick band of duct tape encircled her head, covering her mouth. Her eyes were frozen wide with horror. Blood was everywhere. Bolinger moved closer.

"Watch it, Sergeant!" cried a scowling tech as he darted toward him. Bolinger sidestepped a bloody organ he couldn't identify and crouched down next to the body. There were bruise marks around her neck, and Bolinger found himself involuntarily hoping that was how she died. On the couch were what he presumed had been the girl's clothes. Oddly, they were folded. That told him she probably got naked on her own and that she knew whoever did this pretty well. Carefully, he poked through the clothes. There was no underwear or bra anywhere, and Bolinger wondered if there was a reason or if it had simply been the girl's style.

There was a scuffle in the entryway accompanied by Farnhorst's bark. Bolinger looked up to see a large man with long dark hair. He pushed his way into the living room. Bolinger stood up to face him. Before he could speak, the man, who wore faded jeans and cowboy boots, froze in his tracks and let out a maniacal howl that made Bolinger reflexively draw his gun. The man's face was contorted and he pulled at his own hair. When Farnhorst and his partner got hold of either arm, the man burst into a wild flurry of arms and legs. Farnhorst, who weighed in at about three hundred pounds, went flying like a lawn chair. The other cop, too, went sideways into a lamp, and they both crashed to the floor.

The maniac's howl turned to a bloodcurdling scream, and he shot toward the door. Bolinger was after him with Farnhorst and his partner in tow. The man bolted out the door and down the driveway, screaming all the while.

"Stop him!" Bolinger shouted.

Halfway down the drive two patrolmen brought the man down like a pair of linebackers. But even the shock of his head hitting the pavement did nothing to take the fight out of him. He bucked the patrolmen up into the air and spun himself around. As he rose, one of the cops took out his baton and struck the back of his neck. As he went down, the big man yanked a revolver out of the other patrolman's belt. Bolinger was two steps away on a full run when the man jammed the gun into his own mouth.

Instinctively, Bolinger dove for the pistol, jamming his fingers between the hammer and the chamber just as the man pulled the trigger. Bolinger cried out in pain but didn't let go. With his other hand he grabbed for the gun and wrestled for it, but the maniac had clamped down on the barrel with his teeth for all he was worth.

When Farnhorst hit the guy with Mace, Bolinger got a good shot of it, too. Blood was running freely down his hand now, but still he kept his fingers jammed beneath the gun's hammer. With his eyes shut tight against the burning Mace, Bolinger rolled with the punches until he realized that he'd been separated from the melee and he alone held the gun. He rolled over on the pavement and sat up coughing and crying from the Mace. His eyes cleared enough to see that even with a set of cuffs on his wrists and another shot of Mace, the man continued to struggle violently. Bolinger could only think he was whacked out on PCPs.

Before he knew it, the guy was up again and surrounded by four policemen, two wielding their batons. Blood streamed down the man's face from his nose, his eyes were swollen half shut, and still he screamed. Abruptly, he dropped to his knees, hung his head, and let out a dismal sob. Then he dropped to his side and cried almost as violently as he had fought.

"It was Lipton!" he bawled. "It was Lipton! She said she was afraid! She told me she was afraid of him! Lipton! Oh my God, Lipton!"

And then his words were so garbled that Bolinger couldn't understand him. Carefully, the cops loaded the man into the back of a cruiser and let him sit.

"Shit," Farnhorst said, helping Bolinger to his feet. "You all right?"

"Yeah," Bolinger said, stooping down to pick up a wallet off the ground. He leafed through it.

"Donald Sales," he said to Farnhorst, holding up the wallet and wiping the tears from his face on his sleeve. "Girl's father?"

Farnhorst shrugged. "Jesus, I guess. You think he was the one who killed her?"

"I have no idea," Bolinger said, his lips pressed tight. "Take him in and chain him up to the floor so he can't hurt himself. Let him sit for a while, and then I'll talk to him. He said something about someone named Lipton."

"Sergeant?"

Bolinger spun around. It was Alice Vreeland from the ME's office. She was a stubby redhead and the best they had.

"Rough day?" she asked.

Bolinger shook his head. "Didn't start out that way, but it looks like that's how it's ending up."

"Looks like the photos are finished," she said, eyeing the cameraman, who was loading his equipment back into his van.

"When the crime lab is done, you want me to remove the remains, or is there anything else you need to see?" she asked.

"No," Bolinger said. "I've seen enough."

At six feet five and two hundred sixty pounds, Sales was an imposing man. Cuffed and chained to the floor, with his face swollen and bloody and his pale eyes burning with hate, he looked downright scary.

"Cigarette?" Bolinger asked.

Sales nodded and Bolinger stuck one into the other man's mouth. Sales sucked greedily when it touched the proffered flame. Besides being big, Bolinger guessed that, cleaned up, Sales was a handsome man. His tan skin had a reddish cast that suggested Native American blood somewhere close by in the family tree. Bolinger already knew that Sales was a decorated veteran who'd served in Southeast Asia and that since his return he'd been self-employed as a carpenter who specialized in building docks around Lake Travis. Just after he'd arrived home from the war, Sales had been arrested in separate incidents on charges of disorderly conduct and assault. Both had been pled down to lesser charges. The red flag was that Sales had undergone treatment at the VA hospital for post-traumatic stress disorder. It wasn't an uncommon thing for veterans, but Bolinger knew it wasn't an uncommon thing for psychopathic killers, either.

Bolinger lit a Winston of his own and looked candidly at Sales through the smoke.

"You want to sit down?" the sergeant asked.

Sales jangled his chains and snorted disdainfully but sat down anyway on the cell's concrete floor. Bolinger sat on the bench against the wall. Beside him, he put down a tape recorder whose rectangular red light glared accusingly at Sales.

"What brought you to your daughter's apartment?" he asked quietly.

"Ha!" Sales barked. His face crumpled in pain, and tears began to stream freely down his face. He shook his head from side to side as if trying to make everything go away. "Ha! My daughter! Oh God! Oh my God!"

Bolinger waited. In ten minutes, the big man's crying subsided enough for him to take a deep breath and say,

"We were supposed to have dinner together. I was taking her to dinner . . .

"We did that," he explained sadly, looking directly into Bolinger's eyes. "I promised her that if she went to law school at UT I wouldn't be around all the time. I only live an hour up the road. But I told her I wouldn't always be checking up on her. When she was at San Angelo State, I used to drop in on her a lot . . ."

Here Sales looked at Bolinger to see if he understood. Bolinger didn't have kids, but his brother did, so he nodded with commiseration.

"Yeah, so I stopped doing it, but we'd still see each other pretty regular. We were going to dinner— Oh God!"

Sales started to shake and cry again. When he was quiet, Bolinger said, "Where were you before?"

"Home," Sales said dully. "I finished a job after lunch and took the rest of the day off to work around the house."

"Anyone with you?"

Sales shook his head.

"Anyone see you?"

"My house is out in the middle of nowhere," Sales said. "No one ever sees me."

"Would you sign a consent that allows us to search your house and your truck?" Bolinger asked.

Sales looked at him, mystified. "Why?"

Bolinger shrugged and held out a consent form with a pen.

"Ha!" Sales erupted. "Ha! You think I . . . Ha! I told you who did it! It was Lipton. Her professor, he was after her. I told her I'd talk to him, but she didn't want that. He gave her the creeps.

"Give me that," he said in disgust. "I'll sign anything. You can look anywhere you want for anything you want, but you better have someone go get this guy!"

Bolinger talked with the father for over an hour, pumping him for every bit of information from every angle he could think of. At the end of that time, he excused himself and reported to his lieutenant.

"I'm letting him go," he said.

The lieutenant raised an eyebrow. The father was all they had. They could book him and hold him on charges of assaulting an officer and resisting arrest. They didn't need to let him go anywhere. They could sit on him for another day if they wanted, unless he started barking for a lawyer. But Bolinger cut through all that. He was a man who'd built his reputation on instinct.

"He didn't do it," Bolinger said. "He's calmed down now, and if he blows his brains out, then he does. But I don't think he will. I think he just lost it. If I book him, then I'll have to deal with some lawyer, and I'd rather be able to talk to this guy straight. He may be able to help us, I don't know."

The lieutenant nodded and said, "You going to go home and get some rest?" It was after ten, and Bolinger had gone on duty that morning at seven.

"No."

"Didn't think so. What next?"

"The professor. According to Farnhorst, the girl's criminal law professor is a guy by the name of Eric Lipton, a well-known academic. Besides teaching at UT, he travels all around the country giving seminars on defendants' rights. He's the one the father thinks did it."

"Holy shit," the lieutenant moaned, "a law professor. That'll be fun. Anything prior on him?"

Bolinger shook his head. "Clean as a whistle."

The lieutenant paused for a moment before asking, "You ever look at the crap that builds up on the inside of someone's whistle?" He'd spent the first two years of his career in the traffic division.

"No," Bolinger said, "but I'll take your word for it."

Professor Eric Lipton lived in the fashionable neighborhood of Terrytown. It was where a lot of the old money lived, expensive real estate directly adjacent to the wide, placid stretch of the Colorado River running through the center of Austin. Lipton's place was a big white contemporary speckled with GlassBlock cubes that allowed light without compromising privacy. A wrought-iron fence surrounded the property. Although it was night, landscape lights illuminated the house and the lawn that sprawled under carefully manicured trees cut into geometric designs. It was a big-money place, and Bolinger could tell by the shape it was in that Lipton was the kind of person who squeezed his toothpaste out of the tube from the bottom up. White gravel crunched under Bolinger's tires as he pulled into a semicircular drive and underneath a tall, flat-roofed portico supported by a cluster of narrow white columns.

Lipton came to the door in a white satin sweat suit and expensive Polo leather slippers. His glare was hostile. He was a tall, angular man whose figure suggested that of a swimmer. He had none of the usual stoop for someone of his height and age. His hair was a wavy faded blond, flowing back from his face as if he'd just come out of the wind. His skin was tan, but its orange tint told Bolinger he was the kind of person who'd spent time under an ultraviolet light. His high, rugged cheekbones, perfect teeth, and the weathered skin around his bright blue eyes reminded Bolinger of the tennis pro who had tried to teach him how to serve on his last vacation in Fort Lauderdale.

"Can I help you?" the professor asked with a disinterested sniff.

Bolinger knew that was not what he meant. The last thing on earth he wanted to do was help. Something about the professor didn't smell right.

"Professor Lipton? I'm Sergeant Bolinger," the detective said. "One of your students has been killed, and I wanted to ask you some questions about her. Would you mind coming downtown with me?"

Lipton looked him up and down. A light, airy laugh spilled from his mouth.

"Do you know my area of expertise, Sergeant?" he asked snidely.

"Yes, sir. I do."

"Then you shouldn't have even asked if I would go with you. This is my world, Sergeant. My view of the police is a . . . an adversarial one . . .

"However," he continued as if he were lecturing a class, "I don't wish to imply that mine is a hostile or secretive nature. You can come in, Sergeant. You can ask me whatever you like. I'm a reasonable man . . . I'll give you five minutes."

Lipton looked down at his watch, marking the time, then said simply to Bolinger, "Anything more would be a waste of my time and yours. My knowledge of Ms. Sales is quite limited."

"How did you know it was Marcia Sales?" Bolinger said, his blood racing and his eyes narrowing at the sound of her name coming so unexpectedly from the professor's mouth.

Lipton's eyes flickered with panic, for a moment, nothing more. Then he said calmly, "Why, Sergeant, you told me."

"No," Bolinger said with a crooked smile. "No, I didn't."

"Get the hell out of here!" Lipton said, flaring up angrily. "Don't you come here to my home making insinuations! You forget that I know my rights! I'm not some street thug. I don't have anything to say to you! You want to talk? Call my lawyer!"

The door slammed in Bolinger's face, but still he smiled. He had his man.

A slip of the tongue wasn't much. Bolinger knew that getting a warrant based on that alone might not float. But it was enough for him to stake out the house. And he was confident that by the middle of the next day the crime lab would come up with something.

When they didn't, Bolinger felt his stomach sink.

"Cleanest crime scene I've ever seen," was what the crime lab's captain told him.

Bolinger had twenty men working under him on this one, and so far, no one had turned over anything concrete. He knew it was Lipton. But he needed something solid. A hunch never convicted anyone. That took hard evidence.

Ten minutes later, Farnhorst burst into his office with a mammoth grin.

"Got what you need, Bob!" he said, waving a paper triumphantly in the air. He slapped it down on Bolinger's desk and said, "Did a computer cross-check on the area and I came up with this!"

Bolinger followed the detective's thick finger to the spot on the page that chronicled a code ten-seventeen, a hit-and-run property damage. Apparently, the day before at two-thirty in the afternoon, a woman whose car was parked on the street opposite Marcia Sales's address had seen a maroon Lexus sedan back out of the driveway and into her car. The driver, whom she couldn't identify, sped off without stopping, but the woman had noted the license plate number as the car tore down the street. The car belonged to Lipton.

"Yes!" Bolinger said, slapping the paper. "Get me a warrant, Mo. I want the house and the car turned inside out, and I want him under a light before lunch."

Bolinger closed the door to his office, then opened the window before taking out a cigarette and lighting up. He rubbed his eyes and gulped down what was left of his coffee, taking time to crush a few grounds between his teeth. Sleep was something that would have to wait. This was how it was done, classic detective work. Most homicides were solved in the first forty-eight hours or they weren't solved at all. He'd known when he saw him that Lipton smelled, and now he had him.

Earlier in the morning, Alice Vreeland had confirmed for him that the girl hadn't died of asphyxiation but from having some of her insides cut out. She had bled to death. Alice told him he was looking for a pretty sharp knife.

"Sharp enough to shave," Vreeland had commented.

"By the way," she had continued, "I've got to go back to the house. I thought they had everything, but I can't find her gall bladder. No one picked one up, did they?"

Bolinger rubbed his eyes some more and wondered

again at her macabre comment. Unsure of whether or not
she was trying to be funny, he hadn't reacted. Now he
wondered if, instead of an oversight, there was some reason the gall bladder was missing. H'd never heard of anything like it, but he'd never seen a body like that, either,
half choked to death and split open like a butchered cow.
Bolinger shuddered at the thought. An image came
screaming into the forefront of his mind. It was the look
on Don Sales's face and the sound of his horror when he
walked into that room. How deep must that pain be?

Bolinger picked up the phone. He wanted to give the
father something, an offering of condolence. The only
way he knew to do that was to show how hard he was
working to pin down the killer. He wanted to call Sales
and tell him about the apparent hit-and-run. Then he
thought better of it. He'd wait until they had Lipton in the
bag. There was no reason to build the man's hopes on circumstantial evidence. Who knew? They might get lucky
and find the knife with the girl's blood all over it, although from the cleanliness of the crime scene, he
doubted it. Whoever killed the girl knew what they were
doing. A crime scene that clean was almost unheard of.

Bolinger worked up some paper. It was nearly two
hours before Farnhorst returned.

"We got him, Bob," he said triumphantly. "Guy was
getting ready to take a little trip. He'd booked a ticket to
Toronto and was already on his way north on Thirty-five
towards the airport when I caught up with the surveil-
lance team to bring him in. When we tried to pull him
over, he made a run for it. Wrecked his car, then hopped
out and ran into some woods. He didn't get very far. Had
a couple bags packed, his passport, and about twenty
thousand dollars in cash."

Bolinger stuck a pen in his mouth and started to chew on it. "Shit, good job."

"But this is what you're really gonna like," Farnhorst said, holding forth a plastic bag containing what looked like a woman's underwear.

Bolinger took the bag and looked at it quizzically.

"We found this stuffed into the bottom of his duffel bag . . ." Farnhorst said. "It's a woman's bra and panties . . .

"There's blood on them, Bob," he said quietly. "I wanted to show you before I send them to the lab . . . I think they might be hers."

CHAPTER 3

ONE YEAR LATER

And he wants me to represent him!" Casey said.

She spoke in a tone just this side of obnoxious but still loud enough for everyone else at the table to hear. It was an elegant political fund-raiser for the governor at a thousand dollars a plate. Women in gowns and diamonds, men in tuxedos and gold Swiss watches turned their heads. Casey tossed back her titian hair and laughed frivolously. Her own diamond necklace danced in the candlelight.

With her long, pretty fingers draped loosely over his shoulder, she said to her husband, "Tony wants me to go up to Minnesota and represent a rock star. A rock star! What next?"

Polite chuckles filled the air, but everyone's interest was piqued. It wouldn't surprise a single one of them if Casey Jordan represented a rock star. They only wanted to know which one.

Tony looked up sullenly from the remains of a bloody prime rib and said, "Pierce Culpepper."

General murmurs of acknowledgment filled the air.

"He lives in Minnesota?" someone asked.

"That's where he's from originally," another person answered.

Dessert arrived: strawberry shortcake made with fresh berries and cream. Casey watched jealously as Tony dug into his own and took hers aside for himself as well. Her days of having both dessert and a real waistline were over. At thirty-seven, her body still demanded a second look, but it came only at a price.

"He was arrested for assault," Tony dutifully explained through a mouthful of calories, "and he wants Casey to represent him."

"Did he do it?" someone from the other end of the table asked.

Tony shrugged. His thick eyebrows, like his hair, were graying. He was a portly man with thick jowls anchoring his basset hound face. Its greatest distinction was a small, neat goatee. But his voice was deep and soothing, and his many years in front of judge and jury had left the indelible marks of confidence and wisdom on his brow. And what he lacked in looks he made up for in flamboyant dress. His clothes weren't only expensive, they were colorful. Some people would even say loud.

"Innocent until proven guilty," he said. "We all know that."

"Maybe we should talk to him," Casey said as if she were casually considering the move.

Tony knew her game, not that he minded. He was an outsider in this setting, just as much as she was, probably more. She, at least, had married into the upper crust of Texas society, the Vanderhorns and the Watts, the Gardeners, the Rienholfs, and, of course, her own husband's family, the Jordans. They were rich, every one of them, and most of them had earned their money the old-fashioned way: They had inherited it. The ones who could took great delight in drawing a direct line to some distant fore-father who manufactured paint or firearms or had owned one particular county or another. A snobbish, worthless group in Tony Cronic's estimation, but he was almost used to them by now, and he knew how Casey loved to impress them.

He didn't fault her for it. He knew how deep she wanted to bury her modest beginnings, a small, dusty farm outside Odessa. The clear image of her family in at-tendance at her grand wedding came suddenly into his mind. They were a worn-out, sad-looking bunch, and their ill-fitting formal clothes were so far out of style that they might have been a troop of comics. But there hadn't been anything comical about them. They drank too much and grew louder as the evening wore on. Casey, everyone knew, had been mortified. A lesser woman would have been reduced to tears when her father stood on his chair in the midst of Texas society and flipped his middle fin-ger to the band when they were unable to play a rendition of "The Devil Went Down to Georgia."

But Casey came through it like she came through everything else, with her chin held high. She had run from her past in search of a glamorous life. All anyone had to do was look at her now to know she had made it. Still, there were times when Tony thought she was overeager to please a set of people who paled in compar-ison to her. He had subtly suggested on more than one oc-casion that she not demean herself by pandering to them, but she would only slap his arm playfully and say, "Oh, Tony," the way she did when she was refusing to talk about something. So he'd given up years ago. In fact, he'd given up on the day that she married into that "society."

He supposed that if she had to join the company of such an overrated bunch that at least she'd taken the best they had to offer. Her husband did something anyway, or at least he pretended to. Taylor Jordan never stopped talking about the deals he made all over the globe. But Tony looked at the man and had to wonder. Right now, he was covertly leering past the centerpiece at old-man Rienholf's twenty-eight-year-old blond bride.

Who knew if he was really doing deals in the first place? Tony wouldn't be surprised if he simply used his "deals" as an excuse to gallivant around the globe. And, if he was really at work and not play, how hard was it to do deals when you had a couple hundred million in your trust fund? Either way, Tony afforded Casey's husband only nominally more respect than he did the rest of the cast of characters.

Casey herself was a different story altogether. Tony had known she was special from the first day he saw her in the DA's office, more than ten years before. It wasn't her stunning beauty, either. If anything, her perfectly petite frame, her big brown eyes, and her delicate nose were detractions for a female lawyer. Arguing in front of a jury wasn't a beauty contest, Tony could attest to that.

But Casey had an innate fire that burned so fast and so hard that you knew the minute she opened her mouth that you were dealing with someone who was as formidable as she was smart. In Tony's experience, pretty women had a hard time being aggressive. He thought it was a biological thing, a protection against warding off the most desirable males. But Casey shot his theory to hell.

There was only one man he'd ever seen her want, and

that was the one she got. Jordan was the handsomest rich man in Austin, if not all of Texas. Outwardly, he was so nearly perfect that Tony had never really trusted him. He'd been with Casey the first time she met Jordan. She told him that very night that the polished socialite would be hers. It sounded as strange then as it did now, a woman openly staking her claim on a man.

But after ten years of knowing Casey, there wasn't much that surprised him anymore. The first surprise she'd given him he'd never forget. His chin had dropped when she said she'd join his practice. Over a lunch he had gone on and on about the nobility of defense work, about every man's right to a fair trial, the integrity of the system and how it broke down if the common man had no defense against the ominously powerful state. When he finished, she looked at him with those beautiful incandescent eyes and simply said yes.

"I'm at the DA's office for the experience," she explained, stabbing her fork into a braised scallop. "I have no intention of being a prosecutor for the rest of my life. Besides, I like your style."

That conversation hadn't taken place right away. It was only after a year of licking his wounds that Tony had been able to bring himself to talk to her. She was a twenty-six-year-old junior attorney only three years out of law school when she whipped him in her first rape case ever. That hurt him. But once he got over the shame, he had his epiphany. She could be the most notable trial lawyer since F. Lee Bailey. He could train her. She had all the raw materials and he knew all the tricks. He also knew how to sell.

And Casey knew, as he did, that she couldn't reach her goals from the prosecutor's side of the bar. Prosecutors were limited to the cases that came to them from the crimes committed in their jurisdictions. A defense lawyer could go out and get cases anywhere. A photogenic, savvy female lawyer could go from one big media case to another if she had the proper training and the proper handling. And Tony had known that Casey Woodgate—she was Woodgate at the time—could make them both very rich.

It wasn't that Tony Cronic was a slouch. He was a respected attorney who had at one time served for three years as the president of the Texas Trial Lawyers Association. He had been making a comfortable living, but it was nothing compared to what he was doing now. With Casey as his partner, he had been able to focus on acquiring the clients and handling the media. That let her focus exclusively on trying cases, and she was proving to be one of the very best.

Today, that perfect symbiotic relationship had opened yet another door. Tony had spent the past day and a half on the phone with Culpepper's brother, who was also his manager, trying to sell him on the notion of Casey as his attorney rather than the one his agent, Harvey Weissman, was recommending.

"I've got seats on a plane first thing in the morning," Tony told her.

"I have closing arguments Monday, you know," Casey replied.

Tony had completely forgotten. Suddenly he realized that her reserve hadn't been entirely feigned. She was working on the case of a young woman named Catalina Enos. The young Mexican-American woman had electrocuted her husband by tossing a boom box into his bathtub. As she sometimes did, Casey was representing the woman for free. Pro bono legal work was something every lawyer thought was a noble endeavor; few ever really did much of it.

But Casey was a ferocious defender of the rights of the accused. She believed, as Tony did, that in order for justice to be served, every person accused of a crime deserved competent legal representation. Although she didn't mind her rates being exorbitant for those who could afford them, Casey also insisted on offering her services to those in need as much as her cramped schedule allowed. It was an annoying reality that Tony had presumed would wear away after time, but it hadn't. Casey was still doing her pro bono work as devotedly, if not as frequently, as their paying work.

"We'll be back tomorrow night," Tony argued. "Look, you don't get a chance like this very often."

Tony knew that despite Casey's noble disposition, she, like most people, could be persuaded at least in part by the thought of a remarkably profitable undertaking. And if they were to represent Culpepper, it would be profitable not only in itself but in what it could lead to. While they had represented notable businessmen, politicians, and even a couple of professional baseball players, they had yet to represent a legitimate major entertainer. Since their ultimate goal was to be the legal team of the stars, they might one day look back on this case as the linchpin of their success.

Tony didn't even try to hold back his smile when Casey said with feigned indifference in a hushed tone, "I presume he's innocent."

"No one did it until they're proven guilty, Casey," he said glibly. "You know that. That's our motto."

"Yes, I know that's our motto," she whispered. "But I mean it, Tony. I don't want to do this if he did it."

Tony tugged at his goatee. The prospect of losing a deal this big was intolerable. He knew Casey would represent someone even if all the odds were against them. As long as she thought there was a chance a person was innocent, she would represent them with all her considerable means. He also knew that she was particularly sensitive when it came to sex crimes.

"I doubt he did it," Tony muttered. "He's denied it in the newspapers."

"I don't like these kinds of cases, Tony," she said, still in a low tone, regretful now that she'd opened their discussion in a public forum. "You know that. I heard about it on the radio. I don't want to represent him if he's as bad as he sounds. I really don't."

"Will you go up there with me and at least talk to him?" Tony whispered, conscious of the gaping onlookers and trying not to beg. "You know how these things can be. People like Culpepper are targets. This is what we've been waiting for . . ." His speech ended with a nervous laugh that he tried to make sound offhand.

Casey looked at her husband. He made a smooth transition from his prolonged assessment of the young Mrs. Rienholf to a noncommittal smile. He was proud of his wife. In truth, though he would never admit it even to himself, she was his greatest achievement. And, while they both knew she would do whatever she damn well pleased, he did appreciate the public show she made of consulting him on important decisions.

"You'll do the right thing," he told her. His standard line.

After a pause she said to the table, "I'm sorry, would you excuse us?"

Tony followed her outside into the warm darkness. The quiet night was a sharp contrast to the buzz of the immense dining room. They stood away from the door on the walkway, where they could be certain of being alone.

"I want to go," Casey said, glad to be free to speak in a normal tone, "but it can't be until after the trial."

Tony frowned. "We've got to go now, Casey. If we wait, he'll get another lawyer. Weissman, the agent, is trying to get him to go with Devon Black out of Chicago. But I've got the brother on our side, and he said if we get there this weekend, he knows he can get Pierce to go with us."

"But I've got a woman who could go to jail if I can't lock up the jury with my closing argument," Casey argued.

"Is it really that critical?" Tony asked doubtfully. He knew she'd spent much of her time the past month working on the case, but he didn't get very involved when there was no money at stake.

"Yes, it's that critical," Casey countered. "Van Rawlins is the judge . . ."

Tony winced. Rawlins was the former DA, one whose career as a prosecutor Casey had practically destroyed. After working in his organization for only a short time, she had electrified the city by joining Tony and immediately turning around and whipping her old boss in a major murder trial. The blow had cost him the next election, and Casey presumed she'd seen the last of him. But Rawlins, a political animal, had recently wormed his way from a struggling private practice into the Republican nomination for a vacated seat on the bench. If Rawlins was given a chance to foil Casey, he would.

"And," Casey continued, "the DA had all the good witnesses. My God, Tony, that house was like a prison. Catalina lived in that house with her husband's entire family. She was like a slave. She had no one, and they're all lined up against her.

"No," Casey added, "that girl is counting on me. I've got to be back."

"There are plenty of flights," Tony said. "We can leave in the morning and get back easily by early evening."

Casey considered her partner's face. More than anyone, he had helped her become exactly what she'd always wanted to be. She lived in a big, elegant home that other people cleaned. Her clothes came from a personal shopper who scoured the finest stores in Austin and Dallas, seeing to it she was always dressed in the latest fashion. Her jewelry, although she wore only a few pieces at a time, had to be kept in a vault. She drove the latest, biggest-model Mercedes. And, more important, people admired her. Wasn't she one of only a handful of women invited regularly to tea at the governor's mansion by his wife? Didn't she always have to choose from a broad selection of the women who wanted to play tennis with her at the club?

Yes, Casey was everywhere and everything she'd always wanted to be. And much of that had evolved from her partnership with Tony. Her husband was important, of course. But Casey didn't know if she would even have met Taylor if she hadn't joined forces with Tony. It was Tony who had cultivated her confidence in the big city. She had always been able to shine in her tiny hometown outside Odessa. She was everything back there, the class president, the valedictorian, the homecoming queen. And why shouldn't she have been? It was a squalid little farm town in the middle of nowhere. But Austin was a big city, and Casey needed a mentor like Tony to help give her the confidence that she could still shine at a much higher level.

She smiled fondly at her partner and said, "I'll go."

Then, turning toward the door, she remembered her husband's words and added, "I think it's the right thing."

CHAPTER 4

"My God, it's freezing," Casey said. She wondered aloud how anyone could choose to live in the north. Not only was it cold, but the roiling gray clouds spit fitful bits of ice and snow and rain at them. Despite the proximity to noon, the horizon was inky and flat.

Tony stamped his feet on the dirty concrete and huffed into his hands. The raincoat he wore was like nothing in the cold wind whipping down from Canada. Although it was nearly April, a sudden cold snap had left the ground outside the airport frozen and lightly frosted with snow. The driver who met them at the gate had gone around for the car. Tony and Casey had made the mistake of walking out to the curb to wait for him.

"Let's go inside," he said with a shiver.

"Here he comes," she said. She, too, was dressed for warmer weather in a light coat that covered a classic blue pinstripe business suit and heels. Her shapely legs, bare from the knee down except for dark stockings, were chilled to the bone.

Casey had spent the entire plane ride, as well as the

time during their layover in Chicago, going over her closing-argument notes for her trial the next morning. But their car ride to Pierce Culpepper's side of town was spent going over the facts of the rock star's case, as Tony knew them. Casey nodded silently and let him finish before asking, "What's his legal history?" She already knew the star's background: a suburban kid from St. Paul and one of the few white rap artists to not only thrive, but take his unique sound to the top of the charts worldwide.

Tony shrugged. "The paper talked about a couple of incidents when he was back in college, but nothing that he did any jail time for."

"That's comforting," she said flatly.

Tony rubbed some of the moisture off the window with his palm as they drove through an imposing set of iron gates. Culpepper's home was a three-story fieldstone mansion. The architect had given it myriad gables and turrets that hinted at the notion of a castle. It looked like a home the governor would live in. Years ago, such a place would have intimidated Casey.

She could still remember the home of the president of the Bank of Texas in Odessa. As a little girl of eight, she'd gone there with her father in his pickup truck to buy an old piece of machinery from the man who took care of the bank president's cars. They had entered the estate through a dusty service gate in the back. When her father went into the enormous garage to conduct business, Casey had wandered up the tree-lined path toward the main house.

It rose from the ground amid an old stand of oaks like a brick fortress. Its shutters and columns were brilliantly white, and on the lush green back lawn, the family, dressed as if they were going to church even though it was Saturday, was playing croquet. From behind a tree, Casey had peered at the children. They were close to her age, and happiness to Casey from that moment on was defined by the image of those well-dressed children pocking away with wooden mallets at the colored balls in the shade-mottled grass.

Then her reverie had been destroyed. The greasy hand of a scrofulous boy in ratty jeans and a grimy Astros hat spun her rudely around.

"They don't want no white trash around them," the boy sneered.

"I'm not white trash, you!" Casey piped back at him defiantly, kicking him in the shin.

The boy howled and grabbed her in a headlock, wrestling her to the ground. Before she knew it, the banker himself was upon them, and Casey quivered at the sight of his big, red face and the strong, musty smell of his expensive shaving lotion. He pulled the two of them apart with an expression of disdain and ordered, "You get back to your daddies and don't let me see you around this house again!"

As the limousine rolled through the front gates, Casey fingered her Cartier watch and wondered how it was that the shame of such a small moment could last so long.

"Nice place," she said, feigning complacency.

The rock star made them wait in his study for nearly an hour before he wandered in wearing a baggy pair of pants and a scruffy T-shirt. In less than a minute, Casey sensed that what Tony thought was a done deal was far from done. It wasn't even close. In fact, after a couple of probing questions, she was nearly certain that Culpepper had decided to go with a different attorney.

"Can I ask you a simple question?" she said.

The rock star shrugged. "Sure."

"Why are we here?"

"I don't know," Culpepper said, looking to his brother, a younger, scrawnier version of himself who sat in a big chair in the corner with his feet dangling over the arm.

"I told Tony," the brother said defensively, "nothing was guaranteed. I just said that if you wanted to represent Pierce that you'd better come up here and see him in person."

"My brother likes to jerk people around," Culpepper said in disgust and walked out of the room, absolving himself of the entire situation.

"Hey," the brother said somewhat belligerently after staring blankly for a few moments at the door. "I told you, Tony, Pierce has the final say . . ."

Casey was going to rip into the brother, then she decided to rip into Tony before giving it up completely. It would be a waste of effort. Tony did things like this from time to time, and she didn't want to hear his rationalization about how hard it was to sell their services. It made her feel cheap because deep down she knew it was true. Not that she was a hard act to sell, but beyond Austin, Texas, there was a whole battalion of good trial lawyers trying to represent the big-name stars. She was one of the many, and that was something she would have to live with until the day she became the biggest name in the legal profession. That was her goal, and she believed that one day it would happen. In the meantime, she had to get home. With a look of complete irritation, she made for the door.

Tony wanted to defend himself, and he trailed Casey down the hall and through the house, patiently calling her name. Outside, everything was glazed in ice. Even in the gloom of the storm, the trees shone like glass. The thin layer of freshly fallen snow was also sheathed in ice. On the front steps, Casey slipped but saved herself a broken leg with a desperate grasp at the railing. Tony carefully helped her regain her balance, and they both shuffled tentatively to the car.

"I'm sorry," he said. "I had no idea, really."

"I know you didn't, Tony," she muttered. "Let's just get out of here."

As soon as they were in the backseat, their driver began to fret out loud about the ice.

"It's not good at all," he said, driving with pitiful slowness.

Casey implored him to hurry. "I can't miss this flight."

"I doubt there's going to be a flight," the driver said with an uncomfortable glance in the rearview mirror. "It's real bad, ma'am, and getting worse."

The driver was right. By the time they got to the airport, the flights that weren't being delayed by several hours were being canceled outright. Rain and ice continued to fall from above. Casey plaintively watched the ever-darkening sky from a seat by the window at their gate. At the rate things were going, she wouldn't be home until well after midnight, and she wanted to be fresh for the trial. By seven, a good night's sleep was the last thing on her mind. The airport had closed down completely.

"Come on!" Casey barked after hearing the news. She grabbed Tony by the sleeve and jerked him toward the main terminal. "We can drive."

"Casey," Tony complained as he jogged along beside her, "you can't drive in this. Even if you could, we couldn't make it back if we drove all night."

"I've got to do something," she said in distress.

The rental counters were abandoned anyway.

Casey approached a young skycap who was sitting on a bench with his face in his hands. "Is there any way I can get a car?" she asked him.

The skycap shook his head sadly and said, "Nobody's getting out of here now. Everyone who had the chance got out about two hours ago. I got caught up helping a guy with his stuff. He promised me he'd drop me off in town, but by the time we got his bags in the car, we couldn't even get out of the lot. Everyone here now is here for the night . . ."

"Catalina," Casey whispered to herself at the finality of the news. "I've got to get to a phone," she said to Tony, frantically searching the terminal with her eyes. "I've got to tell Patti. She'll have to do the closing argument . . ."

Patti Dunleavy was Casey's understudy, a capable, vivacious attorney. The problem was that while Patti was the only other lawyer intimately familiar with the nuances of the Enos trial, she was only recently out of school and had never tried a real case before.

"The judge will delay the closing arguments," Tony said, forgetting for a moment the bad blood between Casey and Rawlins.

"He can and he should," Casey replied, grinding her teeth. "It would be wrong to proceed. It would be unethical. But we're talking about Van Rawlins. He hates me, Tony . . . That girl could go to jail. Of course he should delay the closing arguments. But he won't. God-damn him to hell, he won't!"

CHAPTER 5

Donald Sales held his wife's hand mirror as far away from himself as he could and critically assessed his mangy blond wig, thick plastic glasses, and the makeup he had applied to lighten his complexion. He was wearing a dark suit. It seemed that until recently, the only time he ever wore a suit was for a funeral. No one would recognize him now. He smiled grimly at himself and returned the silver mirror to the top of the bureau. This would be a funeral of sorts.

In the top drawer he fished among his socks for a clip, popped it into his Browning 9mm, and slapped a shell into the chamber. On the neatly made bed was a fake leather briefcase he'd purchased at Wal-Mart. Using a handkerchief, he wiped the pistol as well as a can of Mace free of fingerprints before placing them both in the case.

In the tiny room, an iron bed sat on a plank floor, bare except for a small handwoven Navajo rug. Once a brilliant red, it was now faded nearly pink. On the walls were stark black-and-white landscape photographs in barnboard frames. A fragile antique chair sat wedged into the corner, its seat covered with a delicate lace doily. Sales took pride in the fact that, except for the color of the rug, the room hadn't changed in twenty years. When his wife died, he had made a pact with her spirit that their bedroom would remain sacrosanct, that it would always be their place, and so he had never shared it with another woman.

A hall ran through the middle of the cabin, and Sales stopped at the door to his daughter's bedroom. With his hand on the knob, he hesitated, then kept going, past the kitchen and on into the great room. The walls rose all the way to the pitched roof. They were crowded with trophy fish and the heads of wild animals. A walnut gun cabinet stood against the wall. Over the stone fireplace was a Comanche war ax.

The weapon had been given to him by his mother. It had belonged to the men in her family as far back as anyone could remember. She'd given it to him the day he enlisted for the war in Southeast Asia. Before that war, the Sales family had had great hopes for him. He would be the first to go to college. He would become a doctor or a lawyer; no one knew which, they just knew it would be one or the other. But then the army came to the high school and whipped up the young men about the need for patriotism, for saving their country. They would be drafted anyway, one officer forewarned. No one in Sales's family knew of or even talked about exemptions.

So Sales went and did what he was told. When he returned, he realized that it had all been a lie, why they were there and what they were doing. He decided that he would live his own life, his own way, by his own rules. He didn't need to become anything just to please someone else. Those same people, parents, teachers, and coaches, had cheered for him as he boarded the bus that took so many young men away from the sanity of life in rural Texas to the hell of a jungle in a faraway land.

So he got a job as a carpenter and learned a trade. He fell in love with a young girl out of high school, a waitress with dreams of becoming a country western singer. Together they would go to the local dance hall on Friday and Saturday nights. She would sing with a band of old-timers and he would watch, drinking cold bottles of beer until the sound of her voice blended with the night in a perfect harmony of sight and sound.

Everyone told her she could do much better than Sales, a half-breed veteran with a stale and tattered dream of going to college. But she loved him as much as he loved her, and he worked as hard as any man to make them a home. By day, he was a dependable contractor. At night, under the lights of his pickup truck, with his young wife-to-be singing sweetly away with the radio, he toiled at erecting this cabin, raising it from the dust so that they would have a place they could call their own. An uncle who owned a corner store at a crossroads to the north had signed on the note to buy the land, an old, unwanted mining tract. Sales had never missed a payment. Theirs was a happy story, two handsome young people working hard, side by side, to build a simple life together.

He walked out onto the porch and into the shade of the midday sun. His pale green eyes glowed luminescent beneath the thick lenses of his glasses. The terrain around the cabin was rocky and rough except for a gurgling creek to the north. At one point, a stone dam from before the turn of the twentieth century checked the water, giving life to a small stand of pecan trees before it continued on its way to the Pedernales River. To the south rose a forbidding cluster of hills studded with juniper and mesquite. Sales stooped to shift his wet bathing suit from the shade into the sun where it would dry faster, then left the comfort of the porch and climbed into his dusty Ford pickup.

To keep his clothes clean and his wig straight, he rode with the windows up and the AC on. From the tape deck, George Jones bawled on about his broken heart. A bitter smile crept across Sales's face. No one could know how badly life had damaged him. Broken wasn't the word.

He craned his neck to look at his face in the rearview mirror. Even without the disguise, his appearance had changed dramatically over the last thirty-odd years. There was nothing more than a fleeting shadow left from the hopeful days of his youth. But what could he expect? Anyone who had done the things he'd done and seen the things he'd seen would be the same, maybe worse. At least he had the ability in his quiet moments to occasionally slide back into the past, to hear his wife's sweet voice singing in the soft light of the dance hall and just float away, safe from reality.

Some people called it daydreaming, and that's what he did until he was off the highway and jerking to a stop at a red light in the midst of the hectic concrete maze of downtown Austin. At the corner of Eighth and San Jacinto he pulled into a parking garage and got out. He was only a few blocks from the public safety building. He soon came to a corner where the light signal read DON'T WALK, but after checking the traffic he crossed the street anyway, walking confidently with his head held high. He had the same demeanor when he strode into the court-yard, which was busy with police cruisers. Near an ob-

scure door in the side of the concrete building, several
people stood in a silent cluster smoking cigarettes in a
slice of shade. Sales took up his usual station and casually puffed a Winston down to its filter.

He wondered if anyone would remember him. He'd
been here once a week for the past two months, blending
in like a lawyer who had business to do. Around the public safety building and the courthouse, a suit and an air of
confidence were as good as being invisible. Sales had
used the time to reconnoiter the layout of the building and
the tunnel that connected it to the courthouse and also to
check the scheduled court appearances. They were posted
one week in advance in the main hallway of the courthouse.

Passing through the front doors of either building re-
quired a trip through a metal detector. But if you knew
where you were going, the ease of circumventing the security was laughable.

By the time he'd stamped out his second Winston, the
turnover of smokers left him with a new set of faces.
Without speaking, Sales entered the building through the
door that had been jammed open by his fellow smokers.
After a quick check to make sure the stairwell was deserted, he descended the stairs into the basement. A couple of turns and a couple of doors later, he was in the
tunnel that was used to move prisoners from the lockup
to the courthouse. Halfway down the hall was another
stairwell whose door had a small window. With a glance
either way to ensure the tunnel was empty, Sales took a
handkerchief out of his pocket. He quickly covered the
door handle to prevent leaving fingerprints and let himself in.

Quietly, he shut the door and listened to the sound of

his own heavy breathing. After pulling on a pair of surgical gloves, he used his handkerchief to wipe the briefcase clean and place it on the floor. With the hint of a tremble in his hands, he took out another cigarette. There were burn marks on the floor, a sign of other desperate smokers that told Sales he could light up with impunity. The stink of latex filled his nose as he smoked. He checked his watch. Court appearances were at three. It was two-forty. They'd be coming any minute.

His hand was now trembling enough to shake the ashes free from the butt, and he cursed under his breath. He'd spent the entire morning wanting a drink. But determined to be sharp, he'd abstained. Maybe he was too sharp. He took one last big drag, made a burn mark of his own, and leaned back against the wall under the stairs where he could get the best view of the coming prisoners.

When the first guard's head appeared in the glass, Sales's heart leapt in his chest. He bent down and removed the pistol and the can of Mace from the briefcase. By the time he was upright again, Lipton's face was bobbing past the small window. Another prisoner passed immediately behind him. Then, after a slight pause, the second guard went by without a sideways glance.

Sales took a deep breath and plunged through the door. As the second guard turned his head, Sales hit him with the Mace and pushed him to the floor. When the rear prisoner saw the Browning, he yelled and tried to push his way past Lipton. He tripped on his own chains and they both went down. Sales leveled the gun at Lipton and fired three deliberate shots into his body before a slug from the first guard's .45 droned past his ear. Lipton was screaming in agony, and his orange prison clothes were splattered with bright red blood. Sales was certain that he'd scored a kill.

He was then acutely aware that the guard's gun was aimed directly at his head. The gun went off. Sales ducked and spun at the same instant, falling toward the floor. He caught himself and, with the Browning still in hand, took off down the tunnel. Three more shots ricocheted past before the guard stopped shooting to check on his fallen partner. Sales ran free down the long tunnel. Past the bowels of the safety building, he veered off into another tunnel that took him all the way to the municipal records building two blocks away.

After racing up the stairs and out onto the street through a side stairwell door, Sales pulled up into a brisk walk. He never looked back. The gun was now tucked snugly into his pants and covered by his jacket. His ungloved hands were steady and he was strangely calm. He'd done what he had to do. The pickup truck was parked on the garage's second deck. Once inside the vehicle, he pulled off his wig and fluffed out his long dark hair. A handful of baby wipes took the pale makeup from his face and neck, and he switched the thick old plastic glasses for a sleek pair of wraparound prescription sunglasses. As he tore off the suit coat, shirt, and tie, he assessed his face in the mirror and smiled grimly. Wearing a fresh white T-shirt, he rolled down the window and pulled slowly out of the garage.

Sales didn't waste any time getting back to Lake Travis. Not far from the marina, he pulled off onto a dirt road that led to an uninhabited summer camp. With his truck nestled into some trees behind the garage, Sales stripped down to his swimsuit and scanned the shoreline. No one was in sight. Slung over his bare shoulder was a tightly packed nylon net bag containing the gun, his disguise, and a ten-pound hunk of steel. In his other hand was a diving mask. He put the mask on and quickly jumped off the end of the dock.

His tank and gear were on the lake bottom next to the dock's deepest pier, right where he'd left them. With the regulator in his mouth, he could afford to take his time and fix the tank comfortably on his back. Using the compass on his watch for direction, he began his long swim toward the middle. After going for what he estimated to be half a mile, he cautiously poked his head out of the water to reconnoiter. He was only two hundred yards from his boat, a stripped-down twenty-one-foot Larson with a distinctive custom aqua green canopy. Confident that he was in over fifty feet of water, he let the nylon bag slip from his hand into the impenetrable depths.

Once alongside the boat, Sales shifted out of his diving gear and, stepping on the outdrive, hoisted himself up over the stern. Breathing hard, he peeked up over the gunwale and turned in every direction to see if anyone was near. It was a quiet day on the lake and, as far as he could see, only a few distant fishermen and a single pontoon boat shared the water's surface. He immediately began bringing in his lines. One had a good-size striper on it, and that was all the better. With everything in order, he fired up the big V-8 engine and headed for shore. Just to make sure he was seen, he stopped for gas before replacing his boat in its slip.

"Get anything?" drawled the crusty old gaffer who worked the pump.

"Striper," Sales said in his typically taciturn way.

The old man nodded and peered into the boat. He was

surprised when Sales took the time to lift the fish out of the cooler in a neighborly way for him to see.

"Nice 'un," he said.

Sales nodded, but his attention was on the driveway that came down from the main road. When the tank was full, he couldn't keep himself from asking, "You see me out there all day?"

The old man gave him a funny look and said, "Yup." After an uncomfortable pause he continued, "Fact is, me 'n' Kent seen you out there and were talking on it. Not like you to stay in one spot so long . . ."

Sales gave the old man an uncharacteristic smile and, before pushing off, said, "Fell asleep. You believe that? Must be getting old."

Sales wasn't home more than an hour before he heard a car pull in. From his place in the kitchen he looked across the tiny bar and out through the front window to see Bob Bolinger mounting the steps. Bolinger stopped at the top. There were two bathing suits hanging on the rail, one wet and one dry. Tentatively, he picked the damp one off the rail. When he glanced up, he saw Sales staring at him through the window. He replaced the suit with an awkward smile before knocking on the door.

"It's open," Sales bellowed, returning to his fish on the stove as if he'd been expecting a friend.

The pungent scent of onions in a hot skillet flooded Bolinger's mouth with saliva. It was nearly dinnertime. He'd been in the squad room bullshitting with one of his men about an arson when word came in about Lipton's being shot. Since it was just downstairs, everyone and his brother had responded. Because he was so familiar with Lipton's case, Bolinger had been given the lead. And although the witnesses' descriptions of the shooter didn't match Sales, his gut told him that was the place to start. If Sales didn't pull the trigger, he probably knew who did.

Bolinger assessed the great room, its bare timbers, its stuffed animal heads, the weapons in the case and on the wall. Despite all that, it was a comfortable place, with aging leather furniture and Indian rugs that were worn without being shabby. Knowing how much money people were putting into their lake houses these days, it didn't surprise Bolinger that Sales was making a decent living.

"Keep coming, Sergeant," Sales's voice echoed from the kitchen.

Bolinger paused in front of the gun case against the wall before rounding the bar and taking a seat at the small circular table wedged into the corner of the kitchen. Without speaking, Sales left his fish long enough to take two Coronas from the icebox. He set one in front of the detective, took a swig of his own with a knowing look, and returned to the stove. Bolinger just watched. Sales didn't appear rattled in any way. Was it possible that someone could attempt such a daring assault without being shaken up? Possible, but rare.

"How're you doing?" Bolinger asked. He was quite aware of the pain Sales had endured over the last year since his daughter's death. Working on the case against Lipton had brought the two men together on several occasions.

"You know, I'm getting along," Sales said without looking up from the stove. "I keep busy with work. I'm in a little lull right now, but it's been busy enough not to have too much time to think."

"Sometimes I wish I'd done something with my hands," Bolinger said. "Seems like it would be a hell of a deal to fall asleep at night because you're tired out from working with your hands . . . When I fall asleep, if I fall asleep, it's usually because my mind is burnt right down to the filter."

Without asking if Bolinger was staying for dinner, Sales took out two mismatched plates and split the fish. He slid a loaf of Italian bread out of a paper bag and cut off two thick slices before setting the plates down on the table. Without bothering to protest, Bolinger muttered a quiet thanks. After returning to the stove for his beer and some forks, Sales sat down across from the detective and asked, "What's up, Bob?"

After a pause in which he assessed Sales's eyes, Bolinger said, "Lipton was shot today."

Fierce hatred and delight burned brightly in Sales's pale eyes.

"Good," he said.

"He's not dead," Bolinger told him.

A look of consternation slowly bent the father's mouth into a sneer. After a while he said, "That's too bad . . . Who did it?"

"I thought you might tell me," Bolinger shot right back.

Sales took a long pull on his beer before shaking his head and saying, "No, I didn't do it and I don't know who did.

"I wish I'd done it," he added, staring intently at Bolinger. "I wish I'd thought of it. It should have been me. And I wish whoever did it killed him."

Sales took up his fork and began to eat.

"It was pretty bloody," Bolinger said, following his host's lead. "He looked dead, took three slugs from a big gun at close range, blood all over the place. One in the shoulder, one through the chest just above the lungs, and one grazed off his rib cage without even breaking the bone. He'll be out in three or four days . . ."

Sales chewed carefully, but Bolinger could tell that he'd lost whatever appetite he'd possessed.

"This is great," the detective said.

"Caught it this afternoon," Sales said with a mischievous grin.

"That's where you were?"

Sales nodded and carefully recited his alibi.

"You got a lot of guns," Bolinger said. "Any pistols?"

"A Colt forty-five from the service and a Glock I picked up at a bargain," Sales said. "Oh, and a little thirty-eight. The rest are just rifles and bird guns . . ."

Bolinger accepted this and finished his fish along with one last slug of Corona.

"Not supposed to have one on the job, but sometimes you've got to let it slide," he said, standing up. "Thanks for the fish. You going to be around for the next week or so?"

"Sure. You want coffee?"

"No. Thanks," Bolinger said. "I may want to ask you some questions in a few days or so. So if you decide to take a trip or something, let me know, okay?"

"I'll be right here. The trial's two weeks away. Is this going to move that off?"

"No," Bolinger said, pausing at the door. "That'll still happen."

Instead of driving directly back to the city, Bolinger pulled his car off to the shoulder, right next to where Sales's drive entered the main road. He sat there smoking for a while, then got out of his car and took the long, winding dirt road back through the brush to the cabin. Like a peeping Tom, he peered through a window. Sales wasn't doing anything unusual. He sat in front of the TV in a cloud of smoke, rising only to replenish his beer and another time for a fresh pack of cigarettes.

Now Bolinger's gut was uncertain on this one. His experience told him Sales had done it. Who else would have? But if Sales was guilty, he was putting on a pretty good show. If his story checked out and no physical evidence was discovered in the tunnel, Bolinger doubted this case would be solved, and that would bring down some heat. It wasn't that anyone cared about Lipton's taking three slugs. After what he did to Marcia Sales, there wasn't a cop alive who would mind much if he'd bought it. Bolinger had to admit that he'd felt a vague pang of disappointment when he learned that Lipton's life had been spared. But the chief and everyone else would be on the hot seat for the lapse in security, a man shot right underneath their noses. Personally, Bolinger was surprised something like it hadn't happened before. The tunnel was an incident waiting to happen.

Bolinger walked back down the dirt drive to his car. He would follow through with the investigation of Sales the way he would on any other case. He'd go by the numbers, and if there was any evidence linking Sales to the attack, then he'd have to act on it. And if there wasn't? Well, Bolinger certainly wasn't going to harass the man. God knew Donald Sales had been through enough already.

CHAPTER 6

Casey's appointment with Judge Rawlins was for ten. It was nearly twelve. If she were working for a paying client, it would have been nearly a thousand dollars wasted. But because it was for Catalina Enos, Casey was eating it.

Finally, she was admitted through the towering dark doors into Rawlins's chambers. As she entered the room, she averted her eyes, momentarily blinded by a beam of sunlight emanating from the high, arched window. Her nose was filled with the smell of warm, musty books.

The judge, his back lit by the sun, cut a ghoulish figure. The harsh combination of too much sun and too much coloring had left his stringy hair an odd burnt orange, and the greasy shock that lay across his forehead gave his dark eyes a strange cast. His wizened face, mottled with liver spots, sat like a shrunken head amid the splendor of his flowing robes. The nails on his bony fingers were stained from years of smoke and bourbon.

Rawlins was smiling absurdly at Casey's frazzled state.

His eyes, like the extensive gold dental work that filled the back of his mouth, sparkled with malicious delight.

"How can I help you, Ms. Jordan?" he drawled. His accent, like his political connections, was old Texas.

"You can commute Catalina Enos's sentence," she said flatly, taking a seat in the shadow of the wall even though none had been offered.

"Please, sit down," Rawlins said sarcastically. "Now why would I want to do that, Ms. Jordan?"

"Because if you do, you won't have to go through the embarrassment of having a mistrial declared at the appellate level," Casey said without bothering to hide her disdain. Rawlins was an age-old enemy and each of them knew where the other stood.

"I don't believe that's a concern of mine," he said complacently. "Oliver Wendell Holmes himself was turned over on appeal several times, and I don't believe it damaged his credibility very much."

Casey snorted at the mention of the great justice's name in the chambers of someone as tawdry as Van Rawlins.

"I believe Chief Justice Holmes was overturned in his younger days only on points of law," Casey said. "I believe it would have done him a great deal of discredit to be overturned for a procedural error."

"And what procedural error would we be talking about?" Rawlins asked, raising his eyebrows in mock surprise, goading her.

"I had a legitimate reason for not being at the conclusion of that trial and you know it. The precedent is clear. A defendant cannot be put at a disadvantage if her lawyer missed part of the trial because of an ice storm."

"Oh, I think the substance of the trial was quite over by

that time," Rawlins replied. "The closing argument wasn't much more than a wart on a toad's ass. Justice was served in my mind, Ms. Jordan. And if you were so damned concerned with your client, I think you would have made it a priority to be there.

"But then," Rawlins added with a nasty grin, "we all know how important your life is. You're a celebrity after all . . ."

The barb hit its mark. Inwardly Casey fumed, but still she maintained control.

"What I do is irrelevant here, Van—"

"I am a judge!" Rawlins bellowed, slapping his palm against his desk's leather blotter. With an imperious finger pointed her way, Rawlins boiled. "You will address me as such, young lady."

"Your Honor," she said firmly, "what I do is of no import. We're talking about a woman's life here, an innocent woman's life!"

"Ms. Jordan," Rawlins said quietly, "Catalina Enos was found guilty in a court of law. She is a convicted felon . . ."

"Judge Rawlins, I know how you feel about me," Casey said. She could feel her emotions mounting behind her hard-set visage and hoped she could go on without embarrassing herself. "But you know, you know that this will be overturned. I'll get another trial. It will take me a year of work. It'll cost me ten thousand dollars in copying and filing fees. I know that's what you want here. You want to punish me. But in the meantime, Catalina Enos will be in jail.

"Now please listen. I've been embarrassed by this whole thing. I've lost the case. It's been in the papers and on the news. You've done what you wanted to do. If you'll commute her sentence, and you have that latitude, then I won't appeal, you won't be overturned, and I will donate the money it would cost me in time to process this appeal—I figure about fifty thousand dollars—to any charity of your choice . . ."

Rawlins's face was stone. The brass pendulum of an old wall clock tick-tocked, but otherwise the chambers were quiet. Outside a police siren wailed three blocks away. Then a small smirk tugged at the corner of Rawlins's mouth.

"Are you trying to bribe me, Ms. Jordan?" he whispered.

Casey's face fell. It was a game to him. She was beaten.

"Not only will I not commute Ms. Enos's sentence," Rawlins continued, balancing a pair of reading glasses on the end of his nose and frowning at the record he had removed from his desk, "but I see that she has a prior felony . . ."

"Possession of a forged instrument, for God's sake," Casey moaned, knowing what was next.

"A felony nonetheless," Rawlins said perkily. "And so she will receive the maximum sentence. A shame for a girl so young, but like my momma always said, Ms. Jordan, you can't have a fricassee without killing a few chickens . . ."

Casey was up on her feet now. She was shaking all over. Rawlins knew from testimony at the trial that Catalina's abusive husband and his family had probably forced her into the bad-check business. As a judge, Rawlins knew that multiple-felony sentencing guidelines were intended for dangerous criminals. Catalina was hardly dangerous. To treat her as such was outrageous. "Goddamn you! Goddamn you to hell!" she cried, finally losing her control.

Rawlins was on his feet, too. "You're in contempt! Goddamn it, I'll have you arrested for contempt! Get back here, young lady! I'll lock you up, too!"

Casey answered him with the resonating blast of a well-slammed door. She stormed through the clerk's office. On her way into the hallway, she bumped squarely into a gray-suited lawyer. His files and the papers in them flew into the air like a flock of gulls. He was a tall, thin man with a large nose and a receding head of blond hair. As he stooped to pick up his papers, his glasses clattered to the granite floor as well.

"I'm so sorry," Casey said, bending to help him. When she realized whom she'd run into, she said, "Oh, Michael, I'm sorry. I didn't even recognize you."

Michael Dove was a fellow attorney. In fact, although several years older than she, he was a classmate of Casey's at UT. Dove was the closest thing Casey had to competition when it came to her reputation of being the best trial lawyer in the city. His pale skin was flushed, and Casey noticed that a rash had crept up from the inside of his collar to the back of his neck. Dove, Casey knew, was a solid individual, a good attorney with fierce religious convictions. In Casey's opinion, it was only those convictions that kept him from being her equal. She knew, as most people in the legal community did, that Michael Dove's zealous notions of morality sometimes caused him to commit tactical errors. When he spoke to her now, it was obvious to Casey from his quavering voice that he was upset about more than spilled files.

"No, no, that's all right. I'm fine. I'll just, I just, I'll just get these files. I need these files. Were you in with Rawlins?"

"Yes," she said, handing him a stack. "I'm afraid I didn't leave him in a good mood."

Dove forced a nervous chuckle. "It wouldn't matter. He wouldn't like what I'm going to say to him if it was Christmas morning."

Casey looked at her counterpart's face to see if he was going to tell her what that was. When it didn't come, she didn't ask. Part of being a lawyer meant silence when it came to legal issues that could affect a client.

To diffuse the tension, Casey casually inquired about Dove's latest high-profile case. "How's Professor Lipton's case coming along, Michael? I heard about what happened. You've got to be about ready for trial. Has the attack delayed anything?"

The effect of Casey's words proved to be worse than an unfriendly snub. Dove gave her an anxious, bewildered look, shrugged, and pushed past her into Rawlins's chambers with barely a good-bye.

Casey was still shrouded in melancholy when she returned to her office. There she sat, alone, in her high-backed leather chair with her back to the closed door. Only an occasional tuft of cloud interfered with the bright sun burning down on the city of Austin, the brilliant green Colorado River that snaked through it, and the western hills that loomed beyond.

When she was upset, it typically made Casey feel better to look out her window. Hers was a spacious top-floor corner office, prime real estate. But the reason she had such an affinity for the view wasn't that it cost a mint to lease, but because of the perspective it gave her. It put the world in order. She was in a tower, a tower she had created for herself. She was safely above the fray. Down below was the courthouse. The people who lived as far as the eye could see came there to have justice meted out. And it would be. Even Catalina Enos would get justice. Casey would help set her free. In the meantime, she reasoned, the girl's plight in jail would be no worse than the life she had led before her husband's death.

Despite her contemplation and its positive affect on her attitude, Casey still brooded through the following weeks. It wasn't that she didn't have a lot to keep her busy. She did depositions and took lunches, went to the symphony with Taylor and their friends, and played tennis at the club. But she needed something to put her back on track. For a long time she'd been on a roll, representing bigger and bigger clients, negotiating her way through the legal world to their advantage, steadily climbing the ladder of her career. Copping a plea for a senator's nephew accused of statutory rape, for example, seemed tawdry. She wanted something spectacular, something that could distract her from all that had gone wrong with the Enos case.

"Preferably," she mused aloud, "a paying client."

That would take some of the pressure off her for the hours and the resources she would have to devote to proceeding with Catalina's appeal. Casey never considered her husband's personal wealth a financial safety net. She wanted her practice to be a successful entity in its own right. She liked having her own bank account and credit cards that had nothing to do with the hundred-year-old Jordan money.

With a sigh, she looked at her watch and resigned herself to business as usual. That meant she was back to billable hours. There was a stack of uninspiring files on her desk that ranged from the shoplifting wife of a NASCAR driver to a bank vice president's assault on his groundskeeper. Still, it was work, and when her stout, dark-haired secretary, Gina, said that Casey's sister was on the line, Casey only thought wistfully about how long it had been since they'd caught up before she told Gina to take a message.

Now was not the time, not when she was sensing the beginnings of a slump. Hearing about her sister's uninspiring relationship with her farmer husband or the latest on their parents' trials and tribulations in their attempt to collect their fair share of FEMA money from last year's tornado were issues she wanted to avoid. Although Casey loved her sister dearly, she still reeked of Odessa. Casey had never been happier than when she learned that she'd been accepted at UT and even gotten some scholarship money.

From the beginning, Casey had wanted out. She'd spent even her early life being ashamed of the way they lived. Although they lived outside Odessa, the school Casey went to was shared by an outlying suburb. The girls from the suburb lived in new houses that didn't leak. Casey associated a hard rain with a living room floor that was cluttered with pots and pans. Casey would visit the other little girls after school and silently marvel at their nice trim homes. It made her ashamed of her own way of life, the linoleum that covered their floors, the old furniture layered in paint, and the discarded farm implements that littered the high grass surrounding the faded house.

She sighed, glad that she hadn't accepted the call. She had work to do. She began to go through her files the way a bricklayer might begin a massive wall, with skill and efficiency but devoid of any real passion.

She was on her way out the door to have lunch with a judge whom she considered the antithesis of Van Rawlins when Gina raced up to her at the elevator.

"There's a call I think you'll want," she said, out of breath.

Casey raised one eyebrow. "Who?"

"It's your old professor, Lipton. The one who killed his student."

CHAPTER 7

I'm entirely innocent. My case is a classic study of the all too typically overzealous police mentality and, quite frankly, circumstantial bad luck."

Casey looked across the plastic-topped table at her former professor. It was surreal to see him here, dressed in a flame orange jumper with the back of an armed guard's head bobbing in the window outside the door. Although she knew he'd been shot, Lipton showed no signs of the distress or fatigue that would normally accompany such an episode. His face was the same as it had been nearly fifteen years ago, those brilliant, piercing blue eyes, the rakish wavy blond hair. Maybe the hair, like his suntan, had faded, but she didn't know if that was from his incarceration or from age. His demeanor, too, was the same. He sat bolt upright with his chin held high and spoke in snappish commanding phrases.

"You'll take the case, of course," he said. He took out a pair of reading glasses that she didn't remember him having. Still, they were fashionable and did nothing to detract from his appearance. He looked down at the files he'd carried in with him and shuffled through them in a businesslike manner.

"Why did Michael Dove withdraw?" Casey wanted to know.

"Is it appropriate for an attorney to inquire into the privileged discourse between her client and a third-party attorney?" Lipton demanded. He was glaring over the tops of his glasses.

"No," Casey said, shaking her head. "I suppose it isn't."

"I thought not." Lipton sniffed indignantly. He looked back down at his papers before saying, "If it's a matter of money, I know your rates."

Casey didn't know how to respond to that. While it was true that money was on her mind, the way he broached the subject was almost insulting.

"Did my original choice of Michael as my counsel wound your pride?" Lipton inquired archly.

"Of course not," Casey said quickly.

"Of course it did," Lipton corrected. "You always had a thing about being the best, not the best you could be, but first, to win the prize. You always liked prizes, Casey. Well, Michael got the prize this time. He was the one the renowned law professor chose to come to his defense, and you didn't like that one bit, did you?

"No, I suppose you didn't," Lipton continued pensively. "But now it's yours. For reasons we shan't discuss, he is no longer the appropriate person to handle the situation. You, my dear, are just what I need. The evidence against me is insufficient and I will be acquitted. You will see to it."

Lipton passed the files across the table to her.

"I have done the major part of your work for you," he

said, patting the stack of papers with paternal affection. "But your gift is with the jury."

Casey's cheeks showed a hint of pink.

"I have to tell you," she confessed, "that my relationship with Judge Rawlins leaves a lot to be desired."

"All the better," he said. "Maybe he'll do something stupid. That wouldn't be unheard of. If he does, it will give us more to work with if we need to appeal. But as I said, I'm certain you'll win."

"I'll want to start from the beginning," she said in her most professional manner. "I'll ask Rawlins for a six-month extension with the right to resubmit all motions."

"You'll do nothing of the sort," Lipton countered. "My trial begins a week from Monday, and that's all you'll need to prepare."

Casey began to protest that it was almost unheard of for an attorney to have so little time to prepare for trial, but Lipton's halting, slender hand cut her off. "Every motion is in order. I oversaw everything and Michael is no slouch."

"I have to familiarize myself with the case," Casey interjected. "I have to develop a strategy for witnesses, for the entire trial . . ."

Lipton smiled demonically at her and in a hushed voice said, "My dear, I told you. I have everything right here. This is the strategy. These are the witnesses. I am the director. You are the player . . ."

Casey pressed her lips together, thinking. Part of her wanted to wipe the smug, assuming look off this man's face, to politely get up and leave. Another part of her never could. As insulted as she might be, she was also fascinated and challenged. What he said about the prize was painfully true. She remembered the stab of resentment she'd felt when she read about the case and learned that her old professor had chosen Dove and not her for his defense counsel. She had the better reputation of the two, if not by much. And more important, as a female she would have a natural advantage when it came to convincing a jury that her client was not guilty of a heinous crime toward another woman.

And now that he was offering her the case, he was doing so with restrictions. She was fairly certain she knew what he was up to. It was the game within the game. The decision to proceed with the trial was more than just his desire to get out of jail. It was a strategic move, and it made her wonder if Lipton had somehow forced Dove to rescind the case. If Lipton were found guilty, the chances of getting another trial on appeal would be good with a switch in attorneys so close to trial. Van Rawlins wasn't the kind of judge to insist on an extension under normal conditions. He certainly wouldn't do so now, knowing full well that such an extension would make Casey's life easier.

"There are some questions I do need answers to," Casey declared.

"And there are some I'll answer," Lipton replied curtly. "Others I won't. I'm not your usual client, my dear. I am your teacher. You are my pupil. Don't expect to enjoy the usual prerogatives you have with a sniveling criminal. I am neither sniveling nor a criminal."

"Why did you try to escape?" she asked, refusing to be baited.

"I wasn't trying to escape," he told her sternly. "I was there that day. I saw her body. It was horrible. I wanted to get away from everything . . . I loved her."

"She was your . . ."

"We were lovers," he said with a cryptic smile.

Was he suggesting that he was a prize Casey had wanted as well? She felt vaguely disturbed. When she was a student, she had certainly admired him, but many of her classmates had felt the same way. He was considered one of the preeminent authorities on criminal law. His book *The Letter of the Law* had been such a smashing success that he traveled the country giving seminars.

And in the last fifteen years, there were very few attorneys who had ambitions of becoming trial lawyers who hadn't been exposed to either one of his seminars or his book. Essentially, it was a practical guide to winning. After a preamble that described the nobility of criminal defense work, the book went on to describe the most effective tactics for winning a case. Its disregard of moral considerations was stunning and had made the book every bit as controversial as it was popular. Like many great ideas it was simple, and therein lay its brilliance. So there she had been, a young law student awed not only by the notoriety but also by the overwhelming intellect and charisma of the man.

Lipton's strange, almost knowing smile struck a nerve with Casey, but it quickly disappeared and he got back to business.

"I was upset," he continued, his words almost lifeless. "Anyone would have been. I wanted to get away. I had no idea anyone saw me leaving her apartment."

"You ran into another car," Casey pointed out.

Lipton shrugged. "Most people are mindless. For someone to have the perspicacity to see my license plate was an unusual coincidence. Otherwise, I would have taken my leave without arousing suspicion."

"Her father thinks you did it," Casey said.

"The father is mad," Lipton said, flaring up for the first time. "He was behind the attack on me, if it wasn't him who actually shot me." Lipton's hand instinctively sought out and caressed the healing wound not three inches above his heart. "It happened so fast, I don't know.

"He was the one who killed her, you know," he continued, narrowing his eyes malevolently. "He was jealous of what I had with his daughter."

"Did you tell this to anyone?" Casey said, incredulous. She vaguely recalled the father from the newspaper accounts, but nowhere had she heard or read of him as a suspect.

"Of course not!" Lipton scoffed. "I was their suspect. Once the police machine sets its sights on a person, that's it. They're like dumb animals. Beyond a very brief initial interview, I've said nothing to the police. I know better than that. But all this is in the files. You're wasting my time."

Casey thought about asking what other important things he had to do, but didn't.

"What about the underwear?" she asked, averting her eyes from his cold gaze.

"A sexual proclivity," he told her. His voice was quiet, almost syrupy. "A trophy of sorts."

"And the blood?" she asked.

"Old," he said. "Marcia liked to be tied up. She was what I call a dominant woman. Young, but still dominant. She was smart and headstrong and ambitious as well as very beautiful. I find that dominant women often like to be tied up . . . to restore the natural order if you will . . ."

Casey looked up. Lipton's eyes were gleaming now. He was playing with her, staying just barely within the bounds of decency.

"That doesn't explain"—Casey stopped, cleared her throat, and continued—"that doesn't explain the blood."

"Part of the bondage she craved was to have her panties stuffed into her mouth," Lipton responded in a clinical tone. "She bit her tongue. It's that simple."

"And speaking of sexual proclivities," he continued, "Michael Dove has my computer and I want you to get it from him immediately, and by that I mean today. The police took it when they arrested me. After they went through it, along with everything else I own, and found nothing, he was able to get it back. There are some very personal files that I've hidden on the hard drive that could be very damning if they were to get into the wrong hands. Their sexual content is irrelevant. That's my private business. But if a prosecutor got them in front of a jury . . . well, not everyone has our enlightened view when it comes to the First Amendment, especially when it comes to sex."

Lipton was leering at her now, and Casey's skin began to crawl. The air vent hummed. A fly came down from the ceiling and conducted a haphazard march across the tabletop between them before retreating to the glass panel on the door. More than anything, Casey wanted to get out of the room.

"I'm sure I'll have more questions after I read these," she said, rising and gathering the files. "I'll be back tomorrow."

"I'm looking forward to seeing you, Casey, on a daily basis, I mean. It's been quite a while," he said, rising himself and extending his hand. Casey took it, and her old professor pressed his long, cool fingers into her flesh until she twisted free.

*　　*　　*

"Then don't take the case," Tony told her. He was standing next to her Stairmaster machine in a royal blue suit with a crisp white shirt and a bold orange tie. Casey dabbed her sweaty face with a fresh white hand towel and stared hard at him. Her hair, pulled back from her face with a black cloth band, had gone from wavy to curly in the heat of her workout.

"Right, Tony," she huffed sarcastically. It was six-thirty in the morning and she was almost finished with her workout. The small exercise room was adjacent to her office. It came complete with a shower and a small set of free weights. Casey was obsessed with being mistaken at the beach for a twenty-one-year-old. Working out every morning kept her that way. She claimed it also gave her time to think about the coming day. It wasn't unusual at all for Tony to wander in about this time with his second double cappuccino of the morning. His idea of starting the day off right was to have his shoes shined while he drank his first double and scanned the morning paper.

Casey presumed he wasn't serious when he said she should drop the case. When Lipton had first been arrested over a year ago, Tony had implored her to contact him.

"Let him know you're available," Tony had said. She refused, and then when she lamented Michael Dove's being hired by Lipton, Tony only made it worse by saying that if she'd taken that first step of contacting him, she could have had the case.

"The first step is every bit as important as trying the case," Tony was always saying. "Without the first step, there is no case."

"That's your job," she'd responded.

"He wasn't my law professor," Tony had countered. "He was yours. You could have had the case. All you had to do was ask. I tell you that all the time, Casey. You have to ask."

Now that she had the case, she certainly wasn't going to give it up.

"I'm not saying I don't want it. It would be great," Tony said, stepping aside as she got down off the machine. "The media will be like bums on a bologna sandwich for this one. It might even get some play nationally. And the guy can pay our top rate. He's loaded. Those are all good reasons to take it, but I really mean it when I say don't take it if you're not comfortable."

Casey studied his face.

"Do you really think I'm that mercenary?" he asked. "I don't want you working with a client if it disturbs you. Besides, one week to prepare is almost unheard of. I don't know if you could do it."

His last words were spoken with an ingenuous expression. Whether they were actually intended to challenge her or not, Casey responded that way.

"I can do it," she said with a snort, hoisting a pair of dumbbells and beginning to crank out a set of curls as if to accentuate her confidence. "I could walk in on a case in a day if I had to."

"What about the fact that it looks like he did it?" he asked, sitting down on the padded bench and bracing his elbow against one thick knee.

"Innocent until proven guilty," she said. "Remember?"

"But tell me you don't think he did it," Tony said. As he continued to speak, he counted off on his fingers. "Come on. The guy was seen leaving the scene. He lied about it to the police. He had her bloody underwear in his bag, for God's sake! And they caught him heading for the airport with a reservation to Toronto. Oh, that's good,

Casey. That's overzealous. Tell me how you explain the guy out of all that."

"You're talking like a prosecutor," she said.

"Hey, I started there, too, you know," he reminded her.

"You're so far from the DA's office that you . . . I don't know. You're just far."

"Okay," he said, "so we're back to representing defendants until they're proven guilty? That's good. I thought we were going to have to start chasing ambulances."

"Funny," she said, switching her dumbbells to an overhead press. "But Lipton didn't say he did it. That's the difference and you damn well know it. If a client tells me he did it, I won't represent him. I don't care if it's the pope. But Lipton says he's innocent, and he deserves to have someone plead his case."

"Hey, go easy on the pope. This guy's no pope."

CHAPTER 8

A troop of towering white thunderclouds was pressing down from the north, threatening to ruin Bolinger's day off. He'd rented a pontoon boat for the day, and he sat now waiting by himself in the morning sun while the boat bumped steadily against the marina's aluminum dock. His brother, Kurt, was bringing his family. Only last night, Bolinger had been informed that that would also include Kurt's wife's sister from Atlanta and her new husband, whom Bolinger had never met before. He wasn't thrilled.

"Hey, he's a good guy," Kurt had told him. "You'll like him. He's a cop."

"Great," Bolinger had replied, "we can talk about bad guys, like the mailman going for a walk on his day off."

"You'll like him."

Bolinger shook his head at the thought. He didn't like anybody. Kurt, on the other hand, thought everyone was swell. He lived in a nice suburb, had a nice wife, a little on the heavy side but she could cook, two kids, one boy and one girl, and a job as an accountant at a telemarketing company with a great 401(k) plan. Although Kurt was younger and taller and had thinning blond hair, the two of them looked like brothers. But it was almost comical how different they were. When they were children Bolinger had teased Kurt by telling him that he was adopted.

With both their parents dead, they were all each other had in the way of family, and as they got older that seemed to mysteriously transcend any differences. When the silver Volvo wagon pulled into the gravel lot, the kids piled out like excited puppies. Their joy was infectious. Even Bolinger had to smile. Renting a pontoon boat was something beyond Kurt's scope. Too much wind, too much sun, too many things that could go wrong with the outboard motor with no way to fix it. So it was with great pride that Uncle Bob came up with schemes that his niece and nephew would look back on as memorable.

Bolinger got up from the captain's chair to catch the kids as they shot off the dock and into his arms. He kissed his sister-in-law, Luanne, as she stepped boldly onto the bow and shook hands with her sister, Eileen, a pretty little dish with bleached blond hair that was pulled back tightly into a ponytail. The last time Bolinger had seen her, at Kurt's wedding, she had been a skinny little kid with freckles and teeth too big for her head. Time went fast. The cop husband was bringing up the rear with Kurt, lugging more than his half of a big, shiny blue cooler. He was short like Bolinger, but much younger and pumped up like a gym rat. His hair was like Bolinger's, too, cut really short, only black instead of gray.

"I told you I had everything taken care of," Bolinger said without disguising his surly nature. He took the cooler from the two men and set it down disgustedly on the deck beside his own rusty green Coleman model. He didn't like people cutting in on his territory when he was the host.

"It's gonna rain, Bob," Kurt fretted, casting a baleful eye at the sky.

"Maybe not," the young cop put in, gazing northward himself. "Maybe it'll pass right over."

Bolinger nearly smiled, and held out his hand. "Bob Bolinger," he said.

"Vince Cubbins," the young man said. "But call me Cubby."

"How about a beer, Cubby?"

"I've got wine coolers," Kurt offered, dramatically zipping his Polo windbreaker against a gust.

"Beer sounds good," Cubby said.

Bolinger reached into the green Coleman and pulled out two cans of Foster's from under a stack of cellophane-wrapped bologna sandwiches. He opened them with a satisfying hiss, took a long swig, and began unmooring the boat.

He eased the boat away from the dock and made his way through the chop to a secret spot in the lee side of a cove where he had had some luck before. By the time they got there, everyone was spray-soaked. The sudden calm allowed the sun to warm them, but that only lasted long enough for Bolinger to set up the kids with some battered old fishing rods. The tall clouds blotted out the sun and rain sprayed down from above in warm, heavy sheets. The kids were gleefully drenched, while their dad was tucked in a dry corner of the boat under the roof next to his wife. Kurt had that I-told-you-so look on his face, and Bolinger thought he heard him mutter something about the whole thing being ridiculous. He was relieved when Cubby suggested another beer and Eileen got right in there with them. Whenever the call for alcohol came from a guest, it got Bolinger off the hook for looking like he had a problem.

For nearly an hour, it rained as hard as they drank. The downpour drummed the boat's flat tin roof like a thousand tap dancers, forcing them to raise their voices to be heard above the din. Bolstered by the children's glee, the beer, and his newfound ally, Bolinger ignored his brother's whining pleas to head back to shore. Then, as suddenly as it had begun, the clouds stormed south and the sun shone brightly. The fish stopped biting, but the beers tasted better and better, and the laughter of Cubby's wife, Eileen, rang out clear across the cove, echoing off the rocky hillside. Even Kurt joined in by telling a funny story about how he'd tried to return a cordless phone he'd had for over a year.

Soon the whole crew was hungry, and while Kurt and his wife spooned yogurt from plastic cups, the rest of them threw down Bolinger's sandwiches, a simple selection of bologna on white bread sloppily dressed with either brown mustard or ketchup. By mid-afternoon it became unexpectedly warm, warm enough for a dip. Eileen stripped to her underwear and went in. Cubby followed in his shorts, while the kids tittered and pinched each other until the boy, who was ten, threw his older sister in. Bolinger sat in his own sweat smoking and smiling and forgetting about everything until Eileen thrust herself out of the water and onto the bow, where she stood soaking in the sun, a dripping-wet goddess.

"You're livin' right," he said later to Cubby. The two of them were sitting by themselves on Kurt's patio, trying to outlast the night.

Cubby only nodded. Everyone else had gone to bed

long ago, and the conversation had finally begun to wane. A shooting star streaked across the vast dark sky, briefly outshining the mosaic of constellations.

"What's the worst you ever saw?" Cubby asked pensively.

"What do you mean?" Bolinger said, drawing on his Winston hard enough to make his face briefly glow in the orange light. His eyes were dark like empty pits.

"I mean, what's the worst thing you ever seen on a job?" Cubby asked, staggering out of his chair and over to the bushes where he could pee. Over his shoulder he said, "I mean you been at it a long time. You must have seen some bad shit."

Bolinger nodded. "Yup."

Cubby shook himself, zipped up, and began to pace back and forth. "I guess I'm wondering if you ever get used to it, or if there's things, some things, that you just never forget."

Bolinger considered. He hated to see the day end like this, but the kid really wanted to know, and Bolinger already had an affection for him. "I guess it depends on you. Some guys just start to laugh about it. They get hard on the inside. Hard and cold, but they seem pretty cheerful 'cause they're always looking for the humor in it, the dark humor. But me? I guess there's a couple things I'll never forget. Yeah, that's how I am. I just carry it around. I'm not saying it's a good way to be, probably not . . ."

Cubby nodded and was silent for a moment before he blurted out, "I saw a woman who was taped up and strangled and she was cut open like one of those frogs you dissect in high school biology class. Her guts were all over the place."

His voice was on the edge of hysteria and he spoke

fast. "It was like a doctor or something operated on her. I can't get it out of my head. We heard the call, and I wanted to go on break, you know, get a coffee, we were due. But my partner, he was into that kind of stuff. He said we should go check it out." Cubby's voice broke off here like an adolescent's. "Everyone was there, but we got to the scene before the lab closed it down, and I got in there and saw it. I . . . I . . . Do you have something like that that you just can't let go of? Goddamn, it was almost two years ago, and it's affected everything for me, even my marriage. I used to be . . . you saw Eileen. You know what I'm saying? I think about it when I see her naked. It just comes into my mind and it . . . it affects me . . ."

Cubby was standing now in front of Bolinger, swaying drunkenly, with tears running down his face.

"I'm sorry, man," he said, suddenly coming to himself. He sat back down beside Bolinger and quietly opened another beer. They sat for quite some time. Bolinger began to think Cubby might have fallen asleep. Then he suddenly took a swig from his beer, and Bolinger said in a voice so low it was almost a whisper, "You don't know, do you, if her gall bladder was missing?"

"How'd you know that?" Cubby said, staring suspiciously at him.

"Did she have anything to do with the law, not police work, but lawyering?"

"She was in her third year at Emory Law School," Cubby said, after a shocked pause.

Bolinger felt a shot of energy go through him. Most people thought that law enforcement agencies from around the country had some clearinghouse for information. But unless it was a federal crime with the FBI in-

volved, bizarre crimes even within the same state were
never matched up with similar crimes unless by rare
chance. Cops searching for similar crimes and desperate
for clues would often send out a Teletype to neighboring
jurisdictions soliciting information, but typically such re-
quests went unanswered. Then, every once in a great
while, things got matched up by sheer luck. Bolinger got
up out of his chair.

"Where you going?" Cubby asked.

"To make some coffee," Bolinger told him. "I gotta go
to work."

CHAPTER 9

"I need a favor."

Tony looked at Casey across the room with a wry smile and said, "I'm supposed to be the one who asks for favors."

"I know, but I need you to do some digging for me," she said. She had spent the entire weekend with the Lipton files, coming out of her office only for a dinner with her husband and some friends. "I know how I can win, but I need some serious background information."

"On who?" Tony said.

"Donald Sales," she said.

"The dead girl's father? Why?" He was incredulous. He knew one of her favorite strategies was to suggest to the jury a viable alternative to who committed the crime. "You're not going to try to pin it on him, are you?"

"He very well could be the killer," she said. She didn't mention that the idea had originated with Lipton.

"Oh, give me a break!" Tony scoffed. "Come on, Casey, if that's the best you've got, you might as well start asking the DA for a plea."

"Look," she said, "I don't tell you how to get the TV cameras to a press conference. I want you to look into him for me, and I want you to do it now. I know already that he's not mentally stable."

"In what way?" Tony asked, stroking his beard.

"He's a Vietnam vet who was treated for PTSD."

Tony nodded. He knew that included a wide range of possibilities.

"And he has a history of violence."

"Violence? Like what?"

"Assault. Disorderly conduct," she replied.

Tony twisted his lips doubtfully.

"I want you to find out about his relationship with the daughter," she said. "The DA is going to put him on the stand to implicate Lipton. He claims that the girl told him she was afraid of Lipton. I'll have a chance to impeach him in the cross, and I not only want to tear him apart, I want that jury wondering if it wasn't really him that killed her and he's trying to pin it on Lipton."

"That's what you think?" Tony asked.

"I don't know what I think," Casey replied. "It's possible, yes. What I want is for you to get me everything you can on him. Call every PI you know and start digging. I want to know everything about Sales and the relationship he had with his daughter, especially if he ever hit her or hit one of her boyfriends or something like that. Lipton thinks Sales was the one who shot him."

"Probably was," Tony said, thinking of his own daughter, a teenager who lived with her mother in Kansas City. "I'd want to kill him, too, if he did that to my daughter."

"Lipton thinks it's because he was jealous. He was the girl's lover, you know."

Tony let out a low whistle. "I didn't read anything

about that. Don't you think that's something we would have heard about?"

Casey shrugged. "Let's forget about what might have been or what's been written in the paper. This is my theory, and if I'm going to run with it I need some ammunition. I want you to get it."

Tony looked past Casey, staring blankly out the window.

"What are you thinking?" she asked.

"Just about fathers and kids and a custody case I did for a guy once," he said, still in his trance.

"What's that got to do with this?"

"Just that this guy's wife had the little girl saying the dad touched her in her private areas. He said he didn't do anything any father didn't do when he's giving his kids a bath. I didn't know what really happened, but I'll tell you, I couldn't help looking at the guy differently. I still did my best, but inside me, I don't know. I just looked at him differently. Well, the wife and her lawyer made a big stink about it, and the judge choked this guy's visitation off to almost nothing . . . Shit, they got him investigated by the social services people."

Tony refocused his eyes on Casey's face and said, "I saw the lawyer a couple of years later at a conference, and over drinks he told me that after the case, the mother told him that it was all bullshit. She made it up to screw her husband. My God, Casey."

"What?"

"I don't know," Tony said. He shook his head and looked past her again, out the window, unwilling to meet her eyes. "Just think, if Lipton really did kill that girl and you tear the father apart on the witness stand. It's not good."

"Goddamn it, Tony!" she said, boiling over. "Whose side are you on? I say black, you start talking about white. I say I don't want to represent someone, you say we should. I say okay, you go back the other way. My job is to exonerate Professor Lipton. I'm not worried about Donald Sales or his feelings. My God, leave me alone already! If he's not the killer, he'll get over it."

"He'll get over it?" Tony looked at Casey with an expression she had never seen before, and it cut her to the quick. "Listen to yourself. Get over it? The man's daughter was brutally murdered. You're going to put him up on that stand and suggest he was the killer. You think he'll get over that?"

"Are you going to help me or not?" Casey snapped. "Because if you're not, I have to find someone who will."

Tony sat silently for a minute, contemplating his tie. After a heavy sigh he rose from his seat and said, "No, I'll do it. If you're going to do it, I might as well be the one to help you."

"I mean really help," she said curtly. "I don't want you to pull back because you don't like what I'm doing."

Tony stopped on his way out the door and glared at her. "Excuse me?"

Casey kept her mouth closed and dabbed at the sweat that was rolling down her face. She waited.

"Have I ever not done a job all out?" Tony asked.

"I just want to make sure, Tony," she told him. "I don't have any time. I'm in this thing. I'm not looking back and I wish you wouldn't, either."

"You're right," he said. "I'm sorry. It's a bad habit of mine, always looking at the other side of things. I'll get what you need or it can't be gotten."

"Thank you, Tony," she said.

A few minutes later, as the shower's cold water pounded down on her, Casey purged her mind of all the extraneous considerations in the Lipton case, the father, the dead daughter, all of it. It didn't matter to her. It couldn't. Her job was to win the case.

CHAPTER 10

Judge Rawlins's large courtroom evoked a stern tradition of justice. The dark wood, the heavy beams and columns, and the worn white marble floors gave it a feeling of permanence, as if it had always been there and always would be. Casey much preferred the former judge, who had presided there until a heart attack forced him from the bench. Walter Connack had been the antithesis of Van Rawlins, a big, powerful black man who was respected as much for his compassion as he was for his sense of justice. But all the wishing in the world wouldn't change the fact that the bailiff was calling for everyone to rise for the Honorable Van Rawlins.

After the usual formalities, Glen Hopewood, the DA, began his opening argument. While a competent lawyer, he was a heavy man who tended to sweat and whose black plastic glasses slipped down his nose every few minutes only to be reset by thick, doughy fingers that fluttered to his face from the distant regions of his paunch. It was a distraction that Casey knew had an effect on the jury. Still, he painted a grim picture of a diabolical killer whose exceptional knowledge of the law and whose intellectual arrogance made him think he was beyond punishment. Sitting there between Casey and Patti Dunleavy, as dapper and handsome as a distinguished model from *GQ* magazine but also just as aloof, Lipton did nothing visually to contradict the prosecutor's image.

Hopewood then went on to chronicle the crime. Taking advantage of his position as her professor, the DA claimed, Lipton had convinced Marcia Sales to allow him into her apartment. Once inside, he strangled her until she was unconscious, bound her with duct tape, and cut her to pieces. What was particularly shocking was evidence that proved the girl wasn't dead when the killer cut her open and began to remove her insides.

While the DA conceded that the crime scene itself was bereft of any concrete evidence linking Lipton to the murder, he told the jury that Lipton, like most people who think they are above the law, had made a crucial mistake. In his rush to abandon the scene, the professor had struck another automobile on his way out of the victim's driveway. Although he fled the scene immediately, the other driver was able to get a description of Lipton's car as well as his license plate number.

"But you will hear police testimony that Lipton claimed not to have been in the area," Hopewood dramatically stated. "And then, after lying to the police, he tried to escape. He was followed and caught on his way to the airport with packed bags, a passport, twenty thousand dollars in cash, and a plane reservation to Toronto.

"And while Lipton may have left nothing behind at the exact scene of the crime, that doesn't mean he didn't take something with him. He took a trophy, ladies and gentlemen, something to remember his victim by, something

not uncommon to a particularly depraved sort of psychopathic murderer. Yes, the most chilling evidence in this
case, ladies and gentlemen"—Hopewood paused to look
them over, then, pointing his finger back at Lipton, said
in a seething tone—"is that this man . . . this . . . man,
when the police arrested him, had Marcia Sales's underwear in his possession. And they were covered, ladies and
gentlemen, covered with her blood . . ."

The jury's collective gasp made Casey shudder. She
stole a look out of the corner of her eye at Lipton. He
seemed unfazed and stared disdainfully at the prosecutor.
Then Hopewood made a tactical error. He went on longer
than he should have about the details of other evidence
and the witnesses he would produce. If Casey had been
on the other side, she would have stopped after the jury's
gasp. But Hopewood hammered away, unnecessarily bur-
dening them with the minutiae of the case and putting
some comfortable distance between the emotional shock
of the bloody underwear and Casey's own version of the
events surrounding Marcia Sales's death.

In fact, when Hopewood finally sat down, Casey
waited until Rawlins impatiently asked if the defendant's
counsel was waiting for Christmas.

"No," Casey replied calmly to the judge before standing to face the jury. "No, I was just wondering if the prosecutor was finished with his story . . .

"You see, ladies and gentlemen," she said, opening her
arms with palms facing up, welcoming them to her point
of view, "that's all Mr. Hopewood's words were, a story.
Oh, we've all heard stories before. In fact, we're barraged
with stories every day. Most of them are in the news.
They come to us by way of the media, which sensation-
alize and twist reality to give us something we can sink

our teeth into, something salacious, something scandalous, something shocking, violent, or horrible.

"And sometimes these stories have a semblance to the truth," she continued, moving closer to them now, addressing them one by one, face to face. "But sometimes they don't. You see, Mr. Hopewood's job is to tell you a sensational story that will get you to convict someone. That's how he wins. He gets a conviction, he chalks up a win. An acquittal to him is a loss.

"But you . . . you, my friends, are seeking the truth. You want justice. And in order for you to find that truth, and mete out that justice, you have to realize where the police and the prosecutor and even the victim's own father stand. Where do they stand?" Casey asked, with her eyebrows raised.

Then, gesturing toward Lipton, she said in a gentle tone, "Professor Lipton is an intelligent man with a peerless reputation in the academic world. He is financially secure. He works with the best and brightest that this state has to offer in the legal field and they revere him. I revered him, Marcia Sales revered him, nearly anyone who has taken his classes at the University of Texas School of Law feels the same way. He has been a champion for the rights of an individual unjustly accused by the police and public prosecutors and they don't like it.

"Now not all police are corrupt or malignant, we all know that," Casey said, eyeing the white members of the jury. Then, with special connection to the five minority jurors, she said, "But some of us also know that there is an underside to the police, a vicious, mindless beast that only wants to punish someone, anyone, for a criminal act. And it is that very beast, the one he has railed against, that has been unleashed on Professor Lipton.

"Yes, he was at Ms. Sales's apartment the day of her death, but not as the killer. No. He was there to visit her as a friend, a confidant, a lover. And what he found shocked and scared him beyond reason. He raced from that place, and when he was faced with the bullying, accusatory attitude of the police, he was frightened. You see, Professor Lipton knows only too well how many innocent men and women have spent lifetimes in jail, or have even been executed, killed, murdered by the state in the name of police justice.

"How many times have we heard stories of people being freed after years on death row because truthful evidence finally emerges? Well, this man is intimately familiar with almost every one of those cases. That's his field of expertise! So when he realized that the beast was poised to strike out against him, that it had fixed its eyes on him, despite his innocence he panicked. He ran! Anything, he knew, was better than spending years or maybe all of his life in jail, hoping, praying each day that the truth would finally be revealed. And then they say they're sorry, but that didn't help Henry Tasker, a man we all heard of in the news recently who was released after spending thirty years of his life in a state prison. And sorry wouldn't help Professor Lipton, either, so he ran.

"You'll also hear from another man during this trial, and I want you to consider his story as well . . ."

Casey paused to look back toward the first row behind the balustrade in back of the prosecutor's table. Donald Sales sat staring malignantly at her. His jet black hair was pulled back into a ponytail. His large frame and pale, scowling eyes cut an angry and imposing figure. Although his glare was exactly what she wanted, its intensity made Casey swallow involuntarily before she went on.

"While those of you who are parents will naturally identify with Mr. Sales's grief," she told the jury in her most compassionate voice, "I must ask you to remember that anything he says will be clouded by unfettered hatred for Professor Lipton. And that hatred, ladies and gentlemen, did not spring from his daughter's death. No, that hatred burned long and hard before the day of the unfortunate tragedy because Mr. Sales was enraged over the affair his daughter was having with her professor. So when he tells you his story, you have to realize it's just that, another story . . .

"Finally, the prosecution will make much of Ms. Sales's underwear . . ." Here Casey paused to look modestly down at her own feet. "Now . . . I have a sex life. You have your sex lives. And we don't expect that anyone else will be privy to that part of our existence, do we? No. No, we expect that what goes on in the privacy of our bedrooms will stay there. The way we look, what we say, what we do . . . we expect these things to be private. But remember, the DA is telling a story, and won't it make people sit up and listen if he talks about a man with a woman's underwear? And if there's blood on that underwear? How sensational! What a story!

"But . . . what if that garment was nothing more than a private bedroom thing between two adults? What if it was no one's business? What if the blood came, not from the commission of a crime, but from someone wiping her mouth after biting her tongue during some lively consensual sex."

"You bitch!"

The words rang out in the courtroom, leaving a tremendous silence in their wake. Donald Sales was up from his seat and over the balustrade before anyone else could move. Casey instinctively retreated back toward the bench. Luckily, the bailiff, who was a young, tubby three-hundred-pounder, hadn't yet fallen asleep, and when he stepped forward, Casey ducked behind him to screen herself from the raging father. The bailiff grabbed the storming Sales in a bear hug and held tight until help could come from the hallway. Rawlins hammered indignantly with his gavel while two armed officers helped the bailiff subdue Sales in a scuffle in which no one threw a punch.

"Get him out!" Rawlins wailed. "Get that man out of my courtroom!"

Out-muscled and realizing his mistake, Sales allowed the officers to lead him out of the court without resistance.

"Would you like to go on, Ms. Jordan?" Rawlins asked derisively. "We have a trial to conduct here."

Casey checked herself from rebuking Rawlins. It was absurd to continue without at least a brief recess, but Casey quickly decided to turn the situation to her advantage. She wouldn't try to hide the tremble in her voice. She wanted them to see she was frightened, that Sales was an uncontrollable, vicious, and violent man capable of almost anything.

She stood, shaking and scared, until Rawlins badgered her again.

"Please, Ms. Jordan," he barked. "Continue if you have anything more to say. If not, I will direct the prosecution to proceed with its case."

Casey drew a breath, cleared her voice, and said, "As you see, Mr. Sales is a furious, unpredictable man . . . And, as I said, you will hear from him and the police and the prosecutor and all of his other witnesses in an attempt to construct a story that is far from the truth . . . But you must remember this: The most important charge the judge will give to you will be the words 'beyond a reasonable doubt.'

"That means, my friends, that a reasonable person would have not a single doubt that the prosecutor's story is true. But you will see, I will show you, that his story is remarkably doubtful. I will show you a police force so aggressive and a father so bent by hatred that you will understand why they were so eager to point the finger at Professor Lipton. At first glance, yes, his actions are suspicious. But as I said, there are good reasons for why he acted as he did. They make sense, and they will convince you that he is nothing more than a man in the wrong place at the wrong time."

CHAPTER 11

The DA used the first two days of the trial to unveil the evidence that linked Professor Lipton to the scene of the crime. For the most part, Casey did little on cross-examination. She wanted to lull the opposition into a false sense of security before she poured it on. Except for the actual murder, Casey was conceding that Lipton had done everything the police said. Her theory was that, yes, he was at the scene. Yes, he raced away, hitting a car in the process. Yes, he lied to the police and he even tried to flee.

The only point she got aggressive about had to do with the blood on Marcia Sales's underwear. Casey wanted it clear that the women's underwear Lipton was carrying might not have any connection to the murder at all.

"So," she had asked a witness from the crime lab, "while you know this blood belonged to Marcia Sales, you don't know when it got there, do you?"

"No," the tech had answered.

"It's perfectly possible," Casey continued, "that this

blood came from a bite in her tongue or the inside of her mouth, isn't it?"

"Yes."

"So it's possible that Marcia Sales, gagged with that underwear as part of a sexual idiosyncrasy, bit into her tongue or her cheek and bled on that underwear, isn't it?"

The lab technician had to admit that it was possible.

At the time, Donald Sales had twisted his face into a silent snarl. Rawlins had allowed him back into the courtroom after giving him a strong warning that another outburst like the first would land him in jail. Since then, he had spent his time shifting his hateful glare between Casey and Lipton and sometimes even Patti. Instead of avoiding eye contact, Casey stared right back at him, taking in his hatred and allowing her own anger to smolder. She would bring it to a flame when she cross-examined him on the witness stand. And with the information that Tony had gathered, it was going to be a hot flame indeed.

It was the night of that second day when Casey received an unusual call at home from the judge's clerk. Casey was requested in chambers before trial the next morning. The clerk wouldn't say what it was about.

"What's the matter?" her husband asked her absently from his side of the plush velvet couch when she hung up the phone. It was nine-thirty at night. Casey was sitting with him dutifully in their cavernous walnut-paneled den while he watched a rented action movie that she had no interest in.

"I just don't like being called to chambers without knowing why," she said.

"Yeah," he told her, "I know. It'll all work out."

Then his attention was back on the movie. Casey knew

he hadn't even really heard her. It was his mantra. It'll all work out. That was how he dealt with any unexpected bumps in Casey's world. He dismissed them, presuming she could take care of it.

She wondered if it was some deficiency in her that caused the people closest to her to act that way. She'd experienced the same thing with her parents while growing up. Whether it was an award for something she did in sports or school, half the time her parents weren't even there. And just recently, after she had won the Texas Trial Lawyers Association's highest honor, her father had responded over the phone by saying, "That's real nice. What'd they eat at the dinner?"

"Did you ever think you might like to know why or what I'm upset about, Taylor?" she asked, suddenly mad at her husband for a lifetime of underappreciation.

"Yeah," he said. "Sure." But his feet remained on the coffee table, his eyes on the screen.

"Can you shut that off for a minute?" she said.

"Honey, it's a good part right now," he told her, eyes still glued to the set. "Give me a minute . . ."

"Fine," Casey said. She shot off the couch and stomped all the way up the broad spiral staircase to get ready for bed. When she was in her nightshirt, she went to the top of the stairs. She could faintly hear the movie echoing through the long hallways and off the marble walls of the magnificent entryway. He was still watching. She returned to the bedroom and lay down but couldn't sleep. He was obviously going to watch to the conclusion. She was in the middle of an enormous case, a case everyone in all of Texas was talking about, and her husband couldn't even pause his sophomoric action movie to discuss her concerns. It was infuriating.

When he finally did come to bed, she gave him a good dose of silence and the stiffest body language she could muster. He kissed the back of her head anyway, pulled on his sleeping mask, and dropped off to sleep like a champion. Casey twisted under the covers in an attempt to wake him and let him know she was still unsettled, but to no avail. Taylor was out. She lay alone for almost an hour and then felt her way past the fluted columns supporting the archway into the bathroom. She carefully closed the door before feeling for the light switch. Beside the sink on her side of the bathroom, she fished through the ornately carved cabinet until she found a sleeping pill. It wasn't something she liked to do, but with the trial tomorrow and the mysterious conference in chambers, she needed some sleep.

In the morning, it was obvious to Casey that Taylor was now mad at her for being mad at him—so she was mad right back.

On her way into town, Casey turned up the music on the radio louder than normal. She found a song she could sing along with and tried to lose herself in the music, but it kept coming back to her. Her marriage was a farce. It wasn't the fight. It was what was behind the fight. There was nothing there. He didn't really care about her. She was a trophy. She had to face that fact. Her career, her efforts, her cares and concerns were simply interesting novelties for conversation at dinner parties. She saw the way he looked at other women. She was no fool.

Or was she? Had she been kidding herself when she brushed off his roving eyes as a man who simply appreciated beautiful things? There had been other signs as well, now that she allowed herself to think about it. Sometimes he would go on trips and she wouldn't hear from him for a day or two. Then there were phone calls to the house late at night. When she answered, the callers would hang up. Was that just chance or was something there? When they argued, how could it not affect him if she was the only thing in his life? Well, maybe she wasn't the only thing in his life.

That wouldn't be fair. He was the only thing in hers. Yes, she was attracted to the notion of hobnobbing with the social elite. She felt comfortable with his set of friends and the things they did, weekends in New York, holidays in Tahiti or Paris, cocktail parties at the Ritz. And his friends accepted her. She liked that, and she liked his suave manner, his money, and his good looks. But those things were frivolous charms. Beneath all that, she really loved him. She loved him and now she wondered for the first time if he loved her back. Tears began to spill down her cheeks. Without a sniff she wiped them away and turned the music even louder.

Casey was thankful when she finally reached the courtroom steps. Most of her waking hours were spent being a lawyer, and in that world, despite its inevitable disappointments, she was a happy woman. She locked away her haunting suspicions and focused on the unusual request by the judge to see her. When she entered his office, Hopewood was already sitting opposite the judge's imposing desk. His hands were folded patiently across his prodigious belly. His smile told her something bad was coming.

"Sit down," Rawlins told her.

Casey did.

"Glen has some information that he wants brought into evidence," Rawlins said, looking down his nose through his reading glasses at a document on his desk. "Obviously, you need to know about it."

Rawlins looked at the DA, who unfolded his hands and said, "We have a like crime that we've linked Lipton to. About six months before Marcia Sales was murdered, a young woman was killed in Atlanta. Like Marcia Sales, she was a law school student. Like Ms. Sales, she was disemboweled and her gall bladder was missing. Also as with Marcia Sales, the crime, although heinous and bizarre, apparently wasn't sexual in nature."

"You have hard evidence linking my client to that crime?" Casey demanded, cloaking her distress in hostility.

Hopewood looked at Rawlins, then back to Casey before saying, "Not physical evidence, but the girl attended a seminar given by Lipton two months before her death. It's a crime so similar that even you would have to agree that there is only one killer . . ."

"I agree to nothing," Casey said tempestuously. "You have no basis to submit this into evidence."

"Well, that, Ms. Jordan," Rawlins interjected, "is for me to decide. I am the judge . . ." He let his scowl sink in before saying, "I'm adjourning the trial until tomorrow afternoon. I'll hear arguments from you both at one o'clock."

"How can you even consider a hearing?" Casey cried. "This is totally immaterial! If you let him parade that out in front of a jury, they'll take it as a propensity. Thousands of people attend Professor Lipton's seminars every year."

"I'd like to have it admitted as a common plan," Hopewood told her. "To show the common scheme here. The pattern is quite relevant."

"Both of you save it for tomorrow afternoon," Rawlins barked. "I told you there's a hearing, so there's a hearing. Now, I have work to do."

With that, the judge dropped his head like a puppet and began going through his mail as if neither attorney was even there. Casey shot a dirty look at Hopewood, then got up and left.

Lipton had been moved from the county jail to the public safety building across the street for the trial. And although it irked her to give in to his overbearing demands to know every detail of the case, this was a development any client had a right to know, so Casey went directly over to apprise him of the situation. As she crossed the street in front of a police cruiser with two officers who'd stopped to gawk at her legs, she wondered if what Hopewood was saying was true. She really believed Lipton's story, not just because it was her job. She thought his story was quite credible. But now, even though she was confident that she could have the information about the dead girl in Atlanta suppressed from the jury, the knowledge of it made her own convictions about his innocence seem almost ludicrous.

Because he was at the safety building, Casey had to talk to her client through a glass window in a smelly little cubicle whose corners were dark with ancient scum.

"What's going on?" he demanded even before he was in his seat on the other side of the glass. He already knew from the guards that he wasn't going to court that morning, but he didn't know why.

Casey looked at him carefully. While his facial expression and body language were under control, there was a wild light in the professor's eyes that she hadn't seen before.

"The DA found a girl in Atlanta who was killed the same way as Marcia Sales," she said, watching him closely.

Lipton showed no outward reaction. But while he digested the news, Casey could see from his eyes that his mind was spinning. She thought that was a bad sign until he said, "So, they know now that it's not me."

Casey was confused and couldn't hide it. It was the last thing she had expected him to say. She thought she read guilt in his eyes, but the words he spoke were stunningly innocent.

"If it happened again," he said, with the smile of a man who has learned a small trick, "and I'm in jail, then whoever it is, is still out there. I am exonerated."

"No," Casey said, shaking her head, but understanding that she had neglected to say when the girl had been murdered. "The girl was killed before Marcia Sales, six months before . . . and about two months after attending one of your seminars at Emory."

Lipton furrowed his brow and brought his hand up to his chin, a professorial pose.

"It must have been Sales," he said, looking up. "Who else could have done it? He must have planned to kill Marcia well in advance . . ."

Casey didn't know whether she could buy that idea or not, but she didn't want to waste her time thinking about it. It was improper of her, really. The professor was her client, and she was sworn to advocate for him as best she could.

"Maybe it was him," she admitted. "But, as you know, I don't think there's any way even Van Rawlins would allow that information into court, even if they had conclusive proof against you, which they don't."

"Listen," the professor said. "They're going to use *People v. Molineux* to try and get it in under common plan or scheme. It's an old case from New York around the turn of the twentieth century. But you're right, it shouldn't succeed, although with Rawlins we'll want to make your brief airtight. Go right to *Krulewitch v. U.S.*, it's a Supreme Court decision, and make sure you pay careful attention to Jackson's concurring opinion. From there, well, you know how to search out other relevant cases . . ."

Casey nodded that she did. She couldn't help being impressed by his instant recollection of specific cases on an isolated legal issue. She had always known he was brilliant. Students at the law school invariably said he had a photographic memory. She had doubted that until he appeared at a third-year student's graduation party one May afternoon. After a few drinks, Lipton began to show off his memory by answering questions about the phone book. Casey didn't believe it was anything more than a trick until she took the book and showed him page 187 for all of three seconds. After taking the book away, Casey eyed him warily and asked what was the number of Alan Cutler. Lipton rattled it off at once.

Suddenly she was ashamed of ever having doubted her former professor's innocence. She hoped the suspicion in her voice hadn't been noticeable.

"How is everything?" she said haltingly, hoping to rebuild any rapport she might have damaged with her suspicious questioning. "I mean, in here, in the safety building."

"Oh, it's not unlike the county jail," he told her with a forced smile. "But I'm looking forward to being out. I"— a silly little chortle escaped Lipton's throat and he looked at her slyly—"I'm looking forward to having a woman again, my dear. I am a man of passionate humors. I want a woman and a good Cuban cigar, a Cohiba to be exact, and a bottle of Opus merlot.

"Is it difficult for you to think of my earthly desires?" he said, laughing softly again. He was obviously enjoying himself.

"Of course not," she said uncomfortably. In truth, any talk about someone else's sex life made her cringe. Just as unsettling was his sudden gleeful conviviality, and she wished she'd never taken their conversation into personal territory. During all their previous interactions, he had maintained the detached posture of a pedagogue, treating her like an eager student. She much preferred that, however, to his intimacy.

"Good," he said lightly. "I like a woman who isn't a prude. Is your little assistant a prude?"

Casey was stunned by the question.

"I don't think Patti's personal characteristics are anything we need to discuss, Professor Lipton," she said reservedly.

"But why not?" Lipton said. "Why can't we have a little gossip between us? It's always business, but we know each other well enough now to be beyond that. Is she an aggressive young woman? I know she is subordinate to you, but I presume she must have some tenacity or you wouldn't tolerate her."

"Really, Professor," Casey said with an uncomfortable laugh that was aimed for levity. She got up from her chair and said, "I have work to do. I'll see you tomorrow afternoon for the hearing."

"What are you going to do about the media?" Lipton asked her before she could get away.

"In what way?" she asked, turning.

"Hopewood will leak this story," he told her, "about the girl in Atlanta. Rawlins won't let this into the hearing, but everyone will know about it. People will pass judgment, the same way you did . . ."

"I . . . I can't help you there, Professor," she said. "I can only win your case."

"Yes, well, a good word from you on the record might go a long way," he said wistfully, "for when I'm out . . ."

CHAPTER 12

After her expected victory in the hearing on whether to allow the Atlanta killing into evidence, Casey focused all her energy on preparations for the prosecution's final witnesses. Since the silence between her and Taylor had continued, she didn't bother to call, even though she didn't get home until long after he was in bed. With the help of Tony and Patti Dunleavy, she went over every possible turn the following day might take. She knew Hopewood had saved the best for last.

The next day, the prosecutor played his two final cards. Donald Sales was his ace. He would go last and hopefully elicit the jury's inexorable desire to punish someone. But first up was Detective Sergeant Bolinger. He was as credible a witness as Casey had suspected he would be. A seasoned cop who'd been on the stand hundreds of times, Bolinger came across as tough and smart, the kind of police officer people wanted out there keeping the streets safe.

Casey watched him carefully. With Hopewood's lead, the two of them wove a perfectly cohesive tale unveiling the prosecution's theory as to how Lipton had committed the crime. They skillfully rehashed the gruesome testimony already given by Alice Vreeland of the medical examiner's office, re-creating the picture of a young girl who was choked into submission, horrifyingly bound with tape, and then slowly and painfully eviscerated with a sharp instrument until she died.

When the physical evidence was out of the way, Bolinger then helped the DA paint a damning portrait of Lipton as a lying egomaniac who thought he could outsmart the rest of the world because of his intellectual powers. Bolinger was obviously proud of the way he had noticed Lipton's slip of the tongue, proving his knowledge of the crime during their very first encounter, and of the way the police had been able to match the murder with Lipton's unrelated hit-and-run. Farnhorst had already given a vivid recollection of Lipton's attempted escape, but Bolinger added to that by recounting the professor's snide remarks when questioned about Marcia Sales's bloody panties.

When Casey stood for the cross, Bolinger turned her way with a reptilian gaze that made her waver. But it was only a moment before she honed in on destroying the detective and his testimony. That's what she did best, and even the formidable Bolinger wasn't going to keep her from doing her job. Casey stood up. She had pulled back her hair and piled it high on her head. Her long white neck and her regal bearing made her seem taller than she really was. Dressed in a tailored chocolate suit and heels, she was an impressive sight to the jury. She was a woman in total control.

"You've done this a lot, haven't you, Sergeant?" Casey began.

"What would 'this' be?" Bolinger wanted to know. He wasn't going to make it easy.

"This," Casey said, spreading her arms to encompass the entire courtroom, "testifying in a case, being cross-examined by a defense attorney."

"Yes, I have."

"And you don't like it, do you, Sergeant?" she said.

"It's all right," he replied.

"You don't like having your work questioned by some-one like me, though, do you?"

"No, I don't think anyone likes to have their work questioned."

"You don't like it when an attorney points out all the things you've done wrong, do you?"

"I haven't done anything wrong," Bolinger said, bristling a little.

"No?" Casey said, arching her eyebrow and giving the jury a knowing look. "But we all make mistakes, don't we, Sergeant? I know I do from time to time. You're not telling us you're perfect, are you, Sergeant?"

"No. I'm not."

"Because you make mistakes, isn't that right?"

"I suppose," Bolinger said sullenly. "Like everyone else."

"Yes, that's what I said, like everyone else," Casey said with a pleasant smile. "You make mistakes and you don't like to have them pointed out . . . You made a lot of mistakes in this case, didn't you, Sergeant?"

"No," Bolinger scoffed. "No, I didn't."

"No?" Casey asked.

"No," he replied firmly.

"But isn't it true that Mr. Sales was at the crime scene, Sergeant?"

"Yes. What's that got to do with it?" he demanded.

Casey smiled sweetly at Bolinger, then said to the judge, "Your Honor, I would appreciate it if you'd help me to remind Detective Bolinger that I am the attorney and he is the witness."

"Please just answer the questions," Rawlins said to the cop.

"Thank you, Your Honor," Casey said cheerfully. When she turned to Bolinger, her face clouded over with intensity and disgust.

"Mr. Sales was violent at the scene, isn't that true?"

"Yes."

"He resisted arrest. He screamed. He fought. In fact, he had to be Maced and blackjacked and handcuffed before he could be brought to bay, isn't that true?"

"Yeah," Bolinger said, apparently bored.

"He was in a highly emotional state?"

"Yes. He was."

"And he was a suspect at that time, wasn't he?"

"Everyone was a suspect at that time," Bolinger said disdainfully. "At that time we had no clue as to who killed the girl. You were a suspect at that time, Ms. Jordan."

Casey looked to the judge.

"Detective . . . ," Rawlins said in a warning tone.

"So," Casey said after the appropriate pause, "Mr. Sales was in a highly emotional state. He was violent, and at that time, he was your best suspect."

"I don't know about—"

"He was your best suspect at the time!" Casey cried. "Come on, Detective. Let's not play games with the jury. At that time, he was your best suspect, wasn't he?"

"Maybe at that time. He was the first person connected with her on the scene."

"Yes, he was. And so then you took him into the police station, didn't you?"

"Yes, to talk."

"Did you handcuff him?"

"Yes."

"Did you chain him to the floor?"

"That's standard procedure."

"So you chained him to the floor, didn't you?"

"Yeah," Bolinger said wearily.

Casey now marched back to her table and lifted a stack of papers in front of Patti Dunleavy, who was looking on with widened eyes. "But in all these police reports, I see that in all your investigation, your thorough investigation, that Mr. Sales's clothes were not checked for blood, were they?"

"I could see that he didn't have blood on him," Bolinger said irately. "I have eyes."

"You could see?"

"Yes."

"Detective, you know as well as I do that oftentimes blood is present that cannot be seen, isn't that true?"

"It's possible," he said after a pause.

"Yes, and you certainly examined my client's clothes in a lab, didn't you?"

"Yes."

"And you found no blood on my client's clothes, did you, Detective?"

"No, not on his clothes. Just on her underwear."

"Your Honor!" Casey bellowed in disgust.

"Detective." Rawlins glared. "If you do anything but

answer Ms. Jordan's questions, I can have you locked up for contempt and I'll do it. Do I make myself clear?"

"Yes," Bolinger muttered.

"The jury is to disregard the detective's remark," Rawlins said. "It will be struck from the record."

Casey took a deep breath and huffed out through her nose. Bolinger had broken her momentum, exactly what he wanted to do.

"You've been a police officer how long, Detective?" she asked.

"Twenty-seven years."

"And in your experience, how many times did you fail to examine the clothes of a murder suspect?"

"I can't examine someone's clothes without a warrant," Bolinger said craftily.

"But, Detective, you searched Mr. Sales's home and his vehicle, isn't that true?"

"Yes."

"Because he let you. He signed a consent waiver, isn't that true, too?"

"Yes."

"But you never asked to examine his clothes, isn't that right?"

"Correct."

"And you never took nail clippings from Mr. Sales, isn't that true as well?"

"Yes."

"Because you made a decision that day that Mr. Sales wasn't the killer, isn't that right, Sergeant Bolinger?"

"Yes," he said defiantly. "I had a gut feeling that he wasn't the killer."

"So, acting on that gut feeling, you neglected your duty as an investigating officer, didn't you?"

"I never neglected my duty," Bolinger growled.

"Isn't your duty to be thorough?"

"Yes."

"But you made a final judgment on who was innocent and who was guilty, didn't you?"

"I guess I did," Bolinger said, again defiant.

"But isn't your job to collect the evidence, Detective?"

"Yes, that's my job."

"In fact, it is the jury's job to interpret the evidence, isn't it?"

"Yes."

"Yes, it is. And the jury doesn't know if Mr. Sales had blood underneath his fingernails, do they?"

"No."

"And the jury doesn't know if there were traces of blood on Mr. Sales's clothes, do they?"

"No."

"No, they don't because you didn't do your job!" Casey roared. "You made yourself the jury, didn't you, Detective?"

"No, that's ridiculous."

"What's ridiculous," Casey said, at a boil, "is that you made a decision not to gather all the evidence from your best suspect at the time, and now I have to live with that, my client has to live with that, and this jury has to live with that!"

"Objection, Your Honor," Hopewood complained. "Counsel is simply badgering the witness."

"Sustained," Rawlins said. "Are those all the questions you have for the witness, Ms. Jordan?"

Casey didn't answer. She went back to her table and her notes. She wanted the jury to absorb what she'd just done. She wanted them to consider the detective figuratively lying on the floor, gasping for air, before she stepped on his neck. She couldn't help the surge of pride she felt when Lipton looked at her with admiration. He nearly smiled.

"I'm sorry, Your Honor," she said, turning back suddenly. "I have a few more questions for the detective."

"Then go on," Rawlins told her.

Casey approached the jury and saw that they were right there with her, following her every move. When she had joined them in front of their box, she smiled grimly at them before turning back toward Bolinger. In a clear voice she said, "We've heard the evidence you have against Professor Lipton, Sergeant. But we haven't heard about the evidence you don't have. I'd like to ask you about that . . ."

Bolinger glared at her with a malicious frown.

"You don't have any of my client's fingerprints at the scene of the crime, do you, Detective?"

"No."

"And you don't have the weapon used to commit the crime against Miss Sales, with my client's fingerprints on it, do you?"

"No, we don't," Bolinger said stoically.

"You haven't even found the weapon, have you?"

"No."

"In fact, you don't have any physical evidence linking my client to the scene of the crime, do you?"

"He was there," Bolinger said triumphantly. "He hit that woman's car when he was racing to get away."

"Oh, he was there," Casey said, moving toward the witness now. "That's true. He went there for a consensual tryst, saw the girl's body, and fled in an extremely disturbed state of mind. But what I'm saying is, you don't know for a fact if he was inside that living room where the crime was committed, do you?"

Bolinger hesitated, looked at Rawlins, then said, "No, not for a fact."

"Because there wasn't one shred of physical evidence to prove that he was in there, isn't that true?"

"He didn't leave anything in the living room," Bolinger cunningly replied, glancing furtively at Rawlins to see if he had incurred any more wrath.

"In fact, you don't even have a motive, do you, Detective?" Casey continued without pause. "You never, in everything you told us today, told the jury why Professor Lipton would want to kill Miss Sales, did you?"

"No, but I don't always know the motive of people's crimes," he said.

"But in your experience as a policeman, isn't it true that most people commit crimes for a reason?"

"Sometimes, I guess mostly they do, yes."

"Robbers rob for the money, don't they?"

"Yes."

"Yes, and most people who are killed are killed for a reason, like jealousy or revenge or unrequited love, isn't that true?"

"Yes, I suppose."

"But none of those applies to Professor Lipton," Casey said incredulously. "He had no reason to harm Miss Sales in any way, did he?"

"I don't know."

"Well, you haven't been able to find any reason in your year-long investigation of this case, have you?"

"No," Bolinger said defiantly.

"Detective, I'm sorry, but you just told us you have no fingerprints, no weapon, and no other solid evidence linking my client to the exact scene of the crime. You haven't given us any explanation as to why my client would have committed the crime. And, by your own admission, we know you conducted a sloppy, erroneous investigation, allowing potentially vital information to go uncollected because in your judgment, Mr. Sales wasn't the killer. With that set of facts, can you tell me what the hell we're even doing here?"

"Objection!" Hopewood roared.

"Sustained!" Rawlins said with a rap of his gavel.

"I have nothing more for this man, Your Honor," Casey said with disgust.

Rawlins called an adjournment for lunch. Casey had no appetite. Sales was next.

CHAPTER 13

Like many people Casey had seen, Donald Sales, while imposing and impressive in everyday life, was ill at ease on the witness stand. She liked it that way.

"Please tell us, Mr. Sales," Hopewood began after laying a foundation explaining to the jury that Sales was the victim's father, "the nature of your daughter's relationship with Professor Lipton."

"Objection!" Casey roared, jumping to her feet. "Calls for the witness to speculate on state of mind."

Rawlins twisted his mouth and sighed. "Sustained."

"Let me rephrase the question," Hopewood said patiently. "Please tell us what your daughter told you about the nature of her relationship with Professor Lipton."

"She was scared to death of him, she—"

"Objection! Hearsay, Your Honor! The witness has no idea what the actual emotional state of his daughter was." Casey knew it was a minor technicality, but she wanted to badger Sales as much as she could within the confines of the law.

Rawlins pursed his lips but told Sales, "Please limit

your testimony to the things she said to you, Mr. Sales. Although, as a father, I'm sure you think you know how your daughter felt, it's not legally acceptable for you to speculate in that way."

"She told me she was scared to death of him," Sales said, staring hatefully at Casey as he did so.

"Objection! Hearsay!" Casey barked as she stood.

"Now," Rawlins said, pointing his gavel at Casey, "that's enough, Ms. Jordan."

"It's hearsay, Your Honor," she said stubbornly.

"It is allowable hearsay under the state-of-mind exception to the rule, as you damn well know, young lady!" Rawlins bawled. "Now sit down!"

"But her fear is irrelevant!" Casey protested. She knew better than to back down to any judge. Rawlins might despise her personally, but she would be damned if he wasn't going to respect her.

"I'm allowing it." Rawlins scowled. "Overruled!"

"She told me he gave her the creeps," Sales added defiantly.

"Did your daughter at any time indicate to you that she had any kind of relationship with Professor Lipton beyond the normal student-teacher relationship?" Hopewood asked.

"Objection, hearsay," Casey said.

"Overruled."

"No," Sales scoffed.

"Did your daughter say why she was afraid of Professor Lipton?" Hopewood asked.

"She thought he—"

"Objection!"

"Overruled," Rawlins said tiredly. "The jury has the right to know what gave rise to the girl's state of mind."

"She told me the way he looked at her made her uncomfortable and that when she had gone to see him for something about the class that he asked her out and talked to her in a way that was inappropriate, that he alluded to sexual things . . ."

Hopewood paused and looked knowingly at the jury before saying, "Did you talk to your daughter on the day she was killed?"

"I did."

"And can you tell us about that conversation?"

"We were supposed to have dinner together that night. I was going to pick her up—"

"Objection, the witness is not responding to the question," Casey said.

"Overruled."

Sales continued, "She said she was going to study all day for her final in a criminal law class."

"Professor Lipton's class?"

"Objection, Your Honor," Casey cried. "The class she was studying for is totally irrelevant."

"Overruled."

"Yes, it was his class . . . She asked me"—Sales stopped, choked on his words, then mastered his emotions and continued—"she asked me to take a look around the house before I came in."

"Objection!" Casey practically howled.

"Overruled."

"She said she felt like someone had been watching her through the windows sometimes and that the neighbor's dog had been barking the past few nights and that it never did that unless someone was around. She—"

"Objection."

"Overruled."

"She told me she'd feel safer if I looked around . . ."

Sales's face was contorted now in pain. His eyes welled with tears, but none spilled down his face. He kept his chin held high but avoided looking at the jury. Casey knew it was a good move by Hopewood to put him up there. But then, Hopewood probably didn't know what she had coming.

"But when I got there, the police were already there . . . and I saw her . . ." Sales dropped his face into his hands. His broad shoulders shook quietly.

"He killed her," Sales sobbed. "He killed her."

Casey quickly assessed the jury. She could see that they felt his pain. She knew better than to object now.

"I'm sorry, Mr. Sales," Hopewood said compassionately. "That's all."

"Do you wish to cross-examine the witness, Ms. Jordan?" Rawlins said with as much distaste as he could muster.

"I do," Casey said. She sat waiting patiently for the emotions in the room to ebb.

"Well, Ms. Jordan," Rawlins said. "We're waiting."

Casey slowly rose and approached the father. He glared back at her with unadulterated malice. She positioned herself between the jury and Sales so that they, too, could feel the full effect of his hateful stare.

"You're a violent man, aren't you, Mr. Sales?" she said abruptly.

"No, I'm not."

"But you have been arrested on assault charges, isn't that true?"

"Yes."

"And you've been arrested for disorderly conduct, isn't that right?"

"A long time ago, yes."

"Yes, and you attacked a police officer during that incident the same way you attacked an officer the day your daughter was killed, isn't that true?"

"I wouldn't say I attacked anyone the day Marcia was murdered. I don't really remember."

"But you've seen the police reports that say you struck an officer?"

"Yes," Sales said solemnly, nodding his large head.

"You've attacked a lot of people in your day, Mr. Sales."

"Objection," Hopewood cried. "Badgering the witness."

"Sustained."

"So you are violent, aren't you?"

"You say so."

"Yes, I do," Casey quipped. "And you have a history of mental illness as well, isn't that right, Mr. Sales?"

Sales stared at her hard before answering.

"When I got back from Vietnam I had some problems," he said.

"Mental problems?"

"You could say that."

"In fact, you suffer from post-traumatic stress disorder, don't you, Mr. Sales?"

"That's what they called it. But that was a long time ago. I've been fine for a long time."

"Really?" Casey said skeptically. "You don't attribute your violent behavior to your mental condition?"

"No," he said, spitting the word at her.

"But PTSD is something that can recur at any time," Casey said. "In fact, that's one of the characteristics of the disorder, isn't it? In fact, don't people who suffer from PTSD often lapse into fits of inexplicable violence?"

"Objection," Hopewood said. "Mr. Sales is not qualified as an expert in that area."

"Sustained. You will limit the scope of your questions to those the witness is qualified to answer, Ms. Jordan."

Casey paid no outward attention to the judge. She simply stared right back at Sales without blinking, then abruptly switched tracks. "You didn't like for your daughter to have boyfriends, did you, Mr. Sales?"

"Objection," Hopewood said. "Marcia Sales's boyfriends are irrelevant. The presumption that Professor Lipton fit that description is just that, a presumption."

"I'm allowing it," Rawlins said.

"He wasn't her boyfriend, you . . ." Sales muttered a rancid word under his breath. Casey looked pointedly at Rawlins. The judge's pride in having total control of the courtroom superseded even his animosity toward her.

"You will answer the questions, Mr. Sales," he said firmly. "And I've already told you that I will not allow another outburst from you in my courtroom."

"You didn't want her to have boyfriends, did you?" Casey repeated.

"I didn't care," Sales muttered sullenly.

"Oh no?" Casey said, raising one eyebrow. "But you didn't like Professor Lipton, did you?"

"No."

"In fact, you hated him, didn't you?"

"Of course," Sales sneered.

"And isn't it true that you hated your daughter's last boyfriend as well?"

"No."

"No? I'm referring to Frank Castle. Isn't it true that

you attacked Mr. Castle one night when you found him alone with your daughter in her apartment?"

"I didn't attack him. We got into it a little, but I didn't attack him," Sales said.

"Because isn't it true that you used to sneak around your daughter's apartment looking through her windows at night?"

"I never did that, not like that, no."

"No? But you're familiar with Mr. Castle's deposition to the contrary, aren't you?"

"I saw what he said," Sales said contemptuously. "He was mad when Marcia dumped him. You can't believe what he says. Maybe he was scared because I kept an eye on him."

"Yes, you did," Casey said triumphantly. "You kept an eye on him and he was afraid. And the same was true with your daughter, wasn't it? You kept an eye on her, too, and she was afraid, wasn't she?"

"No. She was not. She was never afraid of me."

Casey looked at him with disbelief, then said, "Isn't it true that on the night you attacked Mr. Castle at your daughter's apartment that you threatened her as well?"

"That's a lie!"

"You were mad, isn't that true?" Casey spoke swiftly now, increasing the pace of the examination, hurrying him along.

"Yes, I was mad."

"In fact, you were enraged because you didn't want her to have a boyfriend, isn't that right?"

"That's not true. It was him I didn't like. He was a little, lying, conniving smart-ass."

"Because he tried to take her away from you, isn't that true?"

"No. He, he was a bad kid, too smart for his own good."

"You don't like smart people do you, Mr. Sales? People like Frank Castle and Professor Lipton, they threaten you, isn't that right?"

"No. They don't threaten me."

"But you don't like them."

"Them, those two I don't like, no."

"So you found your daughter and Mr. Castle alone in her apartment at school," Casey said, pulling up short with her pace, getting him off balance before the final push. "There they were, on the couch. They were kissing and fondling each other, and you burst in on them uninvited. You were enraged at him, and you were enraged at her, too, weren't you, Mr. Sales?"

"No."

"Didn't you say, in your rage"—here Casey paused dramatically, returned to her table, and picked up Castle's deposition, flipping the pages and reading to give it even more credibility with the jury—"after you shoved Frank Castle to the floor, didn't you in your rage tell her that if she didn't stop seeing him that you would kill her?"

Casey glanced at the jury and watched her arrow hit home.

"I never would have hurt my daughter," Sales growled. "Never."

"But you said you would kill her, didn't you? Didn't you?" she said quickly.

Sales hesitated too long before answering, "No."

Casey let the silence reign. She could feel the jury's eyes boring into Sales.

"Mr. Sales, let me remind you that you are under oath," Casey said venomously.

"Objection, Your Honor!" Hopewood barked. "Counsel is badgering the witness. The question has been asked and answered."

"Sustained. Move on, Ms. Jordan," Rawlins told her.

Casey paused, again using the silence and allowing the intensity to build before she said clearly, "Mr. Sales, did you ever have sex with your daughter?"

Sales's face went crimson with rage and he sprang from his seat, cursing Casey in every way he knew how. His own cries were nearly lost in the din of Hopewood screaming his objections and Rawlins bawling for order. The entire courtroom, right down to the jury, had erupted.

CHAPTER 14

Lipton's quiet little chuckle spilled into the sterile room and Casey jerked around in her seat. She was momentarily gripped with panic, so strange was the sound. She was alone with Lipton after having sent Patti for her car while she debriefed the professor before the weekend.

"It was a masterpiece, my dear," Lipton chortled as he strode into the tiny room. "A masterpiece."

Casey only looked back down at her notes and nodded. Whereas before she had felt pride in Lipton's praise, she now felt strangely ashamed. She was a good lawyer, but there was no lasting pleasure in tearing someone apart on the witness stand.

Lipton sat down across from her and folded his long hands neatly on the battered table. He was beaming.

"I saw it in their faces," he said, referring to the jury. "They believe in you. You turned them. It was a brilliant stroke, asking if he'd ever had sex with her. It was even better when Rawlins instructed them to strike it from their minds, a perfect punctuation. I thought he was going to boil over . . ."

"Well, he did boil over," she told him.

"But you go for the jugular," Lipton said excitedly. "Really. It was brilliant, and you know I'm not one for flattery. It's your gift. I said so from the start. I daresay you could win a pardon for even the deadliest criminal . . ."

Casey looked up at him. His delight in her skills seemed inappropriate.

"A pardon suggests a level of guilt that requires forgiveness," she said solemnly.

Lipton smiled at her in a funny way before saying, "I think your skills go beyond guilt and innocence. I think your skills supersede justice . . ."

Casey frowned.

"It's true. If I were guilty of killing the girl," he continued, still smiling enigmatically, "I would still be set free, therefore pardoned by the judicial system. I see that look on your face. But have no fear. I am as innocent as a . . . as a lamb . . ."

His words brought little comfort, but maybe it was her own nagging sense of guilt that was weighing Casey down. Not that she had to feel guilty. She knew dozens of defense lawyers who didn't feel a thing when they ripped someone apart on the stand. She had had an arguable right to pose her final question to Sales. Based on the theory of their defense, Sales was jealous of anyone who enjoyed his daughter's attentions. The possibility of his having a relationship that went beyond the normal paternal affections was a logical conclusion. That was how she had argued her position to Rawlins when he sternly ordered her to approach the bench for a conference. To ask such a question for the sole purpose of fostering the jury's prejudice toward the witness was unethical. But, based on her theory, Casey had a legitimate reason to ask it; therefore it was ethical.

"You still have my computer?" Lipton asked abruptly.

"Of course."

"Good," Lipton said softly. "I want you to deliver it to the office of Simon Huff."

"Simon Huff?" Casey asked, confused. Huff was the kind of lawyer who offered cash to potential clients in his TV ads.

"He's handling my civil action against the county for failing to adequately protect me when I was shot," Lipton said with a sniff. "I want him to have the computer and I want you to deliver it over the weekend. The trial will be over by the middle of next week, and I want it in his hands."

Casey stopped herself from asking why. It was none of her business. Whatever was on the computer was obviously personal and private.

"Of course," she said. "I'll have Patti deliver it first thing Monday morning."

"Very good," Lipton said coolly.

Then, in a more pleasant tone, Lipton asked, "Do you really think Castle will make a good witness?" He was intimately familiar with the old boyfriend's deposition but had never actually seen him.

"I said I did," Casey said. "He's afraid of Sales, and I think that will come out on the stand. He's a smart kid, and credible. I think when they hear his version of what happened that night, they'll believe him."

"It was brilliant to find him!" Lipton exclaimed. "Sales will be undermined completely."

"Yes," Casey replied with a hesitant nod, "he will."

*   *   *

First thing Monday morning, Frank Castle did more than undermine Donald Sales. He undermined his daughter. In a quiet, sincere voice, Castle described the girl as a loner, someone with few social contacts and those few nothing more than casual. From his description, it was quite likely that Marcia Sales could have had an affair with her professor without anyone knowing.

When Hopewood cross-examined the young student, he did a poor job. Castle was too smart and too well prepared by Casey to be baited by the rotund prosecutor. He simply stared with his big, baleful brown eyes at the prosecutor's implied insults, and Hopewood came across as a bully. Neither did the jury miss the unspoken dynamics between Sales and Castle. The younger man couldn't contain an occasional furtive glance at the father. Sales, for his part, never took his eyes off the tall, thin Ph.D. student, and his cold hatred was as plain to the jury as if it had been printed on a billboard.

After Castle, Casey called a retired Dallas homicide detective as an expert witness to further emphasize what she considered to be Bolinger's error in not thoroughly investigating Sales. Next was a patrolman who reluctantly testified as to Sales's maniacal state at the scene of the crime, as well as a second officer who had arrested Sales years before for brutally assaulting another man in a bar fight.

On Tuesday, she called the VA psychiatrist who had treated Sales, an expert on PTSD who testified as to the volatile and violent nature of the disorder and how it could lie dormant for years only to spring suddenly into a critical state. Casey's final witness was Curtis Mulholland, a distinguished-looking former DA from San Antonio. While Mulholland couldn't express an opinion on this specific case, Casey was able to re-create a matching hypothetical case for him to tear down. In the final minutes of his testimony, the former DA stated his own unwillingness to proceed in a case in which there were so many unanswered questions about a second likely suspect.

"Mr. Mulholland," Casey said in conclusion, "would you tell the jury why you would not want to proceed in such a case?"

"I think," Mulholland said in his low, booming voice, "that given the circumstances, it would be impossible to prove such a case beyond a reasonable doubt . . ."

"Objection!" cried the incensed Hopewood.

"Sustained," Rawlins barked angrily. Only procedural requirements had persuaded him to allow another DA into his courtroom as an expert witness. "The jury will disregard the witness's last statement!"

"I have no more questions, Your Honor," Casey said.

Rawlins banged his gavel. "Court will adjourn for lunch. We'll hear final arguments at one-thirty."

Hopewood's close was like a bad sermon. He meandered endlessly. Over and over, he rehashed his argument in barely disguised alterations, losing the jury halfway through. For her part, Casey was crisp and to the point. She bludgeoned the prosecution for its lack of concrete evidence against Lipton and chastised the police for letting the best suspect go uninvestigated.

"Beyond a reasonable doubt?" she scoffed, recalling her final witness's words to their minds. "Ladies and gentlemen, as you have seen, the doubts in this case are so numerous and so large that I'm sure you feel almost as indignant as I do that Professor Lipton was even brought to trial. This case has been a misguided sham and a travesty, and I am confident that you will do the right thing by exonerating Professor Lipton."

Rawlins gave a creditable set of instructions to the jury, and they left the courtroom for deliberations. Lipton excused himself to use the bathroom, leaving Casey alone with Patti in their small consultation room.

"This is the worst part," she told her understudy.

"I know," Patti said. "But you pretty much always win."

Casey rapped her knuckles lightly on the wooden table. "Let's hope. You never know with a jury."

"But you rarely lose," Patti reminded her. She had cut her strawberry-blond hair blunt just above her collar, and the glasses she wore were austere but did very little to hide either her bubbling youth or her unmitigated admiration of Casey.

"No, you're right," Casey admitted flatly, staring aimlessly into her jumble of notes. "I rarely lose . . ."

The jury was back in just under an hour, a good sign. Lipton stood by Casey's side as they handed their verdict to the bailiff, who in turn delivered it to the judge. Casey felt the blood pound in her heart. She was lightheaded. It was always the same. Rawlins frowned and nodded his head. As the bailiff crossed the court, Lipton dipped his head down toward Casey until his lips lightly brushed her ear.

With a shiver, she heard his words just as the judge directed the foreman of the jury to read their verdict on the count of first-degree murder.

Lipton's voice was charged with delight, his words were sickeningly sweet. "I really killed her."

Casey's mind swam. Shock and horror contorted her face. She looked at Lipton. His incandescent eyes were wild with amusement. A greedy smirk shone from his handsome face.

"We find the defendant, Eric Lipton"—uncomfortable with being the focus of attention, the middle-aged foreman's voice quavered—"not guilty."

Patti grabbed Casey, hugging her with delight. In the confusion, Casey gently separated herself from the younger lawyer and stood alone in a kind of personal fog. From the bench, Rawlins shot her a begrudging frown, then in a flourish of robes, he was gone. She looked to Hopewood.

The DA picked up his papers with a sour look and, without acknowledgment of any kind, left the courtroom, surrounded by a small pack of sympathetic underlings. Only Donald Sales gave Casey her due. She caught his eye from across the room. In the row of seats immediately behind the prosecutor's table, he remained standing like a great, dark rock in the ebbing sea of spectators. His pale green eyes, so full of loathing, made her start. Still, she seemed unable to look away, and for several moments his malice was something she could actually feel pressing against her face.

When she turned away, the professor was gone. There was only one last glimpse of his wavy hair and his orange prison suit as he passed through the side door between two guards like a moving flame. There were no congratulations, no thanks, only the resonating words from his diabolical confession, which she prayed was nothing more than a demented joke.

CHAPTER 15

Bob Bolinger farmed out two burglaries, an assault, and an arson before he dug into some paperwork on a fifteen-year-old kid who'd been killed execution-style in what appeared to be a drug deal gone bad. It was an uninspiring case because the killer was a kid himself and wouldn't do more than a few years in juvenile lockup before he was out doing it again. He closed the door, opened the window, and smoked his way through it. By the time he was finished, the big clock on the squad room wall told him it was almost time for lunch.

Bolinger spotted Farnhorst at a desk near the door and invited him for a hot dog on the street. It was a pleasant day outside, and armed with a couple of cans of Pepsi and their dogs, the two detectives found a bench in the green area across the street. The small park was milling with businesspeople who had the same idea.

"How's your boy?" Bolinger asked.

Farnhorst grinned widely and reeled off his sixteen-year-old's latest accomplishments on his way to the state shot put championship. By the time he finished, the only thing left of Bolinger's dog was a mustard skid on his chin.

"How about you, Bob?" Farnhorst asked.

Bolinger lit a cigarette and squinted through the smoke in the direction of the courthouse, where only yesterday Lipton had walked free.

After a pause during which he'd followed his sergeant's gaze, Farnhorst solemnly said, "You don't want to think about that shit, Bob. You gotta forget about it. You told me that same thing yourself. We set 'em up and the DA's gotta knock 'em down. Sometimes they get a strike, sometimes they roll a gutter ball."

Bolinger looked at Farnhorst, then back toward the courthouse before speaking. "I know that. I know what I'm supposed to do and what I'm supposed to think, but the more I try not to think about it, the more it's on my mind."

"But what can you do?"

Bolinger crushed out his smoke and slapped his hands on his knees, then rose from the bench.

"I can call Dean Wentworth."

"From the FBI?" Farnhorst asked, standing as well and jump-shooting his trash into the barrel at the other end of the bench.

"Yeah, I know Dean pretty well," Bolinger said. "The guys in Atlanta hit a wall. Their crime scene was as clean as ours. I spoke to my brother's brother-in-law this morning, and after what happened here, the DA in Atlanta told them to leave it alone. But the FBI, now they could do something about it . . ."

Farnhorst shook his head doubtfully and said, "With all those bank robberies in the news, I doubt they're gonna pull someone away to chase this. It was a loser. That's just the way it is. It happens. Come on, Bob, you gotta let it go. It ain't healthy."

Bolinger squinted up into Farnhorst's eyes and saw real concern. He smiled and patted the big man on the back.

"Don't worry about me," he said. "I don't have a bunch of kids like you. I need something to worry about . . . It keeps me going."

Dean Wentworth was the special agent in charge in the Austin FBI office. He was glad to hear from Bolinger and wanted to set up a game of golf, but when it came to tracking down evidence against Lipton, he politely declined.

"I just can't," Wentworth explained. "The one guy I had to spare was working on some local stuff up in Stratford on a deal where some salesman disappeared from a hotel. The killer didn't leave anything behind but a blood-soaked pillow. The dead guy's brother is Ron Tanner, the number three guy over at Treasury, and I got a request from up top to look into it. But now, even that's by the board, and if I do anything at all, I have to put someone back on that case. Really, Bob, I can't take on anything that's not priority one."

"But this is big," Bolinger argued. "Really big."

"Hell, Bob, I got a call from Washington on Tuesday," Wentworth said. "The goddamn vice president was watching CNN the night before he had a meeting with the director, and he asked specifically about these goddamn bank robberies. I can't spare a single man. Fact is, they're sending me six goddamn guys from D.C. to help out."

Bolinger thought for a moment, then broke the silence

by saying, "Dean, I need this . . . as a favor. I've never asked you a favor before."

Bolinger knew Dean knew what he was talking about. The FBI agent's wife had been dragged in one night for DUI, and Bob had quietly taken care of it. It was a big marker.

Wentworth emitted a bitter sigh into the phone and said, "You're right. I owe you. But I can't go chasing goddamn phantoms when every goddamn agent between here and Washington is wondering why I don't have these bank bandits locked up. Do you know what'll happen to me if those goddamn Texas Rangers get them before me? Can you say early retirement? Those big-hatted bastards are everywhere. They found that boxcar killer before me, and I had to go through hell with my back broke just to keep my goddamn job. I can't, Bob . . ."

Bolinger silently waited.

"Okay, listen," Wentworth said, "this is what I can do. You said you had a body with the same MO in Atlanta, right?"

"Yeah."

"Okay, I know Vittarelli, the number two guy in Atlanta. I'll call him and do everything I can to get him to put someone on it from Atlanta. Is that good?"

"That sounds good," Bolinger said. "I don't care where they're from. I'll help them out, too, calling around to the other cities where this guy's been doing his seminars. I know we'll find something, but I need a Fed to open the case and keep it alive. I appreciate it, Dean, I really do. I wouldn't ask you like this if it wasn't important."

"Yeah, well, if I can get them to do it, we're even, okay?"

"Okay," Bolinger said. "We're even."

*   *   *

Casey knew the letdown on the day after a big trial was as certain as a hangover the morning after a hard night of drinking. What she wasn't prepared for was the severity of the malaise. It began the moment her mind was sprung from an uncomfortable dream. She bolted upright in bed with a gasp. Taylor was tying his tie in the antique full-length mirror in the corner of the room. He looked her way only briefly before finishing the job and proceeding to his bureau, where he unloaded a stack of underwear and socks into a suitcase that lay across the arms of a high-backed chair.

"What are you doing?" she asked after she'd caught her breath.

"Getting dressed," he said indifferently.

Casey looked at the clock. It was early, just light. She remembered him coming in sometime late, very late. She'd been sleeping.

"You're packing," she said.

"That, too," he told her.

Casey felt a bolt of energy dance up her spine.

"Why?" she said, unable to hide the note of panic.

"Business."

"Where?" she asked, relieved and now angry with herself for the way she felt. If he was leaving her, why should she care? She'd come home after a grueling but successful trial, only to spend her evening with a book. He wasn't a real part of her life. If it wasn't evident before this trial, it certainly should be now.

"San Francisco," he answered.

Casey ran through the possibilities in her mind. There was an old flame of his in San Francisco, a society girl who fancied herself an artist. Taylor also owned a small ball-bearing factory outside the city. Why should she care what the trip was for?

"How long will you be gone?" she asked. She got out of bed and made her way toward the bathroom as if she didn't care.

"I'll be back Sunday night," he told her as she passed him.

"Business on the weekend?" she said.

He shrugged. "Some bankers from Hong Kong want to golf in Carmel."

Casey brushed her teeth, secretly watching him in the mirror. In her mind she knew it didn't matter. But a great fear had seized hold of her heart. She couldn't help it. If it didn't work, it would be a failure. She despised failures. She lived to win. She'd won him, and although in her mind she knew he wasn't worth winning, a sick but powerful part of her couldn't let go. Casey spit the paste into her sink and rinsed her mouth. She disappeared into her closet.

When she came out, Taylor was closing the suitcase. He looked up and saw her standing with one hand high on the wall and the other resting firmly on her milky-white hip. Her hair spilled down around her small, muscular shoulders in tangles of red. She wore nothing but white lace and heels, a spicy little setup he'd given her one Valentine's Day. It was something she rarely wore, maybe after some champagne and an evening of rubbing her foot up and down his leg underneath a particularly formal table.

Taylor looked at her hungrily and stopped right where he was. Without a word he undid the tie and began unbuttoning his shirt. He crossed the room and met her lips with his own. Without breaking the voracious kiss, he stripped himself naked and moved her hands toward his waist. When she found him, he emitted a guttural groan and began to grope her with adolescent desperation, finally lifting her off her feet and taking her across the room to their bed.

Ten minutes later, Taylor was back at the mirror adjusting his dark blue windowpane suit. Casey lay sprawled out on her back, watching him from the bed. When he was dressed, he picked up his suitcase and kissed her on the lips.

"That was good," he said.

"It was," she said, trying to believe. "We need to talk."

"Everything is fine." He flashed that million-dollar smile. "I'll be back before you know, but I've got to go now."

"All right."

"I'll call you," he said. "I've got to go or I'll miss my plane. I love you."

"I love you," she said.

Then he was gone. Casey lay alone for a long while, feeling worse about herself than she had the night before. Now, on top of feeling confused about the trial and her entire career, she felt cheap and suddenly helpless. Her life had been all about taking action, knowing what she wanted and getting it. She had gotten the husband she wanted. She won the cases she wanted. What was the saying?

"Be careful what you ask for," she whispered out loud, staring at a wedding picture that sat in a silver frame on the mantelpiece above the marble fireplace. "You might get it." Did she want him or didn't she? One thing she had to admit to herself as she dressed for work was that she didn't want to be cast aside. If it wasn't going to work between them, she'd be the one to pull the plug.

The garage underneath her office building was still nearly empty, but that was nothing unusual. Casey was usually one of the first people in the entire building to arrive. She parked in her spot, and as her heels clicked along on the concrete floor, echoing through the silence, she had an eerie feeling that someone else was in the garage. She spun around and blinked her eyes. Had she seen something move in the shadows behind an empty van? Or was it something within the van itself? She took two backward steps toward the elevator.

The van was tucked up near the bottom of the ramp on the opposite side of the garage. Casey looked around for someone else, but there was no one. Slowly, she edged toward the elevator without taking her eyes off the van. When she reached the elevator and the door opened with a quiet ding, she turned and entered the building, disgusted with her own squeamishness.

The day didn't get any better for her upstairs. The coffee wasn't made, Patti was late, and the first call of the morning was from Simon Huff. His voice was as loud as it was crass.

"Where the hell is my client's computer?" he demanded.

"What are you talking about?" Casey asked venomously.

"You know just what I'm talking about, lady!" Huff bellowed. "My next call is to the bar association. That computer is privileged material. This is more than unethical. It's criminal. What is this? Some kind of fucking shakedown?"

Casey was seething. "Don't you accuse me of being unethical!"

"If the shoe fits, wear it, hotshot," Huff remarked. "I want my client's computer back, and I want it back today! You got that?"

Casey slammed down the phone. When it rang back, she told Gina to say she wasn't available.

"Get Patti in here," she added.

Two minutes later her associate came in with an apprehensive frown.

"Did you deliver Professor Lipton's computer to Simon Huff's office?" Casey demanded.

"I . . ." Patti began hesitantly.

"My God, Patti," Casey growled. "How the hell could you? You think being a lawyer is cross-examining a witness? It goes a lot deeper than that, my friend. It's details! Attention to details! That means when you have something you have to do, something you said you were going to do, you do it. Is that so hard?" she demanded, her voice one note below a shriek.

"No," Patti said, keeping her chin high but visibly fighting back a wave of emotions. "I'll get it over there right away. I—"

"No you won't!" Casey cried. "You won't take it over there. I will. Your chance to do the job is by the board. That's all."

Patti stared back just as fiercely before walking out the door. Tony Cronic passed her in the hall and wondered at her unresponsiveness to his cheery hello.

"I wouldn't go in there if I were you," Gina warned him.

"Hey," Tony said to Gina with his easy, disarming

smile, "it's me." He opened the door and greeted Casey with more of the same.

"Hey," he said, dropping casually into a chair opposite her desk, "congratulations on the win."

Casey scowled at him. "I don't need your sarcasm today, Tony."

"What?" he said, opening his hands and raising both eyebrows in a gesture of peace. "I meant what I said. You won. Right? Or did they get it wrong on the news?"

Tears filmed Casey's eyes, and her mouth turned down. If Tony hadn't know her better he would have thought she was going to cry.

"Yes, I won the case," she said bitterly. "But I think I may have been wrong about him."

"Lipton?"

She bit her lower lip and nodded.

"You don't mean you think he did it?" Tony asked with a flippant laugh.

"He told me he did."

"What?" Tony was incredulous. "When?"

"Just before the jury read the verdict."

"You're kidding."

"I wish I were."

Tony looked at her in disbelief, then turned his eyes to the floor.

"I'm sick about it," Casey said.

"Maybe he was kidding," Tony suggested hopefully. "You said yourself that he was difficult the whole time you were getting ready for trial. Maybe it's just some kind of bizarre mind game."

"I hope that's what it was," she told him, "that he was kidding. He could do that. You're right. But I just don't know. What you said to me about tearing apart the father just sticks in my mind. I mean, Tony . . . I suggested he had an incestuous relationship with his dead daughter."

"You did your job," Tony reminded her. "Don't go soft on me now."

"I never had my client confess to the crime two seconds before the jury acquitted him," she said.

"But he might not have really done it," Tony pointed out. "Don't think about it, Casey. You never have before."

She looked wounded.

"I didn't mean it like that," he said quickly. "Come on, Casey. This is the reason you and I are defense lawyers. It's the process. Everyone needs an advocate and you gave him one. The state has to prove its case beyond a reasonable doubt, and if they can't, then the accused goes free. Our system would rather have ten guilty men go free than one innocent one be punished."

"I know that's what we both say." She nodded. "I know. That's what I keep telling myself, but it isn't helping. And to make it worse, I got a call from Simon Huff this morning accusing me of withholding Lipton's computer to blackmail him."

"Simon Huff?" Tony asked.

"He's representing Lipton in his tort action against the county for when he got shot," she told him. "The weekend before the trial ended, he asked me to have the computer delivered to Huff's office. I told Patti to do it, but she forgot. So Huff called me this morning and made some nasty accusations."

"What's on the computer anyway?" Tony asked, sitting up and forward in his chair.

"I have no idea," she said. "He said there were some embarrassing things on there, some hidden files with sexually explicit things or something like that."

"What were you doing with it?"

"First Michael Dove had it, and Lipton asked me to get it from him. He didn't want it to get into Hopewood's hands, and as we all know, the safest place for something like that is with your attorney. I didn't get into it with him, really. It was the last thing on my mind."

"Where is it?"

"The computer? It's right here," she said, reaching into a drawer and setting an IBM notebook on top of her desk.

Tony eyed it silently for a few moments.

"What?" Casey asked. "What are you thinking?"

"Nothing," he said. "I was just wondering what's in there."

"Whatever it is," she said coolly, "it's privileged information."

"I know," Tony said. "I know that. That doesn't mean we can't look at it. We're attorneys. It's not unethical to look . . ."

Casey stared at him for a moment, then looked down at the flat black rectangular machine.

"It's just that it might be something we'd regret letting go of," Tony said in a low, gentle tone.

Casey heard him, but she wondered if Tony wasn't simply looking for an edge the way he did with everything else, stocking away something that could later help him in his drive for fame and fortune. Her phone buzzed. She stabbed at a button and shut it off. Tony raised his eyebrows inquisitively.

"You're a character, Tony. You're a model of inconsistency. One minute you're for defending the rights of the accused, the next you're ready to violate a client's privacy."

"That's why you love me," he said, grinning as impishly as a man of his girth could. "Look, I just want to do the right thing."

"The right thing?" Casey asked dubiously. She stared intently at the computer.

After a while Tony said, "There was an attorney in upstate New York I read about in law school who represented a guy accused of killing several young girls. They pegged him for one particular murder and put him on trial even though they hadn't found the body. Everyone was pretty sure he did it . . ."

He looked at Casey's passive expression.

"Of course the guy was a defense lawyer, so he took the case. But during the trial the defendant told him the body was lying under a pile of leaves in some woods behind a cemetery. The lawyer went there and found the body. Now of course he never told anyone that he'd found the body, because the information was privileged."

Casey nodded that she understood.

"Wait," Tony said, raising his thick hand. "I'm not finished. A few days later there was an anonymous call to the police. They found the body, and the guy was convicted."

"Anonymous," Casey said, knowing the truth.

"Anonymous," he said with a shrug. "I'm not suggesting that you're going to turn what's on this computer over to the police. But you're done representing Lipton, and once it's gone, it's gone. You know, Casey, sometimes . . . sometimes you just have to do what you have to do."

Tony pressed his hands between his knees and said, "I could just, uh . . . just take a CD and do a disk image of the whole hard drive . . . so we have it if we ever need it. We don't even have to look at it."

"I don't know," she said with a sour look on her face.

She got up and looked at her watch, effectively ending the conversation.

Then, with a duplicitous look on her face, she said, "I've got a meeting with a woman who wants us to support her run for the assembly. I'll be back in an hour or so, and then I'm going to take the computer over to Huff's office."

"Okay," Tony said, but he remained seated as Casey reached for the door. "I'll see you later."

When Casey was gone, Tony took the computer from her desk, and whistling quietly, he headed for his own office.

CHAPTER 16

Two days after Dean Wentworth made the call to the Atlanta offices of the FBI, James Unger landed in Austin. Bolinger was waiting for him outside airport security. Bolinger had described himself over the phone as a short, middle-aged guy with a gray crew cut, then added that he also had a fairly athletic build. He stood there in his tweed jacket, scanning the passengers as they flowed past. When a dumpy-looking man with steel-rimmed glasses and longish hair approached him, Bolinger was sure it was for directions to the john. He was wrong.

"I'm Agent Unger," the man mumbled. "You must be Detective Bolinger."

Bolinger could see now that Unger's greasy dark hair was shot through with long gray strands. He was about thirty pounds overweight. At five feet ten, that was just enough to look bad without having anyone call him fat. His suit was a charcoal pinstripe, and he wore a black-and-gold herringbone tie. But as nice as the suit material was, it couldn't make up for the poor fit. Unger wore the sour look of a man who'd been mostly disappointed by life, and while he was only thirty-nine, he looked to be in his mid-forties.

"Thanks for coming," Bolinger said, shaking his hand and trying not to sound disappointed. "Luggage is this way."

"Thanks for picking me up like this," Unger said, but the words were without enthusiasm. He presumed his trip to Austin was nothing more than an opportunity to visit with an old college roommate who now owned a small car dealership. He hadn't been sent out on an important assignment in over ten years.

Unger's career had somehow drifted into a stagnant pool along the normal stream of advancement in the bureau. By his age, an agent expected at the very least to be in a nominal supervisory role. But Unger had never had that chance. He fancied a good part of his career's stagnation was due to his not kissing anyone's ass. But while that may have been true in part, the main reason he'd been passed over was that he had really never done anything to distinguish himself. And he knew he'd been labeled early on as a guy who really couldn't get the job done if it was a hot case. So it was only natural for him to presume that Bolinger's supposed serial killer case was shabby at best.

"I just thought I'd try to get this thing off on the right foot," Bolinger explained. "Dean Wentworth told me the bureau has an extra car for you at the office, so I knew someone had to come get you, that or take a cab. I really appreciate your coming out and opening this case."

"Doesn't sound like there's much of a case to open," he said sullenly. Bolinger looked at the agent with concern. Despite his appearance and his morose attitude, Bolinger tried to take comfort from the fact that Unger's cobalt eyes were alive with intelligence.

After the agent's big leather valise and his golf clubs were tucked snugly in the trunk of Bolinger's cruiser, they set off toward the city.

Unger turned the air-conditioning vents his way. "I've got an old college roommate who lives here," he said complacently. "He owns a Dodge dealership. He's getting us on at the West Lake Hills Country Club. You ever played there?"

"No," Bolinger said. "Can't say I have. Hey, Jim, you mind if I smoke? I'll open the window."

Unger glared at him indignantly and said, "Listen, Bob, I might as well get this out right up front. I can't stand smoke. It makes me sick, so I'd appreciate it if you wouldn't do it."

"Okay, no problem," Bolinger said, trying not to sound defensive. He stuffed the pack back into his coat pocket. "That's why I asked."

"And I might as well tell you right now that I don't like the name Jim," Unger continued. "My name is James. That's the name my mom gave me and she didn't like people calling me Jim or Jimmy, so I can't stand it myself."

Bolinger felt his face burning with an unusual blend of embarrassment and annoyance. He was about ready to turn the car around and ship this guy right back to Atlanta. But he needed an FBI agent to work with. Alone, he had no jurisdiction whatsoever to go poking around the country chasing down possible leads on a possible serial killer.

Which was what Bolinger thought Lipton was. The more he had thought about the Marcia Sales case, the more he was convinced that she was killed by someone who'd done that kind of thing before. No one, not even a guy as smart as Lipton, could go out and knock someone off that neatly, disemboweling the girl while at the same time not leaving any kind of clues on the scene. You couldn't do that the first time out. A crime scene like that was the result of years of practice. It also made sense that Lipton had never killed someone so close to home before.

The murder in Atlanta, for example, was something relatively safe. Lipton had had very limited contact with that girl, then two months later had returned to commit the crime. Looking back now, it made sense, but for the cops investigating her death, there would have been no logical connection to Lipton. Bolinger felt confident that as he worked his way backward through Lipton's travel schedule, he would find more bodies. But to do that he needed James Unger.

In an attempt to light some kind of fire under the agent, Bolinger spent the rest of his afternoon in the federal building going through the entire case with Unger. There were moments when he thought there was something in the agent's eyes that indicated at least a minimal level of interest. But that was only until he realized that Unger was spending more time looking longingly at the pre-crime photos of Marcia Sales than he was paying attention to what Bolinger was saying.

"Wasn't the lawyer in this case that woman I've seen on CNN? Wasn't it Casey Jordan?" Unger asked with a yawn along about four o'clock.

"Yeah, she represented Lipton," Bolinger told him.

"I remember seeing her on CNN a while ago during that state senator's trial. Remember? The guy who they said killed his mistress? Does she look as good in person as she does on TV?" Unger asked with a leering grin. "I wouldn't mind running into her while I'm in on this case. Is there any reason we might have to run into her?"

Bolinger looked away from the agent in an attempt to hide his disgust. "Maybe you'll run into her out on the golf course," he said. "She lives out at West Lake Hills."

Unger fingered the picture of Marcia Sales once more before saying, "Yeah, that makes sense. I guess that's where a bigshot attorney would live. She's kind of big time, huh?"

Unger spoke with the transparent bitterness that the disappointed typically show when referring to someone rich or famous.

"I guess as far as lawyers go, she is. Well," Bolinger said, gathering up his papers, "I've given you enough stuff for one day. I'm sure you're going to want to get to your hotel and get ready for tonight."

"What's tonight?"

"You said the car dealer was taking you to Sixth Street, right?"

"Yeah. Oh yeah. Yeah, that's a good idea," Unger said, standing and seeing Bolinger to the door. "I've got to check in with Dean, too. Um . . . so tomorrow, I kind of want to get a feel for this West Lake Hills course. How about we get things going around two in the afternoon?"

"So soon?" Bolinger said with a straight face. "Why not take the day to settle in and we can meet on Wednesday morning?"

"Oh, you sure you don't mind?" Unger actually smiled, glad to see that this guy got it.

"No. I'll get to work on this stuff," Bolinger said, patting his files. "What I would like you to do, though, is give my captain a call and tell him you'd like to have my help for the next week or so."

"Why?" Unger asked dubiously.

"You're the FBI," Bolinger said. "You'd be helping me out if you just call him and say you're working on a case that involves the Lipton, I mean, the Marcia Sales murder. If he gets a call from you, he'll let me work on this with you for a few days. That way I can get going on this and take some of the workload off your hands."

"I appreciate that, Bob," the agent said, unable to help feeling slightly suspicious. "I really do. That sounds great. I'll give him a call right now."

By the time Bolinger got back to the station, John Clark, the captain, was asking to see him. The detectives' squad room was in turmoil, but Bolinger was so tuned into getting clearance to work with the FBI that he paid no attention to all the hubbub. He marched straight through it all and into his boss's office. The captain was on the phone but held up one finger and got off after a few curt words to someone whose name Bolinger recognized as a local TV anchor.

"You want to help this guy from the FBI, Bob?" the captain asked skeptically. His face was hard and his bullet-shaped head was bald except for a few steely strands that traversed his flushed dome from ear to ear.

"Yeah," Bolinger said, then lied. "I told Dean Wentworth I'd help him out. He's got this one by himself. Dean's busy as all hell with that string of bank robberies."

The captain nodded grimly. "Well, you can give them some help, but not right away. I want you to get up to the campus and take a look at that kid who was killed. I want you to handle it."

"What kid?" Bolinger said, the energy in the squad room suddenly making sense.

"You didn't hear the call?" the captain asked. "It was the kid who testified in the Lipton case, the dead girl's old boyfriend. I'm surprised you didn't hear about it."

"I've been out all afternoon," Bolinger said hesitantly.

"Well, I'm on my way there," the captain said, rising from his chair and removing his hat from the coat rack behind his desk. "You might as well go over with me. You know the father, right? The father of the girl."

"Yeah," Bolinger said.

"I guess this kid made him look pretty bad at the trial?"

"He did."

"Well, you'll want to have a talk with him, I'm sure."

"Yes," Bolinger said. He was having a hard time believing what he'd just heard. If it was what it appeared to be, then it certainly shot his theory all to hell.

"Yes, I'll want to talk to him right away," he murmured.

CHAPTER 17

Bolinger rode with his captain through the area dominated by student housing. They passed within two blocks of where Marcia Sales was killed and as they did, the captain bitched about the pressure he was going to be under now that another student was dead. The body had been found by a guy walking his dog in Pease Park, a green area near the university that encompassed a portion of Shoal Creek. It was a favorite spot for runners. A dozen police cars, an ambulance, and a fire emergency vehicle lined a portion of the parkway that ran through the park. Bolinger hopped out and followed his boss over the guardrail. As they tromped down a slope into the afternoon shade of the woods, Bolinger paused to light a Winston.

Castle lay in a tangle of brush just to the other side of a hedge that bordered a blacktop path. His clouded eyes stared up at them and his mouth was agog; a nasty rope burn had scoured his neck. Bolinger removed his sunglasses and crouched down next to the student. Like Marcia Sales's, his torso had been split open like a pea pod.

The incision was neat and clean and his innards had been removed. The lab techs were carefully stepping around in the brush, and he heard someone say something about a coyote. Bolinger absently wondered how much of the evisceration was due to the killer and how much was due to any dogs or coyotes that might have gotten into it.

"Lipton," he murmered.

"What's that, Bob?" the captain said, leaning over him.

Bolinger looked up with the cigarette hanging from his lips. "I said 'Lipton.' He did this."

The captain's face clouded over. Bolinger was his best homicide man, maybe the best he'd ever seen. But he was also a hardheaded mule, a man who had a difficult time admitting when he was wrong.

"I want you to look into the father, Bob," he said firmly. "I know how you feel about your instincts. I respect that as much as anyone . . . but I want you to check him out. Keep an open mind. Can you do that?"

Bolinger looked past his boss at a young woman who was sliding what looked like a kidney into a cellophane bag.

"Yeah," he said as he rose to his feet. "I can do that."

Back at the station, Bolinger let the captain out at the curb.

"You going out there now?" he asked.

"Yeah," Bolinger answered.

"You'll take someone with you, Bob?" the captain said, leaning into the car through the window. It was more than a suggestion.

"Okay," Bolinger said.

"Good." The captain rapped twice on the roof of the cruiser with his knuckles. "Let me know what you turn up. I'll be here all night."

Bolinger paged up Farnhorst, who had been questioning a barmaid down on Sixth Street about a knifing on Saturday night.

"But I'm having a sandwich right now," he admitted.

"I'll swing by and get you," Bolinger said.

On the ride out to Sales's place, Bolinger filled in Farnhorst on what had happened.

"My gut tells me it's Lipton," he concluded.

Farnhorst nodded but was noncommittal, and that made Bolinger wonder. He knew better than the captain about his own propensity to be pigheaded. Was he being that way now? They pulled into Sales's dirt drive just as the sun was dipping below the rim of the western hills. It was a perfect crimson orb. With it went the warmth of the day, and Bolinger rolled up his window before he got out.

Together they mounted Sales's porch. The creak of old wood called out amid the din of ten thousand night insects. The tranquil setting was strangely familiar.

"Bob," Farnhorst said in an alarmed tone, "look."

As Farnhorst drew his gun, Bolinger looked down on the porch. There was a spattered line of blood he hadn't noticed that started at the bottom step and ended at the front door. Bolinger knelt down and touched it with the tips of his first two fingers. It was still greasy and moist.

"It's not too old," he said quietly. He looked at Farnhorst's gun but didn't draw his own. Instead he stood and hammered on the door. There were no lights on, and the new dusk made it quite dark inside the cabin. Through the front window, he could see a large form passing quickly through the gloom. The porch light went on suddenly, and Farnhorst stepped back into the shadows with his gun raised. Bolinger stepped aside as well. The door swung slowly open, spilling light into the cabin through the screen. There was no one in sight.

"Don," Bolinger cried out, "it's Bob Bolinger. We need to talk to you."

There was some shuffling inside the cabin, and suddenly Sales appeared in the doorway.

"What do you want?" Sales demanded in a tone that was sullen and much harsher than Bolinger had grown used to over the past year. His expression was hard to read through the screen, but Bolinger could hear the tension in his voice.

"Put the gun down," Farnhorst commanded in a loud booming voice that seemed almost obscene on such a peaceful night. Sales had a pistol in his hand, and although his arm hung straight down with the gun pointed at the floor, it made Bolinger swallow hard.

"You put yours down then." Sales glowered. "I don't need someone pointing a gun at me in the doorway of my own house."

"Put it down," Bolinger gently told his partner. "We need to talk to you, Don."

"Talk," Sales said. Some of the tension left his voice at the sight of Farnhorst's weapon by his side.

"We want you to come downtown with us," Bolinger said. "Will you do that?"

"Why?" Sales asked. "What's the problem? I didn't do anything."

"I know, Don," Bolinger said. "But Frank Castle was killed last night. Someone cut him open."

Sales stared blankly at the detective. He sighed resignedly and said, "Let me get my coat."

Without waiting for a reply, Sales turned back into the house, then emerged a minute later emptyhanded, wear-

ing a black suede jacket and a matching cowboy hat.
Farnhorst kept his gun ready, and when Bolinger asked
about the blood on the porch, he tightened his grip. But
Sales only laughed at them and held up his left hand.
There was a blood-soaked bandage wrapped tightly
around his index finger.

"Cut it to the bone," he explained. His mouth was
twisted somewhere between a grimace and a smile. Then,
pointing to the small shop on the side of the cabin, he
continued, "Band saw."

The two detectives nodded silently and followed Sales
across the dusty front yard. They piled into their car just
as the headlights from his pickup cut into the coming
night. Sales waited until they got turned around, then followed the police cruiser as it snaked its way to the main
road.

"I didn't like that gun," Farnhorst complained.

"Man has a right to protect his own house," Bolinger
pointed out. The lighter popped out on the dash, and after
removing it he touched off the Winston that dangled from
his mouth.

They hadn't been driving for more than three minutes
before Bolinger, who had been keeping a casual eye on
Sales in the rearview mirror, saw the dome light illumi-
nate the truck's cab. Bolinger's instincts told him it meant
something. When the light went off, however, he relaxed.
But two minutes later, Farnhorst heard him utter the
words "Oh, shit."

"What's the problem?" Farnhorst asked, but before
Bolinger even answered, Farnhorst was thrown into his
door when the sergeant slammed on the brakes and
flipped the wheel, skidding around until they were facing
in the opposite direction.

"There he goes," Bolinger muttered as he hit the gas. He slammed the wheel with the palm of his hand. "Shit!"

The two grim-faced cops wove in and out of the thin traffic. Sales was driving like a maniac, passing cars on double yellow lines and narrowly avoiding the oncoming traffic. Bolinger flicked on his lights and the siren, which helped clear the traffic.

"Hang on!" he shouted as the cruiser mounted a hilltop and took to the air momentarily before crashing back to the pavement. Sales was already at the bottom of the hill and had shot around a wooded bend out of sight. When Bolinger rounded the corner, he cursed out loud.

"Son of a bitch!"

There was Sales's truck, driven right off the road and stopped just this side of the trees in some knee-deep grass. Sales shot out of the truck with a bundle under one arm and a rifle he'd wrenched from the rack behind the seat. Farnhorst rolled down his window on the approach and brandished his gun; he screamed for Sales to freeze. Sales never broke stride. Just before he hit the trees, Farnhorst began to fire. Bolinger jammed on the brakes, throwing his partner into the dash.

"Goddamn!" Bolinger cried. "What the hell are you doing?"

"Son of a bitch is gonna get away, Bob!" Farnhorst shouted. He jumped from the car, gun in hand, but pulled up beside the pickup and turned to face his sergeant. The truck's engine was still running. Country music spilled from the cab into the dusk. Bolinger got out of the car and met Farnhorst's eyes with a cold, hard stare.

"You know better than that," he told Farnhorst in reference to the gunfire. Bolinger waded through the grass, already wet with dew. Farnhorst pursed his lips. He did know better.

"Should we try to follow him?" Farnhorst asked, his gaze following the beam of the headlights where they pierced the darkness of the woods.

Bolinger wore a grim frown. "You or I could follow him for a year and we wouldn't get any closer than we are right now."

He met Farnhorst's puzzled look and explained, "The man lives in these hills. He lives in them. He hunts in them. He fishes in them. I've heard him talk about getting back in these hills hunting by himself and not coming home for a week at a time. No, we won't find him."

Bolinger leaned into the truck and flicked on the dome light. On the seat were smears of dried blood. He wondered if they were from Sales's cut finger.

"We better get the lab out here and check this truck out," he said. "There's some blood here on the seat."

"Should we call the sheriffs?" Farnhorst said. "They've got a helicopter. They've got dogs, too . . ."

Bolinger looked past the truck door off into the blackness of the woods and thought for a moment before sighing. With a nod he said, "Yeah, we'd better get them. Tell them he's armed.

"Shit!" he said, kicking up a small spray of dew in the beam of the car's headlights. "A goddamn manhunt. Shit! I didn't think it was him."

"Maybe it still isn't," Farnhorst said, but they both knew he was just being polite.

CHAPTER 18

I still think Lipton killed Marcia Sales, and the girl in Atlanta," Bolinger argued. The captain looked at him skeptically.

"There's not that much I can do with Sales anyway," Bolinger continued. "The sheriffs are out there looking. The Texas Rangers are on alert. I've got a stakeout on his cabin. No one's come up with anything. Unless Sales turns up on his own, I don't know what more I can do with that case. With the FBI I can still investigate Lipton across state lines."

"Traces of that boy's blood were found on the seat of his truck," the captain reminded him. "Bob, admit it. You were wrong."

"I may have been wrong about Sales," Bolinger conceded. "But just because he killed Frank Castle doesn't mean he killed those girls. His own daughter, for God's sake, John. A man doesn't do that."

"You don't do it. I don't do it," the captain countered, "but you or I don't butcher Frank Castle, either. He was killed the same way as the girl. How do you explain that?"

"I think maybe Sales was trying to make it look like Lipton," Bolinger said.

The captain considered that for a moment, then said, "By the way, have you contacted the lawyer?"

"No," Bolinger said sullenly. "I haven't."

"Well, you should," the captain said, removing his reading glasses. He leaned forward to put his arms on the desk. "That's all we need, to have her get bumped and we didn't warn her that Sales is out there killing people involved with that case."

"It was on the news. It's the big story," Bolinger grumbled.

"Bob, talk to her," the captain said. "That's an order. In the meantime, as long as you give me your word you're staying on top of the Sales situation, you can help out the FBI."

"Thanks, John," Bolinger said, standing to leave.

"Why you thanking me?" the captain asked.

"It's better when it's official," Bolinger said with a grin.

"You were gonna do it whether I said you could or not," the captain complained as Bolinger went out the door. "I know you, Bob. You're the most stubborn son of a bitch I've ever known."

Bolinger headed for the law school in an attempt to find out the seminar schedule that Lipton had kept over the past several years. On his way there, he indulged himself with a detour to Lipton's neighborhood. The professor's stately manor was lifeless. Bolinger parked across the street and wandered up the pretty stone drive. On the far side of the house was a landscaper's truck, and from the back, Bolinger could hear the sound of a weed eater.

The rich smell of freshly cut grass filled his nose. As he approached a young Mexican man in a green jumpsuit, he eyed the back of the house for any sign of Lipton. Although wrought-iron furniture adorned the patio surrounding the pool, the pool itself was covered. Bolinger tapped the landscaper's back amid the high-pitched drone of his tool. The man jumped in the air and spun around in alarm. Bolinger disarmed him with a smile. The man shut down the weed eater and in broken English asked how he could be of help.

"Anyone home?" Bolinger asked, casually showing the young man his badge.

The man's eyes widened. He wiped his sweaty forehead with his cap and looked from the cop to the house and back to the cop. "No. No one home for much times."

"Never home?" Bolinger asked.

"No," the man said, fervently shaking his head. "I go here two times every week. No person live here."

"Do you have a card?" Bolinger asked as he removed a cigarette from his pocket. The man looked at him as if he were from Mars.

"Business card," Bolinger said carefully as he lit the Winston. "El nombre de su company."

"Oh, si," he said and led Bolinger to the truck. On the other side was the name Conquest Landscapes along with the phone number. Bolinger wrote it down and thanked the man. He took a tour around the house before he left and saw nothing that indicated Lipton had been around.

No one had seen Lipton at the law school, either. Bolinger got in to see the dean, a stern-looking overweight woman with two last names.

"Obviously, he's not teaching this semester," she told him curtly. She also either didn't know or wouldn't say whether or not he'd be back in the fall.

There wasn't a question he asked that wasn't met with an abrupt answer full of mistrust. The dean apparently had no knowledge of the way in which Lipton scheduled his seminars.

"This is a university," she reminded him, "not a police force. Our professors have private lives outside of the university. Many of them are consultants to businesses or have their own independent undertakings."

In the eyes of such a place, Bolinger thought, he was obviously a bad guy, an overzealous cop, the kind of prying monster that innocent citizens had to be protected from. On his way out of the building, he saw a nerdy-looking kid with a crew cut who reminded Bolinger of his brother when he was a student until the kid opened his mouth.

"You go to school here?" Bolinger asked the kid, who was reading on the steps.

The kid marked his spot in his book with a finger and looked up through his glasses.

"Looks that way."

"You know Professor Lipton?"

"I know who he is, sure, the crim law guy in the murder trial."

Bolinger could tell from his tone that the kid hadn't taken a class with Lipton. There wasn't a hint of the recognition that a student would display for a teacher he'd studied under. Bolinger nodded and said, "If I was a guy who wanted to know about those seminars he teaches . . . you know what I'm talking about?"

"No."

"Professor Lipton went around the country," Bolinger explained patiently, "giving seminars on his specialty, on criminal law."

"Yeah," the kid said, obviously impatient now to get back to his work.

"How would I find out about something like that?"

"What are you, a cop?" the kid said derisively.

"That's me," Bolinger said.

The kid shrugged and, turning back to his book, he said sarcastically, "How about the Internet? You know . . . computers."

"I know," Bolinger said gruffly. "I'll let you get back to your studies so you can go out and sue somebody."

The kid might have been a smart-ass, but Bolinger wasn't above taking an idea from anyone. Back at the station, he looked up Rutlege, the department's version of a computer geek. Rutlege was a muscular guy who did triathlons in his spare time. He was the best the Austin police department had in the way of a hacker. Whenever a crook had a computer, chances were Rutlege saw it.

"You remember when we pulled in Professor Lipton?" Bolinger asked.

Rutlege leaned back in his chair and tilted his head back until Bolinger could see the Adam's apple bobbing in his neck.

"Yeah," he said, dropping his head back into place. "I don't remember everything on his machine, but I remember we looked at it."

"Any chance he had his business records on there?" Bolinger said. "He ran these seminars all over the country, and I want to find out where it was he was going. I wondered if you had anything or saw anything that could help me or if you could find some stuff about his seminars on the Internet."

"I could do a search on-line for you, Sarge," Rutlege said. "But as far as his computer, if anything turned up pertinent to the murder we would have told you back then. I don't remember any office files or anything. There could have been. I'll get you my report. It was just a little four- or five-sentence deal, I think, saying that I didn't find anything that would help in the case. I do remember one thing, though."

Rutlege snickered and said, "The guy had some porn files in there. It was funny. I remember the file name, Roman Empire Limited."

"What do you think that means?" Bolinger asked, searching his brain for some connection and coming up with none.

Rutlege shrugged. "I don't know. You could ask the guys in vice. It's nothing I ever heard of, just a file name, I guess. I thought it was kind of unusual, though, the name. So I opened it, and there was some kinky stuff, whips and leather and shit like that with the professor right in the middle of it all. Nothing too crazy, but I remembered it because I was talking to Delucca about it and he wanted me to copy them off for him. He likes that kind of crap. Well, I went back to the property section to get the machine and it was gone."

"Gone?"

"Yeah, seems Lipton's lawyer showed up and demanded if the DA wasn't going to use it as evidence that he get it back."

"Why would the lawyer want the computer?"

Rutlege shrugged. "I don't know. The porn stuff was kinky, but it's not like the DA could have used it. And it's not like Lipton could have used the computer in jail, either. They gave it back, of course. I didn't know about it until it was already gone. Made me think I must have missed something, you know?"

"Could you have?"

Rutlege shrugged. "I hope not, but you know, people have files they can hide and you can't get at them unless you know they're there or unless you look hard enough. I go through so many machines I pretty much just see what files turn up in the regular directories unless someone tells me there's a chance something could be hidden that's important to the case. Then I'll take the damn thing home with me and hack on it over the weekend."

"Could you hide a whole set of business records?"

"Sure," Rutlege said. "You could hide a dictionary if you knew what you were doing."

"Listen, I want you to go on the Internet and try to find out all the places he gave seminars in the last five years. Don't you think the records from this seminar business that he had have to be on a computer somewhere?"

"Sure they do," Rutlege said. "This guy's computer literate. He was carrying that notebook with him when he tried to get away. That tells you he can't do without it. Now it might not have been on that computer, but I guarantee a guy like that has his records on a computer somewhere. But like I said, they could have been right there and I wouldn't have written anything up on it because it didn't really fit into the case at the time. All we were looking for then was any letters or e-mail back and forth between him and the girl. You get your hands on his computer, you might just have everything you want."

"That's not too likely," Bolinger said. "I can't even get my hands on him."

"Well, meantime," Rutlege told him, "I'll get what I can off the Internet and I'll e-mail it to you."

"E-mail it?"

"You've got a computer, don't you?"

"No," Bolinger grumbled. "Just make me a good old-fashioned Xerox copy of whatever you find and put it on my desk."

Bolinger's next stop was the federal building. He wanted to get at Lipton's credit card records. Unless he used cash wherever he went, that information should give him a trail showing where the professor had traveled over the last five years. He knew getting a subpoena from a local judge for something like that would be a tough nut. They'd want him to show probable cause. But he also knew that the FBI could get a federal judge to do it without batting an eye.

On his way over, he dialed up Casey Jordan's office. Her assistant said she wasn't available and asked if he wanted her voice mail. Bolinger preferred her voice mail. He wasn't calling because he wanted to. He was calling because it had been a direct order.

At the federal building, Agent Unger wasn't in and hadn't been seen all day. The secretary gave Bolinger a vacant look when he asked if she knew where he might be. Bolinger looked out the window at the bright sun, the clear sky, and the dry, warm air, a perfect day to be out on the links.

"West Lake Hills Country Club," Bolinger said out loud in disgust. He wasn't the least opposed to grabbing a round on a beautiful day, but he figured Unger would at least go through the motions. Not to show up at all was totally negligent. He dialed up the agent's cell phone and got a machine. With a sigh, he went down the hall to Dean Wentworth's office.

Dean looked up from a pile of paperwork.

"What's up, Bob?"

"I need a subpoena."

"Have Unger get it," he said.

"Unger's out . . . golfing, I imagine."

"Bob, look, I meant what I said. I can't help you with this goddamn stuff. I got you a goddamn guy, you'll have to use him."

"What you got me is some sorry-ass guy who's waiting to get vested so he can get a government pension and retire."

"Bob, give me a goddamn break. Come on, I know we're friends, but you've got to leave me alone. I got people breathing down my goddamn neck."

"Good, go ahead," Bolinger said sullenly. "Go get your high-profile bank robber, but when I turn this guy over and we find two dozen dead women all across the country, don't even think about sticking your face in front of the cameras."

"What the hell is that supposed to mean?" Dean said indignantly.

"It means you guys are all media whores," Bolinger said, jutting his chin out, "that's what it means. It means you're worried less about catching the bad guys than you are about having a camera there to see you do it."

"Hey, Bob . . ."

"What?"

"Kiss my goddamn ass."

CHAPTER 19

Casey looked at her watch and hurried through the garage. It was Friday and most everyone else had already gone home. In her rush, she was only remotely aware of the sensation that had made her skin crawl the other day in the garage. She scanned the area as she went, but then took her eyes off everything around her as she struggled to fit the key into the door of her Mercedes sedan. After tossing her briefcase onto the passenger seat, she slid in and started the engine.

On her way up the ramp, Casey glanced into the rearview mirror. A figure dashed across her field of vision and her heart froze. She jammed on her brakes and turned around. There was nothing. Was her mind playing tricks on her? She waited and even considered going back, but it was too creepy down there, so she told herself it was nothing and went on with tires squealing through the turns until she pulled up out of the garage and into the evening light.

She already knew about Frank Castle. It was all over the news. She couldn't let that scare her. An attorney had to expect things like that to happen. As a prosecutor, she had received threats as a matter of course. Since she'd been doing defense work, she hadn't had such a situation. Now, she needed to call on the rationale that every prosecutor repeated to herself, talk was cheap. Criminals rarely followed through on their vengeful desires. You were more apt to be struck by lightning.

Still, as she drove along she turned the situation over in her mind. The image of Donald Sales's last hateful stare filled her mind. It had to be him who killed Frank Castle. It was him . . . or it was Lipton. Lipton's confession echoed through her mind. Had it been a sick joke or was it really true? But why would Lipton kill Frank Castle? Only Sales had reason for that.

And if Sales would go to the trouble of hunting down Frank Castle, couldn't he be watching her as well? Casey shivered involuntarily and checked her rearview mirror again. There was nothing there outside the normal evening traffic. Casey thought about the guard gates that protected her community and the extensive alarm system in her home. She was safe. With disgust, she turned her mind to Taylor. They had spoken only briefly during the day, and he had brushed off the news about Frank Castle the way he did everything else. Casey imagined what it would be like to have a man who hurried home from halfway across the world to make sure she was all right. Didn't she deserve someone like that? To be sure, there had been men in her life who would have reacted that way.

When she got home, she changed out of her work clothes, then took a steak from the freezer. While it defrosted in the microwave, she steamed some broccoli. When the meat was ready, she put it on a plate and took it out back to the grill that was built into the stone bar beside the pool. Casey relished a good steak and she didn't mind cooking it herself. Growing up, steak had meant chuck steak, a cut of meat so tough your cheeks were sore the next day from chewing. One of the things she enjoyed most about being financially comfortable was eating well.

As the meat popped and sizzled on the open flame, Casey gazed out across the low shrubs surrounding the pool area to the rippling golf course lake, the lush fairway, and the dusty green hills beyond. Casey took a deep breath of evening air laced with the smell of good steak. The tranquillity of her surroundings sometimes allowed her to relax. She'd come a long way.

She thought back to her girlhood home, a modest farm that revealed its age by a rash of ancient gray wood beneath the pockmarks of peeling paint. She looked back over her shoulder at the towering white edifice she lived in now. Maybe her marriage wasn't as bad as she was making out. Most people had problems. Things were never perfect. She thought of her own mother's devotion to a husband who treated her like a chair. Occasionally, he would take his ease with her. Otherwise, he apparently gave her no thought whatsoever.

They'd never done much of anything together besides eat at the same silent dinner table to begin with, although in the early days there was at least a vitality about them. Her mother's pretty cheeks always seemed flushed with sun or wind, and the muscles in her father's forearms bespoke the sinewy strength of a farmer. But then, as the years passed, each of them went to seed. Her father's belly began to hang over his belt, and as her older brother did more and more of the work, his muscles grew flaccid.

Her mother's face grew pale and drawn, and her hair began to fade to a mousy gray as she shrank in stature. It wasn't long before disinterest grew into disdain, at least on her father's part. Casey's lot was better than that anyway. If nothing else, Taylor still had a strong sexual hunger for her.

Casey flipped the steak and in the edge of her vision saw something move. Someone had ducked back into the woods bordering the fairway. She searched the cart path that looped around the water, back to the tee, and then snaked along the fairway through the cluster of trees on the near side of the course. There wasn't a cart in sight. Neither was there a golf bag or anything that would indicate the presence of a golfer who'd hooked his shot into the thick woods on the far side of the fairway. The sun was low in the west but not yet below the ridge of hills beyond the golf course. It still burned brightly yellow, and Casey had to shade her eyes and squint toward the spot in the woods where she was almost certain she'd seen the strange movement.

What she needed was a glass of wine. She was jumpy and overreacting to an emotional few days. She took her steak off the grill and cut the flame. With several glances over her shoulder, she went back into the house, stopping to lock the sliding door that led into the kitchen. She set her steak on the granite bar and dumped the broccoli down on the plate beside it.

From the wine rack she removed a good bottle of merlot, opened it, and poured a large glass. While the wine breathed, she went back to the glass door and peered outside for several minutes. The sun had dropped down below the edge of the hills, and the sky was already beginning to turn a deep postcard pink. Casey took little no-

tice of the sky. Instead, she carefully studied the woods
that bordered the fairway.

After a while she turned her attention back to her meal.
But before sitting down, she went upstairs and took a
small Colt 7mm automatic out of the dresser drawer. She
set it down beside her plate and took a long sip of wine.
The steak was a little underdone, but she ate it anyway,
relishing the taste of blood with her wine. Half a bottle
later, with her stomach now full, she began to relax once
more.

When the doorbell rang, she jumped. They didn't live
in the kind of neighborhood where people made house
calls. Each house was on its own small estate. Neighbors
naturally afforded one another a considerable degree of
privacy. But no one else should have been able to get into
the development without stopping at the gate. Security
would have called to ask her permission to let them in.
Pistol in hand, she cautiously approached the front door.
Through the ornate beveled glass in the door, she could
make out the shadowy form of a man.

With her free hand on the doorknob she said, "Tony?"

He was the only person she could think of who might
be able to get past the security gate without their calling,
although even that didn't make sense. The fleeting im-
ages she thought she'd seen in the garage and outside
came back to her. Whoever it was rang the bell again.

"Tony!" she said as an edge of panic crept into her
voice. "Is that you?"

There was a sidelight next to the door that was cloaked
in a translucent curtain. Casey wanted to pull the curtain
aside and look out, but something inside her didn't want
to be seen peering out like a timid mouse by whoever was
there. The man rapped his knuckles hard and loud against

the wood of the door. Casey started to feel angry now; angry at her fear and angry at the insistence of whoever was out there. She was no coward. She'd grown up literally fighting like a boy. In that moment, she remembered with pride the shock on her parents' faces when she'd been suspended from school for breaking the nose of an insolent boy. If she had to shoot someone to defend herself, she could do that, too, and without hesitation. Against her better senses, she raised the gun, twisted the lock, and yanked open the door with a ferocious look on her face.

"Ms. Jordan."

"Detective," she said, still angry. "Why in hell are you here?"

"Did I shake you up?" Bolinger asked, eyeing the gun with only mild concern. His badge had been enough to get him through the gates. Bolinger had actually tracked Unger down at the clubhouse. To make the agent feel a part of things, he'd filled him in on the details of his investigation into Lipton's computer, including the titillating details about Roman Empire Ltd., before requesting that Unger process a subpoena.

"No. Yes. You didn't shake me up," Casey explained, dropping the gun down to her side, "but I certainly didn't expect to be disturbed by you at home, my home, without warning."

"Well, I don't mean to disturb you," Bolinger said sarcastically. "But my captain wanted me to make sure you knew about Frank Castle and that we're still looking for Donald Sales and I was . . . in the neighborhood, so to speak."

"I read the papers," Casey said defiantly. Actually, she felt like a fool standing there with a pistol in her big T-shirt and a pair of UT athletic shorts. The last time she'd seen Bolinger, she'd been in a charcoal business suit and heels, and the only thing in her hand was a briefcase.

"That's what I said," he told her, unable to keep his eyes from wandering toward her fine bare legs. "But the captain, he doesn't want something to happen to you and have anyone say that we should have made you aware of the situation so you could . . . so you could be more alert than you otherwise might be. But I see you're already prepared for the worst."

"Are you trying to scare me, Sergeant?" she asked.

"No. You're already scared," he said placidly. "That's pretty obvious. Has something happened?"

Casey pressed her lips tightly together and considered the detective. Irrational or not, she was scared. She was still shaking from the unannounced intrusion and the connection it had in her mind to the shadowy fears she'd already experienced. She cleared her throat and said, "Would you like a cup of coffee, Sergeant?"

"I've been known to drink coffee," he said, stepping across the threshold and into the house.

Bolinger sat at the kitchen table while Casey put the coffee on.

"That's some view," he remarked, looking out past the pool, across the water, and down the dark green fairway of the luxuriant golf course and the blood-red sky still framing the hills. "I never realized getting criminals off was such a lucrative business."

Casey placed two steaming ceramic mugs on the table and sat down across from Bolinger. "I'm not a lawyer because of the money, Detective. I do it because I believe in it. Our judicial system is the best in the world, the best in the history of the human race."

"Wow. That's pretty good," Bolinger said with a mischievous smile. "Do you think the judicial system was working good when you got Lipton off?"

"I didn't free Professor Lipton." Casey sniffed. "A jury did that. I advocated for him to the best of my abilities. That's what I do. That's what people deserve. I know you're not familiar with it, but it's called the presumption of innocence, Detective."

Bolinger shook his head. "Do you think society deserves to have him running around out there, killing innocent young women?"

"Detective," Casey said, glowering. "I invited you in for a cup of coffee, not to talk about Professor Lipton. I'd like to know what's being done to find Donald Sales. I would think you'd be looking for him.

"But," she added sharply, "I'm only basing that on logic."

Bolinger sighed and took a swig of his coffee. It was the flavored stuff that cost fifteen bucks a pound. He swallowed it fast to get past the taste and thought wistfully about the Dunkin' Donuts he would have to visit on the way home for a cup of coffee. "I'm interested in them both. Hey, look, I don't mean to be callous, but I find it pretty ironic that someone who spends her time helping to set criminals free is now concerned about one that's on the loose."

Casey bit back a caustic response and instead asked, "Is there any particular reason your captain thinks that I have a reason to worry about Donald Sales?"

"I don't know," Bolinger said, considering her carefully. "I guess I haven't thought about it too much. I guess not, really. Sales is probably in Mexico by now, or somewhere."

"But not here?" Casey asked.

"No. Not here."

Casey nodded and came quite close to telling him about the things she'd seen.

"There is something I'd like to ask you about Lipton, though," he continued. "I'd like to know about his legal seminars."

"The Letter of the Law," she said.

"The Letter of the Law?" he asked quizzically.

"The seminars, that's what they're called," Casey told him. "He wrote a book, too. They focus on the nuances of our criminal justice system."

Bolinger took another quick sip and fought back a grimace. "Lipton had a computer that we confiscated when we arrested him last year. One of our people looked at it, but not very hard. I was thinking that he probably kept his business records on that computer. Would you agree with that?"

Casey looked at him blank-faced. "I can't really discuss anything about Professor Lipton with you, Sergeant. You should know that. He's my client."

"I thought he *was* your client," Bolinger said. "And . . . if you go by the books, he's been tried and acquitted in the case where you represented him. Technically, you're not his lawyer anymore, and you can talk to me about him and you know it. And you also know that if you have information that could prevent a future crime, you not only can tell me, you're ethically bound to."

"I know the law, Sergeant," she said impatiently.

"He's gone, you know," Bolinger said quietly. "I need to find him, and I'd like to know where it was he conducted these seminars."

"I really shouldn't be discussing any of this," she said.

"Can't you just tell me if I'm right? I mean about his computer. I know you have it. I spoke to Michael Dove. He got it from property and gave it to you when you took the case." Bolinger leaned across the table and dropped his voice in an excited tone, "I'm going to level with you . . . I don't think Marcia Sales or the girl in Atlanta were the only ones. I think there were probably girls before and . . . there'll be girls to come."

"Detective, I—"

"No! You just listen to me," Bolinger said, his eyes burning with intensity. "You don't have to say anything, just listen. I've got a feeling that that computer holds the key to everything, where he was, where he's going. Maybe even a list of women he met over the years at these seminars, a goddamn target list!

"That's how these kinds of people do things," he continued frantically. "They don't stop! That job on Marcia Sales was done by someone who'd done it before, probably dozens of times. He took her fucking gall bladder for a trophy, for God's sake!"

Bolinger was boiling over now. He'd been formulating his theory for months, without telling anyone. It had just churned around in his gut fermenting until now. "That's the kind of crazy shit a serial killer does, that crazy connection. She wasn't raped. She was eviscerated! That's bizarre. It's unheard of. He's probably impotent. He gets off on tying up these women lawyers. He tapes them up, that's his way of controlling them, asserting his dominance. Then he butchers them and takes their gall bladders for a memento.

"That's how these sick fucks think, that's how they get started. They kill someone somewhere, and it turns them on in their own sick way, and then they get away with it.

When they get away with it once, they keep doing it and every time they get better. Then, they get so good they start to play with you. With the police, I mean. They know how it works by then. They know how to leave a crime scene totally clean. They wear gloves. They wear two layers of clothes and shoes wrapped in plastic bags. Their balls get bigger and bigger until they think they're fucking untouchable.

"I think that's why Lipton killed Marcia Sales. He wanted to prove something, like he could do it in his own backyard and get away with it. He would have, too, if he hadn't hit that woman's car. Even then, he got off. He's free, and he's probably got more balls than ever!"

"And what if you're wrong, Detective?" Casey said with just as much passion. "What if I was right at the trial and it really was Donald Sales? Maybe he's the killer."

"What about the girl in Atlanta?" Bolinger demanded. "Why would Sales kill her? There's no connection."

"Maybe that was part of a different perfect crime, the perfect setup," she argued. "He was infuriated with his daughter, maybe enough to kill her. He hated Lipton for his involvement, and he figured he could kill the girl and blame it on Lipton at the same time."

"And go all the way to Atlanta to do it?" Bolinger asked incredulously.

"It's possible, Detective. It's really possible," she said.

Lipton's own confession was ringing out all the while, clear and keen in the back of her mind. Casey wanted desperately to be right. The idea that Lipton's confession was anything but a sick joke was too horrible to admit without a fight.

Bolinger frowned. "If I could get his records, we'd know. If I could find out where he's been over the past

five or ten years, I could check those places for this kind
of crime. If we find one that's connected to Lipton, we'll
know it's not the father. Lipton didn't know Marcia Sales
until she came to school. Sales couldn't have killed
someone five years ago to set him up."

"Well, even if you're right," Casey said, "I can't help
you. Even if I could help you, I don't have his computer,
and when I did have it I didn't even look at it. He just
asked me to hold it."

"When did he get it back?"

"The day after the trial," she said.

"Goddamn!" Bolinger struck his palm with a fist. "I
knew it. He wanted it back!"

"Of course he wanted it back," Casey snapped. "Anyone would want their computer back."

"No, but right away?" Bolinger said. "First thing you
do is get your computer back and disappear?"

"You said he was gone, now you're saying he disappeared," Casey said with concern.

"He has."

"Maybe he's afraid of Sales," Casey suggested hopefully.

"I won't lie to you. I know Sales," Bolinger said, looking at her hard. "He's a dangerous man. I like him, but
he's dangerous. I think this trial, what you . . . what happened to him and to his daughter put him over the edge.
He killed Frank Castle, and I'm pretty sure he was the
one who shot Lipton. I could never prove it, but it was
him. To be honest, I didn't care all that much about what
he did to Lipton because I know Lipton killed Marcia
Sales and that girl in Atlanta and probably a lot more. Unlike you, I figure sometimes justice needs a little shove.

But Lipton lived and now he's free and he's out there and I'm going to get him."

"And Sales?" Casey said.

Bolinger shrugged. "I'll get him, too, if I can."

"If you can?" Casey asked incredulously. "If he killed Frank Castle and shot Lipton, he could be the one that's behind everything."

"You mean the girl in Atlanta, too?" Bolinger scoffed.

"Yes," she urged. "You're right about one thing. There's a killer loose somewhere, a serial killer if that's what you say. And you can go on all you want about Professor Lipton, but it's every bit as likely that Donald Sales is the man you want."

Bolinger looked at her long and hard before saying, "You're trying awfully hard to be convincing . . . But I wonder . . ."

He paused, then said, "Are you trying to convince me? Or are you really just trying to convince yourself?"

CHAPTER 20

By the light of the moon, Donald Sales crept out of the trees and up to the golf course maintenance shed. Along its side lay an eighteen-foot aluminum ladder. Sales spun his shoulders around and swept the area one more time completely with his bloodshot eyes. He then shouldered the ladder and hurried back into the shadows.

Picking his way carefully along the course, it took him nearly thirty minutes to get from the shed to Casey's house. He knew where the cover was and where the open places were. He also knew from two nights of reconnoitering that people sometimes walked along the cart paths at night. At three A.M., however, he doubted he'd run into anyone. But Sales was thorough. So thorough, in fact, that in his mind he'd already formulated a sequence of events once he was inside the house.

The first thing he'd done when he eluded Bolinger three days ago was make his way to a shopping center with a Wal-Mart and a nearby grocery store. He had known that he had only a small amount of time before his face would hit the news, and he wanted to take advantage of his short-lived anonymity to get supplies. Living in the hills wasn't a problem. He knew of a multiplicity of hidden caves that would provide him with shelter. But having a sleeping bag, a flashlight, some food, clothes, and ample ammunition, among other things, would make his existence that much easier. They would also afford him the time he needed to carry out his mission.

If he'd had to worry about hunting for food, he wouldn't have been able to sneak around the shrubbery surrounding Casey's home reconnoitering the situation. After more than a day of watching, he knew her husband was gone. It wasn't that her husband was a particularly imposing obstacle, but his absence made things that much easier.

At the edge of Casey's property, down near the golf course lake, was an ornate little wrought-iron fence. Sales set the ladder down inside the fence, gently felt for the roll of duct tape on his hip, and vaulted over the fence with remarkable agility for a big man in his late forties. With the ladder over his shoulder, he waded through the low bushes toward the house. After skirting the pool, he gently poised the ladder against the small balcony that jutted out from the master bedroom. He knew from the way the lights went out that this was where Casey slept. He had already wrapped the ends of the ladder in rags, so the only sound was the quiet complaint of aluminum as he lifted his two hundred sixty pounds hand-over-hand up toward the balcony. When he got to the edge, he stopped to listen.

His heart pounded steadily in his chest. Otherwise, the night was silent. He could feel a thrill not unlike what he had felt in warfare in the marrow of his bones. With unusual stealth he went over the railing and stood at full height in the doorway that led into the bedroom. The sliding glass door was open. Only a screen stood between him and Casey Jordan. The moonlight at his back was strong enough for him to see her lying there, sound asleep under the thin film of a soft, white sheet. He smiled grimly at the sight of the small black automatic on the table beside the bed. That wouldn't help her. From the back of his belt, he removed the same long, cruel blade that had been used to gut Frank Castle.

After three deep breaths for total clarity, Sales inserted the point of the knife into the corner of the screen. Quickly, he slashed along the bottom of the door frame and then upward so he could pass easily into the room. Before Casey could awake, Sales was on top of her, bearing down with his full weight and with one hand clasped tightly across her mouth.

Casey's eyes shot open as the shocking bolt of panic swept through her entire frame, rending her from a confusing dream. She bucked twice, but the overwhelming pressure on her face and the sharp point of a knife at the base of her throat left her wide-eyed and paralyzed with fear.

Knowing that she was completely subdued, Sales rolled her over on her stomach and swiftly covered her mouth with duct tape by wrapping it around the back of her head. With the back of her T-shirt twisted in his hand, he lifted her off the bed and forced her over to the alarm panel that was above the light switch just inside the bedroom door. With the long knife pricking the back of her neck, Sales commanded her to disarm the system.

Casey's knees were shaking. She looked hopelessly at her gun on the night table. It was only a few feet away,

but it might have been a million miles. Slowly she began
to punch in the numbers. But instead of the last digit, she
stabbed the panic button and held on, triggering the
alarm. She heard the wail of the sirens inside the house.
She saw stars. Then everything went black.

Sales had struck Casey in the back of the head with the
handle of the knife that was grasped tightly in his fist.
Even with the alarm shrieking in his ears, he looked
coolly around the room. As quickly and as neatly as possible, he pulled the covers up and made the bed, finishing just as the phone stopped ringing. He knew after
getting no response to their call, the alarm company
would now call the police. That gave him at least five
minutes, maybe more. He tossed Casey's little automatic
into the nightstand drawer, then crossed the room and
slid the screen door all the way open. That would hide
the tear he'd made from anything but the most careful
examination. He then slid the glass door shut and locked
it.

With Casey's limp body draped over his shoulder,
Sales descended the stairs and found his way to the
garage. As he passed through the kitchen, he grabbed
what he presumed was Casey's purse, hanging off the
back of a chair. The keys were in the ignition of the Mercedes. Sales opened the trunk and tossed Casey inside.
Quickly, he let himself out the back door of the garage
onto the patio. He took the ladder from its spot against
the balcony and simply laid it down along the outside of
the garage behind some bushes.

Back inside, he glanced at his watch and made sure to
lock the door between the garage and the house. Only
three and a half minutes had gone by since the phone
stopped ringing. He had a good ninety seconds at least.

He pressed the button that opened the garage door and got into the car. Carefully, he backed the Mercedes out into the driveway. The remote to the garage door was clipped to the sun visor. Sales closed it, then backed into the street and set out for the main gate.

A sheriff's car was pulling in just as the exit arm swung up, clearing his path. Sales glanced at the guard shack, where the only sign of life was the dim square of light that filled the window. At this time of night, the guard was probably fast asleep in his chair. On the open road, Sales checked the rearview mirror. It wouldn't make sense for the police to be concerned with a car leaving the community. They would be focused on answering the call. A call that most cops would presume to be a false alarm. By neatly locking up when he left, Sales had given them no reason to think anything else.

When Casey came to, her head was throbbing so severely that she could think of nothing else. As her senses cleared, she frantically wondered where she was. She was lying facedown on a rock floor of some kind. Her hands were taped tightly behind her, and her naked ankles were likewise bound with tape. In a panic she rolled over, only to see Donald Sales slumped up against the rock wall of their cave, fast asleep.

Tears spilled down Casey's cheeks as she remembered the horrifying events that had brought her here. She tried to control her breathing, but it was difficult. The tape over her mouth and her shortness of breath were causing her to gasp through her nose. She tried with all her mental powers to stifle the gurgles of panic rumbling in her throat and breathe as deeply and slowly as she could. Still, she was making too much noise. Only the faint sound of birds outside the cave helped to mute the sounds of her distress. Sales suddenly stirred, and Casey froze with her eyes shut tight. After a moment, she opened them and studied her captor's scowling face. It was smudged with dirt and his hair was pulled into a tight ponytail. He was wearing a pair of black jeans and his legs were crossed. His boots stood patiently slumped over beside his feet.

When Sales's breathing again returned to a quiet, regular rhythm, Casey began to worm her way toward the brilliant light in the mouth of the cave. Because her arms were bare and taped beneath her, the grit on the stone floor chafed against her skin. By the time she reached the cave's entrance, she was bleeding. Beads of sweat dripped down into her eyes, blurring her last look at the dozing Sales. She turned her face into the fresh breeze. The morning air filled her nostrils like champagne after the humid closeness of the cave. With a burst of energy, she tried to rise, then gave up and began to roll as fast and as far as she could.

The rocky terrain sloped downhill, and she was able to cover a substantial distance in a short space of time despite the bumps and bruises she sustained. Within minutes she was out in the open and resting on a soft, needle-covered floor in a stand of pines. The distance she'd put between herself and Sales and the exertion from her efforts had cleared her mind enough to think. She needed to free her hands and feet. While she caught her breath she listened, and she knew that she was in the middle of nowhere. There were no sounds of people or traffic or even jets in the sky. There was no way she could travel any great distance bound as she was. She needed to regain her feet.

She heaved herself up into a sitting position and searched the area for some kind of sharp stone. She saw a jagged outcropping of granite uphill and a little off to her left. She lay back down and began to roll toward it. When she reached the spot, she sat back up and searched for the right edge. Struggling against the constraints of her bondage, she worked her wrists up against the stone. She struggled several times to get the right angle and several times slumped to the ground after gashing her skin. Finally, with her feet wedged up against another rock, Casey had just the right position where she could cut into the tape by flexing her legs and shoulders up and down at the same time. After fifteen minutes of exhausting work, she was free.

Her hands were slick and sticky with her own blood, and it was difficult for her to get a purchase on the tape that bound her feet. She fought hard against the instinct to free her mouth first, but she knew that Sales could awaken any moment, and if her ankles were bound she'd have no chance of escape. She tore at the edge of the tape, ripped about an inch into it, but was then hopelessly stopped where the bond thickened. Twice she broke fingernails as she fought to peel back the end piece of tape. Then she got it started and frantically began to unwind her ankles.

Once free, Casey staggered to her feet and stumbled downhill, catching herself against every other tree trunk. Her legs and back ached and barely responded to the commands her brain was sending to walk, let alone run. But the more she moved, the more limber she became, and soon she had enough balance to lope along and at the same time work at the thick gray tape that was wrapped around her head.

By the time she reached the bottom of the hill, she was completely free. A narrow stream cut through the rocks, and Casey, parched from her efforts, slipped down into an oblong pool whose edges were slick with brown moss. She was filthy from her roll in the dirt and the blood that had begun to dry on her hands and arms. She crouched down and dipped her face into the water, drinking long, cool draughts until her stomach sloshed. She absently rubbed some of the dirt and blood off her arms before submerging her head to rinse her hair and face.

The water felt so good and the sunlit spot was so peaceful that a part of her wanted to stop, to just lie back in the water and let it rush over her, cooling her, refreshing her, and lulling her to sleep with its quiet whisper. When she woke up, she would find that it had all been a bad dream. In the water, she became aware of the stinging pain in her feet. She looked down into the clear pool and turned her pale foot on its edge to look at her sole. Tiny red fissures oozed billowing crimson clouds of blood into the swirling water.

She climbed up out of the pool and stood dripping on a rock like a half-drowned rodent. Strands of dark red hair hung like cobwebs on her face until she pushed them back with a weary, bleeding wrist. She stepped tentatively on the large rocks, and the stinging pain made her totally aware now of the damage she'd done to her feet.

She couldn't help beginning to cry. Casey was no woodsman. She had shunned anything of the sort when she was a girl. She had no idea where she was and no idea how to figure it out. The closest help could be to the north, south, east, or west. She could start out in any direction and be wrong. Her body ached from lying bound up on the cave's floor. The throbbing in her head from the blow she'd received the night before and now the bleeding lacerations on her hands and feet were almost too much to bear.

It was a hopeless situation, made even worse because her whole world had been turned upside down. Everything she believed in had been shaken to its foundation. She had spent her life making what she thought were the right moves. She had worked hard and she had learned the rules of the game, the law. Studying the law had not only given order to the world; it had been her means of escape, escape from the chaotic uncertainty of growing up poor and unaccounted for by the world at large. But now, for the first time in her life, she was afraid that the law was nothing more than a useless facade. And if that were true, then couldn't the same be said for her entire existence?

What was happening to her now, this, was real. All her knowledge of the law and its noble purposes could do nothing to protect her. Hadn't the same laws been useless in protecting Marcia Sales and Frank Castle? For a victim, the law was a remote and unimportant counter to what was real. Suddenly, and for the first time, the law seemed to her an insignificant shell, fragile and weak when compared to the visceral realities of life and death.

This was reality. Her rich, handsome husband (who, she became suddenly and painfully certain, was off cavorting with another woman), her bank account, her expensive car, her elegant home, her reputation, what good were they here and now? They were useless. If she could run fast and far she might live. If she tired and lost her

way . . . she would die. Her limbs grew heavy with the
weight of her life's foolish mission.

Yet, when the sound of a snapping branch reached her
ears from about a hundred yards up the tree-covered
slope, Casey felt a burst of adrenaline. Survival instincts
she'd never known she possessed took over. She was
being pursued and she knew how to run. Like a gazelle,
she skipped across the rocks, up the other bank of the
stream, and plunged blindly into the woods beyond.

Casey moved steadily through the wilderness until
cool evening shadows began to chill the surface of her
skin. Twice she thought she recognized landmarks she'd
seen before, but she couldn't be sure. She was exhausted
and hungry. Even the fuel from her fear was beginning
to ebb. As night came, she began to look for a place to
lie down. The best thing she could come up with was to
burrow beneath the soft mat of brown needles that encircled a massive pine tree.

Instinctively, she wrapped one arm around the thick
root of the enormous tree. Her mind slipped unthink-
ingly into the habit of imagining that she was holding on
to the iron limb of a protective man. It was silly. She had
done the same thing as a girl, stacking up extra pillows
in her bed and clinging tightly to them in the night. But
she had no man, not really. She was alone in life, just as
she'd always been. The man who was her husband didn't
afford her protection from anything. He never had. To
the world, Taylor Jordan might look like the perfect life's
companion. But she was now painfully aware that in reality, he was nothing more than a stack of pillows or the
twisted root of an ancient tree.

Casey knew she was as exhausted as she was deliri-
ous. She was so tired that within minutes, despite the

dull throbbing of her feet and head, she was fading off to sleep. But while sleep was a blissful reprieve for her tortured body and mind, it gave her no warning of the ghostly beam of light swinging to and fro like a pendulum as it crept slowly toward her through the trees.

CHAPTER 21

It was the first real sleep Sales had had in three days. So when he awoke, he came from the depths with the gasp of a man desperately breaking the surface of the ocean. His head snapped this way and that for a sign of Casey. She was gone. He yanked on his boots and stood. Without moving, he studied the faint signs in the dust on the stone floor. When he came to the place halfway to the cave's entrance where her skin opened up, a small smile grew from his frown. His racing heart settled. After sliding the knife into the back of his belt, he picked up his rifle and walked carefully out of the cave. By the strength of the light, he knew it was close to noon.

Out in the sun, the thin swatch of blood grew so faint on the rock that he had to crouch low to distinguish it from the various striations in the granite. When it disappeared completely, it took several minutes of casting about before Sales could pick up the trail again. He knew she must have rolled downhill. Even when her general direction became apparent, it was slow work tracking her on the rough ground.

Once he found her first mark in the pine needles, it became easy again. He was several yards away from the rock outcrop when he spotted the shiny gray remains of her bonds.

"Shit!" he said aloud, casting his eyes three hundred and sixty degrees, hoping to catch a sign of her dashing through the trees. He bent down over the spot where she'd cut through the tape. The sharp-edged stone was liberally decorated with her blood. He touched his finger to one of the larger spots and brought it to his lips. It was still sticky.

He stood slowly and carefully examined the scene. The scuffs in the dirt at the base of the tree, a bloody swatch on another rock, and the pattern of blood on the sharp stone told him the story of how she'd been able to break free from the tape. Her resourcefulness and determination were impressive. His brow grew dark as he considered the possibility of her escape. He had expected her to be formidable, even before her bold move to set off the alarm with a knife to her neck. But to have the energy and the will to free herself in this way after a night of being bound up on a cold stone floor? He squatted back down and began to search for the new trail. Only years of practice made it possible for him to follow her.

When her feet started to open up, he knew even an amateur could track her down. Once he had that clear trail, he began to jog through the trees, knowing now the line of her escape was the same as any wounded doe's. She would move downhill in as straight a line as she could, fleeing from him as fast and as far as her injured feet would take her. When a stick snapped under his feet, he cursed, somehow sensing the magnitude of the mistake, and began to move carefully again at a much slower pace.

At the creek, the spot where she'd stood to dry was still evident, although the watermarks were rapidly evaporating in the warm sun. He knew from the sudden distance between her bloody footprints that this was the place where she had stood when he'd spooked her. Sales cursed again, but pressed on, glad at least that she was heading farther into the wilderness and not in the direction of the old mining road where he had stashed her car.

Around noon, he topped a rise in the woods and caught sight of her running well below him through a clearing in the trees. He swung the rifle expertly up to his shoulder, and held her in his sights.

"Bang," he said, with a gleeful smile. Then as she disappeared, he put it down and scrambled to the place he'd seen her last. By three o'clock, he knew he wasn't going to be able to run her down. The harder he pressed, the more distance she covered. At four-thirty, her trail crossed back on itself, and he knew she was completely lost. Sales marked the spot well, took his bearings, and started back for the cave. He was famished.

He stopped at the stream to drink his fill, then climbed the hill to the cave, wary all the while for signs of danger. Although he doubted there was any possibility of his being followed, one never knew. If the alarm company showed up with the police and they had a key to the house, there was the outside chance that one of the cops was sharp enough to suspect that the bed didn't look made quite right. He might notice the cut screen and figure that instead of an electrical malfunction, Casey really had pushed the panic alarm. It would then be well within reason that they remembered the dark blue Mercedes leaving the community. With an APB out for the car, who knew? A kid on a dirt bike or a lost hunter could stumble into the Mercedes and the rest would be history. They'd have a SWAT team in the rocks above his cave waiting to welcome him back with a bullet in the brain.

But as he surveyed the area from behind a tree on the edge of the stony rise that led to the cave, the only other sign of life was the plaintive cry of a male cardinal searching for a mate. Inside, Sales greedily opened a can of beans and slurped them down straight from the can. After resting his feet for nearly an hour, he rose with a long sigh and gathered up his things. Besides the rifle and the knife, he picked up his flashlight and snaked his belt through the roll of duct tape, wearing it on his hip the way he had when he broke into Casey's home.

By the time he reached the spot where he'd marked Casey's trail, the shadows had grown long. Before darkness engulfed him completely, Sales was locked in on her track again. He knew as hard as she'd run that she'd lie down once darkness came. He took his time and moved methodically along the path she'd taken. Every so often he would stoop to confirm that the faint dark smear on a rock or a leaf was really blood from her foot or that a particular twig was freshly broken or that a certain pebble was recently turned up from the earth. She had done nothing to conceal her trail. She was just running.

When his beam of light finally came to rest on her curled-up, bedraggled form at the base of an ancient white pine, he indulged himself with half a smile. He quickly swung the beam up into the boughs of the tree so as not to waken her. He approached her with stealth. Standing above her, he cupped his hand over the light, deflecting the beam and making a dim lamp. Despite her dirty, matted hair and the smear of dried blood on her face, she was still a beautiful woman.

"Goddamn hellcat is what she is," Sales murmured quietly to himself. He knew that to subdue her he was going to have to render her unconscious. With a carotid control technique, he could slip his arm around her neck and deprive her brain of its oxygen. He set down his flashlight. The darkness surrounding its beam was absolute, and he adjusted it so that she lay in its path. The moment Sales touched her, she came alive as if she were in the midst of a fight, scratching and clawing desperately. The light was kicked aside in the struggle, and the two of them fought in total darkness. Sales slowly tightened his grasp, careful not to crush her windpipe or break her neck. He wanted her alive.

After her one last vicious burst of energy, Casey slumped down on the ground. Sales recovered his light, then removed the roll of tape from his belt. Methodically he wrapped her wrists and ankles before gagging her mouth. This time he taped her hands in front so he could carry her over his shoulders like a backpack, with one arm through her legs and the other through her arms. This kept his hands free, one for the light and another to balance himself as he made his way slowly but certainly back through the woods toward his lair.

Several minutes later Casey came to. At first, she tried to struggle, but by flexing his arms forward Sales was able to squeeze the breath, and the resistance, right out of her. For an hour, he marched in a direct line, stopping only once to rest until they reached his hiding place. After setting Casey down, he crossed to the other side of the cave and slumped against the wall, breathing heavily. The beam of the light careened off the rough rock walls, casting about pitch-black shadows. Sales wiped the sweat from his brow with the back of his shirtsleeve and eyed Casey critically. She stared at him in wide-eyed horror. When he spoke, his voice was low and raspy.

"You see this knife?" he said. He passed the long narrow blade through the light's beam. Casey's eyes grew wide and brimmed with tears. Her mouth was dry and swollen beneath her mask of tape. Sales simply stared at her as he twisted the knife in the air. She began to shiver, not knowing whether it was from fear or cold. Her dirty T-shirt had been soaked clean through from the musky sweat pouring down Sales's back, and now it was starting to cool. She looked at him with pleading eyes and shook her head no.

Sales got up and came toward her with the knife. Through the tape she murmured, "No. No, no, no."

Sales rolled her on her side and pulled her bound wrists behind her head. Using the roll of tape, he fastened the bonds on her wrists to the ones at her ankles, then rolled her to her back. Casey squirmed until Sales put his boot firmly in the center of her chest.

"My daughter," he said, spitting the words at her and pointing with his knife, "was cut open from about here to about there . . ."

Casey was sobbing hysterically now. Sales's face was set in a grim sneer. His pale but bloodshot eyes were deep pools of hatred, and his glare promised no mercy whatsoever.

"You," Sales said in disgust. "The lawyer. You and your fucking laws. What good are your laws? The only laws out here are my laws. I decide who lives and dies.

"The law!" Sales said mockingly, and spit on the cave's floor.

"The Comanches would tie up their hated enemies," Sales continued in a low voice, staring into her eyes. "They would tie them to a stake and cut open their bellies with a knife. This wouldn't kill them. The pain of having your stomach cut open with a knife makes you wish you were dead, but it doesn't kill you. Then they'd yank their guts out and leave them to the buzzards. That way they could watch their insides getting torn apart . . ."

Casey closed her eyes against his evil glare and sobbed uncontrollably. She had almost gotten to the point where she was too tired and sore to even care. He had her. He was going to kill her. Part of her had already succumbed to that fact. But now, the horror of hearing him speak stabbed at her core.

"Marcia was alive when she was cut open," he said without emotion. Then, in a burst of violent rage, he screamed, "Open your fucking eyes! You goddamn bitch! Open your eyes before I cut them out!"

Casey opened her eyes. Sales bent down over her and put the point of the knife just below her sternum.

"She died like this!" he wailed at her. "She was cut open and her insides were pulled out of her and she was alive! She felt the pain, goddamn you! She felt it!"

Casey's stomach heaved, and she gagged, choking, and waited for him to plunge the knife into her body, waited to die. Sales raised his head and let out a primal howl. It was the cry of a mind that had been broken, a spirit dashed beyond recognition. His body, too, began to shake. He screamed and tore at his hair, pulling it out in long, thin strands.

"She was my daughter!" he wailed. "She was my daughter! And you! You shit on her! You shit on me!"

CHAPTER 22

Sales threw the knife toward the back of the cave and then threw himself down beside her on the stone floor.

Casey watched him shake. After several minutes he began to tire, and soon he rose to his hands and knees, with his face turned away from her. Sales stood and then wiped his face on his sleeve and retrieved the knife from where it had landed. When he returned, he carefully cut through the tape at her ankles, then her hands. Finally, slowly, he unwrapped the band around her mouth, gently pressing down on her scalp to remove the sticky tape from her hair as painlessly as possible.

Casey rubbed her wrists and blinked at him in the dim light of the cave. Sales sat back against the far wall and hugged his knees to his chest.

"I'm sorry," he said quietly, looking down at the floor between them. Then he looked up at her defiantly and said, "But I wanted you to know what she felt like. I wanted you to know what they all felt like, what the next girl will feel like and the girl after that and the one after that . . . Unless you help me, it won't ever stop."

"What"—Casey cleared her throat and whispered—
"what are you talking about?"

Sales looked at her. The passionate fire in his eyes was
quenched. They were tired now, dull, almost lifeless.

"I'm talking about Lipton," he said. "I didn't kill Marcia. I didn't kill Frank Castle or the other girl. He killed
them all. And he's going to kill you."

Casey wrinkled her face in doubt. She was still trembling. Sales got up and removed a big flannel shirt from
his pile of things. He crossed the floor of the cave and put
it around her shoulders. The kindness of the act was mag-
nified a hundred-fold. The relief she felt was overwhelming. She railed against the inexplicable sudden feeling of
gratitude she had toward Sales. After all, he had kidnapped her and terrorized her. Casey remembered reading that victims of torture experienced similar emotions,
and she suspected this was the same thing. Whatever was
causing it, she couldn't help the way she felt, almost
giddy.

"I'm not crazy," he said, sitting back down and leaning
back against the wall. With profound sadness he continued, "And if I was a killer, I would have killed you for
what you did."

Casey looked at Sales, and the memory of her tearing
him apart on the witness stand was painfully fresh. Tony
Cronic's warning about accusing an innocent man of having sex with his daughter came to her mind. Despite the
complexity of emotions she was feeling, shame jumped
to the forefront.

"Why do you say he's going to kill me?" Casey heard
herself say, the lawyer's part of her mind automatically
probing for information.

Sales shrugged. "Because he's watching you. He has a

white van that he drives. I don't know how he gets in your neighborhood past the security gates, but I saw him."

Casey thought of the white van she'd seen and the shadowy figure in the parking garage at work.

"He disappeared after the trial, you know," Sales said. "He probably knew I was going to kill him . . ."

"You said you weren't a killer," Casey said, unable to keep a hint of panic from seeping back into her voice.

Sales considered her in the gloom of the cave. He looked down as if contemplating his words, then looked up at her again. "Yeah, well that's different . . . You don't have any kids. You can't really understand . . ."

His eyes were alight again. Casey said nothing. She didn't want to think about it.

"You can't love anything like you love a little girl. You can't imagine it," he said emotionally. "Having your child die, having her killed, having her tortured, cut up . . . that's too much for anyone to think about. But I didn't have a choice, Casey Jordan. Lipton did those things to my little girl . . .

"Someone who did that," he said bitterly, his voice rising, "you kill someone who did that, you rip the life from their body. It's not murder . . . It's justice."

"Why am I here?" Casey asked after an uncomfortable silence.

"I told you," Sales said, looking so deeply into her eyes that she felt exposed. "I want your help."

"How would I help you?" Casey asked.

"I want you to tell me how to find him. What he does, how he does it. I know there was another girl. I want to know where. Where was he then, where else has he gone. You're his lawyer. There are things you know about him that no one else knows. I want to know. That's how you can help find him."

"But there's more," Casey said.

"Yes, there is more," Sales told her. "I know he wants you. If I can stay close to you, I'll get a chance at him. Sooner or later, I'll get a chance at him . . . you're the perfect person to help. You're the one who got him off."

Casey looked at him for a long time before saying quietly, "I still don't know that he killed anyone."

"Hah!" Sales snorted. "You don't know? You don't know? Think about it! You know goddamn well he did it."

"Either he did it or you did it," Casey said angrily. "I don't really know. You didn't have an alibi. You could have killed the girl in Atlanta."

"Could I?" Sales said disdainfully.

"Yes."

Sales jumped to his feet, and with his flashlight in one hand blinding her, he brandished the knife with the other. "If I was going to kill anyone, I'd kill you. How come I didn't kill you just now? Explain that away, Casey Jordan. If that's what I do, I'd kill you!" His words resonated through the cave before the darkness could swallow the sound.

Casey wasn't scared all over again. She knew Sales was angry, but there was no malice in his words. He was speaking out of frustration, and what he said was true. She had expected him to kill her. If he had killed everyone else, why wouldn't he have done it? Unless . . .

"Unless you want me to get to Professor Lipton," she said, shielding her eyes from his light with her hand. "You hate him."

"I would," Sales said. "But if that were true, why would I kill Frank Castle?"

"To make it look like Professor Lipton," she said.

"Now you're not even thinking," he retorted. "If all I wanted was to kill Lipton, why would I bother trying to frame him for another murder?"

"Because of what Frank Castle did to you at the trial," Casey said. It was surreal to be sitting there talking about life and death as if they were poker chips.

"Now we're back to you," Sales said calmly, taking his light off her and shining it on the rock floor that lay between them. "If I was going to kill someone over what happened at the trial, you'd have been first on my list. Believe me, you would have been the only one on my list . . . And if Lipton wasn't the killer, he wouldn't be stalking you. And if he wasn't the killer, stalking you, then there wouldn't be any reason to keep you alive to help me find him."

Casey was used to thinking quickly on her feet, and she knew that everything Sales said was perfectly logical. "You said you wanted me to tell you how to find him."

"I do," Sales said. "But if that's all I wanted, I could have gotten it out of you. Believe me, I could have gotten it out of you and then killed you."

"But we have the disk," she responded.

"What disk?"

"A copy of his computer hard drive. It might have information on it."

"I never knew about a computer disk," Sales said.

Casey rubbed her eyes with the palms of her hands. Of course he didn't know about that. She sighed wearily. "I'm exhausted. I just don't know anything right now. Why is Bolinger so convinced you killed Frank Castle?"

"When he came to question me after Castle was killed," Sales said, "I got in my truck to follow him down to the police station. While I was driving, I reached under my seat for a little thing of lip balm that I dropped. I felt a sticky rag under there, and I had no idea what it was. When I put on the light, I saw it was a shirt and it was all covered with blood. The blood was all over my hands and this knife was wrapped in the middle of the shirt . . .

"Don't you see?" he said. "Lipton put it there. The police would've found it and I would've gone to jail for the rest of my life, if they didn't give me the death penalty. That's what he wants. He's afraid of me. I'm the only thing he is afraid of, because he knows he can't kill me. I'll crush him like a bug. He kills women, girls he can overpower, Frank Castle. He's big and he's strong and he's smart, but he still knows that I'll kill him if I get my hands on him. That's why he wants me in jail. Without me he can do what he wants, kill anyone he wants . . ."

"Meaning me?"

"You and others, too. He'll keep killing," Sales said simply. "He won't stop."

"Why are you so sure he wants to kill me?" Casey asked.

"Because I know. I thought so before I saw him going past your house. I saw the way he looked at you all during the trial. I know. It's a sense, but I know."

"How did you know it was him that drove past?"

"I watched your house for two days. I know him," Sales said.

"Why didn't you just follow him then?"

"I didn't have a car," Sales explained.

"What are you going to do with me now?" Casey asked quietly.

"I'm not going to do anything with you," he said. "I'm not going to force you to help me. At best, you'd slow me down. At worst, you'd trip me up. You do what you want. I'll take you to your car. But if you don't help me, you're making a mistake, a big mistake . . ."

Casey sat still, thinking. Sales got up and opened a can of beans. He handed them to her with a spoon. "You must be hungry."

Casey wolfed them down without a second thought. They tasted as good as anything she'd ever eaten.

"I'll hunt him until I die," Sales said vaguely as Casey wiped the last bit of sauce from the inside of the can with her fingers and licked them clean. "The police won't catch me, and I'll hunt him till I get him. But the longer it takes me, the more women he's going to kill."

"Even if I wanted to help you," Casey said wearily, "there's nothing I can do. The police are looking for you."

"They won't get me. I told you that," he said.

"But I can't help you by crawling around in the woods."

"You can help me by staying with me," Sales said. "I don't mean in a cave. You have a car. You have credit cards and money. You can show me that disk you were talking about. Maybe there's something on it that will tell us where he is or where he'll go next. You can help me track him down."

"No. I can't do that," she said. "I can't help someone who's running from the police. That's aiding and abetting a fugitive. That's a crime. In fact, I should tell you to turn yourself in. I'm not saying it just because of legal ethics, either. It's the smartest thing you could do. The police will get you. Sooner or later, they almost always do. If you turn yourself in, there isn't a judge in Austin who wouldn't give you a reasonable bail. I can help you that way if you want. I can help you turn yourself in . . ."

Sales shook his head. "No. That's not happening. I'm not turning myself in and taking that chance. I don't care what you say. The police won't get me."

"The police will be looking for me, though," she said. "That makes it even more likely that they'll find you."

"No," Sales said. "They won't be looking for you. I don't think they will anyway. Does the alarm company have the keys to your house?"

"No."

"So you must have had the alarm go off before," Sales said. "Think about what happens. First, they call the house. When there's no answer, they call the police. When the police get there, they look around the outside of the house. If there's no sign of anyone breaking in and the alarm company doesn't have a key to the house, they think it's a false alarm. They file a report and go away. Unless your husband came home yesterday, which from the size of his suitcase it didn't look like, then there probably isn't even anyone who knows you're gone."

"That's how you planned it," Casey said bitterly.

"That's how I planned it," Sales admitted. "I'm not going to beg you, you know. But if you don't help, there's going to be a lot more killing . . ."

"I can't just help you hunt someone down to kill them," Casey said, shaking her head. "That goes against everything I believe in."

Sales shrugged. "You believe he should go on killing?"

After a long pause, Casey said, "If I helped you in any way—if I helped you—then it would be to bring Professor Lipton to the police, not to hunt him down to kill him.

I can't do that and I can't help you do that. I never would."

"Even if more innocent women are going to die?" Sales said sharply. "Even if he's going to try to kill you?"

"Yes, even if that," Casey said. "I believe in the system despite its shortcomings. We can't just go out and execute people. That's lawlessness."

Sales scoffed at that with a derisive snort. "Look what your system has done. It's nothing to be so proud of."

"That's your opinion," Casey retorted, defending her vocation out of habit, but aware deep down of her own new doubts. "Nothing's perfect, but it's what I believe in. Whatever help I can be, I have to be to the police."

"That's just what Lipton would want you to do," Sales said in disgust.

"Why is that?" Casey asked dubiously.

"Lipton knows how to stay ahead of the police," Sales cried. "They can't catch him any more than they can catch me. What do they do? Stake out his house, the way they did mine? That's a joke. He knows the rules of the game too well. The police can't get to him the way I can. I'm a hunter and I don't have anything holding me back. You should know that better than anyone. The police can't just bust into a hotel room or break into his van, but I can. He can't hide behind the law from me. But he'll beat the police. He beat them before and he's learned from it. He's always learning. He's a piece of shit, but he's smart.

"Listen," Sales continued. "I want him stopped, period. If you help me get him, I won't kill him."

Casey looked at him skeptically.

"If you help me in a way that'll guarantee he goes to jail," Sales added, "then I won't kill him."

"You're lying," Casey said.

"When Lipton told you he didn't kill that girl in Atlanta," Sales said, "did you believe him?"

"Yes," she said, after a pause.

"Why? Because that's what he said, right?"

"Yes," Casey replied. "That's what he said."

"So, I'm saying I won't kill him and I want you to believe me. I won't kill him. If it means you'll help me, then I won't. If that's what it takes, then I'm saying I'll bring him to justice, to the police. Just give me the same deal you gave him. Help me, Casey. I need your help."

"I want you to take me to my car," Casey said after a few silent minutes of contemplation. "I need to go home. I need to sleep. I need to think."

Sales nodded and rose. The mouth of the cave was beginning to fill up with the pale light of dawn.

"I'll take you to your car, Casey Jordan," Sales said. "But will you help me?"

"Maybe," Casey said, rising stiffly, anxious to get away. She was thinking of the computer disk Tony had. Part of her said it would be wrong to use it. Lipton had given her the computer in confidence as a client. But he was a killer. Didn't she have a higher duty to help stop him if she could?

"Maybe I will."

CHAPTER 23

Sales bundled up his things and offered to carry Casey to the car, but she refused. She stepped gingerly on the rough ground, though, and found herself wishing she'd accepted his offer. The cuts on the bottom of her feet opened up again, and as they descended a gently sloping face of bare rock, Casey became aware of how easy it must have been for Sales to follow her trail through the woods.

Sales turned back toward her, looking weary and depressed. "It's not far," he said.

When they reached Casey's car, Sales got behind the wheel.

"I need you to take me somewhere," he explained. "I'll drive. Then you can go."

The long, twisting dirt road seemed to go forever. At its end, it emptied into a decrepit blacktop road that Casey didn't recognize. Their next turn, however, brought them to familiar ground, and Casey realized that they were now less than two miles from where she lived. But instead of heading back that way, Sales turned west.

Casey's stomach dropped, and she blurted out, "You said I could go home."

"You can. You will," Sales told her, taking his eyes from the road. "I need some way to get around, and I've got an uncle out near Lake Buchanan who'll help me. I need a car."

Sales said no more, and despite her uncertainty, Casey fell asleep with her head resting against the window. When the car eventually came to a stop and the engine was shut off, she bolted upright and wiped a line of drool from her cheek. They were parked in front of a dusty, run-down service station at a barren crossroads. As the fine cloud of grit that marked their arrival settled back to the ground, an old man with a cowboy hat bearing a dead horned toad on its band hobbled out through the open doorway. The wiry old man had long gray braids, and his wrinkled hatchet face told Casey he was a full-blooded Native American.

The old man stared accusingly at them through the settling dust, squinting until Sales got out of the car. Then the hint of a smile tugged at the corners of his mouth, and he turned and walked back into the station. Sales smiled wanly at Casey.

"Come with me if you like," he said. "I'll introduce you to my uncle Ben and you can get a drink."

Casey looked up past a faded Phillips 66 sign at the flaming yellow sun and shrugged. Inside, it took her eyes a minute to adjust to the cool, dim interior. There were shelves in the back crowded with an eclectic array of food items. A glass cooler labored noisily against the back wall, sweating in an effort to keep its milk, beer, and soda cold. Sales went to the back and took out two Diet Cokes.

Uncle Ben had planted himself back behind the counter where he could keep an eye on his pumps through a dirty picture window. An old fan blew enough hot air to tug at the ends of his braids. His mouth worked methodically on a bag of sunflower seeds, spitting the shells out into a plastic cup. On the shelf behind him, Rush Limbaugh droned on over the AM static from a little transistor radio with a twisted coat hanger for its antenna.

Sales took two bills from his pocket and slid them across the counter. The old man silently rang up the soda and went right back to his seeds, waiting patiently for Sales to speak.

"This is my friend Casey Jordan, Uncle Ben," Sales said when the transaction was complete.

Uncle Ben looked up sharply at Casey, then inquisitively at Sales. Casey was certain that the old man knew about the trial and her role in it. She briefly averted her eyes in shame. It wasn't just her and Sales anymore. This old man was real, an average person, the kind of person who lived in the place where she was raised. And the way he looked at her was biting. Looking back on it now, seeing it through the eyes of an average person, what she had done to Donald Sales during the trial was so heinous that the ordeal Sales had just put her through barely seemed an appropriate payback. The guilt of actually accusing Sales of an incestuous relationship with his dead daughter and then suggesting that he was the one who killed her shook Casey's convictions to their foundation. Everything she'd always believed in, winning, success, and notoriety, all of that, when she looked into this old man's face, now seemed a sham.

"She's my friend now," Sales told the uncle firmly. "She brought me here."

The old man nodded as if that was good enough for him.

It was true anyway. Casey was his friend. She would be his friend. She wanted to help him. She felt that with sudden certainty. She just had to figure out how far she could go without committing a crime herself. That she wouldn't do.

"The police are after me, Uncle Ben."

The old man snorted quietly, chastising his nephew for thinking that he didn't already know what was afoot.

"I knew you'd be coming," he said in his haggard voice.

"There's a blue pickup in the back for you," he said. His dark eyes were locked on Sales, and Casey had the feeling that the two of them were saying much more than she could understand without the use of spoken words. "It's got a full tank of gas. You need money, too?"

"No, Uncle Ben. Maybe a credit card."

The old man nodded and split a seed with his front teeth before expertly shucking it with his tongue and spitting out the shells. From a drawer he took out a shiny new Mastercard and laid it on the countertop. Sales took it and put it in his pocket.

Uncle Ben narrowed his eyes as a compact car buzzed by and continued on down the road.

"You gonna eat with us?" he said to Sales.

Sales turned to Casey. "Would you like to come to the house and clean up and then eat?"

"No," she said quietly. "No thank you. I have to go."

Sales nodded and led her out of the station into the heat. He handed her the keys.

"I want to help you," she told him quietly. "I just have to figure out how. I can't break the law. I know you see things differently from me, but everything I've done has always been within the law. I'm not proud of what I did in that trial and I'm sorry. But for me to just do things that are wrong to try and make up for it . . . I don't think I can do that. But I do mean it when I tell you I'm sorry . . ."

She stared up into his eyes. They were deep wells of emotion, churning with so many conflicting thoughts and feelings that she didn't know whether her words had evoked gratitude or more hatred. Then Sales put his large, rough hand on her shoulder. She could feel its horny calluses through the flannel shirt.

With a gentle squeeze he said softly, "I know you are. I see it. There's nothing we can do about what already happened. What's done is done. But you can help what will be. If you help me find Lipton, it'll make things as right as they can be . . ."

Casey felt sick. She wanted to help, but she had to think. She took the keys and turned away.

"I don't even know how to get home," she said softly, opening the car door.

Sales pointed east and said, "The easiest way is if you stay straight on that road there. It runs right into one eighty-three. You know how to go from there?"

"Yes."

"I think it'd be better if we stayed together," he told her, "but I have to go to the house. If I didn't, it would insult them and I can't do that. Are you sure you won't stay?"

"Call me in my office tomorrow morning," Casey said. "I need to figure things out and I'll be fine until then . . ."

Casey wanted a shower. She wanted to put something

on her bare injured feet. She wanted to rest. Most of all, she wanted to gather her wits. The bizarre events of the last day had left her feeling as though she were caught in a disturbing dream.

As she drove, Casey found that it was strangely easy to forget about what Sales had done to her. Part of her understood it. He wanted her help, but he also wanted her to know how it felt to be a victim, how his own daughter had felt. Only Marcia Sales's killing hadn't been a game.

Lipton. The thought of him made her shudder. He was a sick killer. She believed now that Sales was right about him. When she hit the highway, Casey dialed information on her car phone and asked for Bob Bolinger's home number. She got it and pressed one for an instant connection.

"Hello," Bolinger said after nearly six rings. It sounded as if she'd just woken him up.

"Detective," she said, "this is Casey Jordan."

There was silence on the other end until Bolinger cleared his throat.

"It's Sunday," he said. "What do you want?"

"I want to know what kind of protection the police can give me," she said.

"From who?"

"From Professor Lipton," she said. "I think he's been following me. I don't know, but I think so."

Bolinger paused again before saying, "Ms. Jordan, are you all right?"

"I'm all right," she said irritably. "Of course I'm all right. If you mean have I been drinking or something like that, no. But I'm not all right in that I think Professor Lipton has been following me, and I want to know what you can do."

"I can't do much, Ms. Jordan," Bolinger said after a long moment of silence. "I can see if someone from the sheriff's department will go by your house a couple times at night."

"I mean something substantial, Detective."

"We don't do that," Bolinger patiently explained.

"What do you mean, you don't do that?" Casey said incredulously. "You told me yourself you were looking for him. Now I'm telling you he's following me. That should be enough."

"Do you see him right now, Ms. Jordan?" Bolinger inquired.

Casey looked in her rearview mirror, even though she knew Lipton wouldn't be there.

"No, not right now," she said weakly. "But I've seen him."

"You're sure?" Bolinger said in a challenging tone.

Casey's innate integrity made her pause too long. Bolinger knew she was talking about shadows.

"I think what happened with Frank Castle has affected you, Ms. Jordan," he said patiently. "I think you should keep the sheriff's number or my number close by and if you see Lipton, or Sales for that matter, you give us a call."

"That's it?" Casey said.

"Ms. Jordan," Bolinger said quietly, "do you know how many people think they need police protection? We're not in the bodyguard business. If we put an officer with every person who thinks someone is following him, even in cases like yours where they have some kind of link to a perpetrator, there wouldn't be a cop left on the street.

"I'll tell you what I'll do," Bolinger said. "I'll give you

my cell phone number. If you see Lipton, you give me a call."

Casey hung up. It was a long drive back to West Lake Hills. When she got home, she locked the house up tight, took a long, hot shower, and climbed into bed. Typically, Casey slept less than most people. She often read late into the night before she dropped off, and sleep during the day was almost unheard of. But after what she'd been through, despite her anxieties she had no problem at all plunging into a deep, dark sleep.

CHAPTER 24

When Casey awoke, Taylor was standing over her, glowering.

"Taylor?" she said sleepily. The afternoon was gone. From the angle of the light falling through the windows, she knew she'd slept all day.

"Where have you been?" Taylor said in a poisonous tone of voice.

Casey got her bearings and thought of everything she'd been through in the past forty-eight hours. She didn't know how or where to begin.

Taylor interpreted her confusion as a play at deception. He was enraged.

"Goddamn you, Casey!" he growled.

He had discovered the flannel shirt Sales had given her. It was in the laundry basket when he emptied the suitcase from his trip. He held the shirt up for her to see and threw it violently at her face. Casey instinctively flinched away, but Taylor grasped her by the upper arm and yanked her toward him until his face was only inches away, his eyes searching. He'd done plenty of cheating in his day, but he had sworn it would never happen to him in reverse. It was one of the reasons he'd married Casey. He'd never in a million years imagined she would do that to him. The hot flame of hatred and jealousy seared his insides, and he squeezed her hard.

"Let go of me!" Casey shrieked. He had never dared to get physical with her before. No man had. "Let me go!"

Casey struggled to free herself from his grip.

"Where were you last night, Casey?" Taylor demanded, unaffected by her malignant stare.

"Who is he?" he shouted. "Who?"

"You don't even know what you're talking about. Let me go!" Casey shrieked. Finally she snapped her arm free and scrambled to the other side of the bed.

"I know what I'm talking about!" he yelled. "You know! I called here last night. I called here this morning. You were out all night! And now, here you are, sleeping at six o'clock! His shirt was in the fucking laundry bin! Who is it? Goddamn you, Casey! I can't believe you did this to me!"

"You?" she shouted. "You? You who went out to San Francisco to be with that slut of yours! You wouldn't marry her, but she's still glad to sleep with you whenever you get the itch. Well, she's trash and so are you!"

"I wasn't with her!" Taylor shouted, but even to his own ears it sounded false.

Emboldened, Casey hissed, "I know. I had you followed by a private detective."

It was a lie, but she wanted him to know that she knew, and she knew as certainly as if she did have someone following him. "I know what you were doing, and if I had a man," she continued scornfully, "then it's too bad for you. How do you like it, Taylor? How do you like having the person you're married to fucking someone else?"

"You bitch!" he snarled. "It's over. You're just a white trash whore from a hick town. That's all you ever were. That's all you'll ever be! Everyone told me. They told me you weren't good enough and you're not even close."

"Ha!" Casey scoffed bitterly. "I'm not good enough? I'm not good enough? Look at you. You're not a man. A man marries a woman and that's enough. A real man makes his way in the world, and he's too busy doing things to go sleeping around. You never did anything. You couldn't even make it in the world if everything wasn't handed to you on a silver platter. The only way you think you can prove yourself is in the bedroom by screwing around with any woman that would have you, and from what I know, you're not even any good at that."

"Yeah," she said caustically, "you're a real accomplished man, Taylor. I bet you feel real good about all the things you've done with your life."

"Get out," he said flatly. "Get out of my house."

"This is my house as much as it is yours," she said. "You get out."

Casey marched past him, and he raised his hand to strike her. She turned on him and caught his eye with a hateful stare.

"If you touch me again, I'll have the police on you so fast you'll think you were hit by a train."

He stood there shaking, his hand in the air. Casey waited, her eyes shining with defiance until he slowly brought his hand down to his side. Without a word, she went downstairs and sat in the living room with her arms folded tightly as she listened to the faint sounds of him packing his bags. Finally, she heard his footsteps on the stairs. He walked past the living room without a word and into the garage. When she heard his car pulling out, she took a deep breath and set her jaw.

She felt a great sense of relief, as if she'd just come through a long-drawn-out illness. That's what her marriage had been, an illness. As she thought about the things that had prompted her to marry Taylor in the first place, she realized that her whole life had been sick. Her priorities were all wrong. She had wanted a husband who was rich and privileged, a man who would give her universal social acceptance. She had gotten what she wanted, but she had also gotten a husband who was untrue and selfish and who didn't appreciate any of the truly good qualities she had. To him, she was nothing more than a pretty ornament.

She had wanted to be a famous lawyer, too, and look where that had gotten her. She was recognized by many, but she was also reviled. She had also wanted to win at all costs, and look what she'd done. She'd bludgeoned an innocent father, besmirched his reputation, salted his deep, bleeding wounds. Worse yet, she had almost singlehandedly turned a diabolical killer free.

Casey twisted a long piece of her wavy red hair until it hurt.

She felt like she had no one now. Her whole life had been her career. It was such an empty feeling to suddenly face the fact that her husband, the person who was supposed to be closest to her in the world, was emotionally miles away. Casey picked up the telephone. She hadn't spoken to her sister in months. She'd been too busy. She hadn't taken her calls, and she hadn't even thought of her. There was a time when they'd been close, but only when they were little girls. By the time Casey was a teenager, her ambitions had been clear in her head, and her younger sister Shelly's lack of the same were just as evident.

"Shelly?" she said at the sound of the familiar voice.

"Casey? Is that you, girl?" came the response in a backcountry drawl that made Casey involuntarily wince. It had taken her years to eradicate the same accent from her own speech.

"How are you?" Casey asked tentatively.

"Me? Oh, I'm just the same as ever," her sister said, talking as if they'd spoken only yesterday. "The kids are growing like weeds, and Gabe's losing his hair faster than you could think of, but I'm just the same. How are you, though? I seen you on the news during that trial. That's all everyone talked about 'round here, my famous sister. God dawg, you should of seen Momma and Daddy. They were ready to bust at church, everyone crowding around them and asking about you . . ."

"What did they say?" Casey asked, with the sudden realization that she hadn't spoken with her parents in a good long while, either.

"Well, you know Daddy, he don't say nothing, and Momma, she just chattered on like a jay bird about Casey this and Casey that, telling stories about when you was young. You know, stuff you did that let all us know you was gonna be something special . . ." Shelly's words were completely ingenuous. She was one of the rare few who go through life without a hint of jealousy, and the goodness of her sister and the life she led gave Casey a sharp pang of dismay.

"I'm not the special one," she said seriously. "You are, Shelly. Look at you, a husband and three kids . . ."

"Oh, that ain't nothing," her sister said bashfully. "I

didn't even get a four-year degree, and you got a husband, too.

"A handsome one with hair," she added with a giggle.

"No, I don't have a husband," Casey said.

There was a painful silence, and then Shelly said sadly, "I'm sorry, Casey. I didn't know. Are you okay?"

"I'm okay," she said, falling back lamely on her habit of indefatigable optimism. "I'm really okay."

"Once means you are, twice means you aren't," Shelly said quietly. It was an adage of their father's, and Casey had never known it not to be true.

"Well, I'll be fine," Casey said.

"How about you come for a visit?" Shelly suggested pleasantly. "It'd be good to see you. I'll get Gabe to watch the kids, and you and I can go out and have a dinner and go to a movie like we did last time you come home. You remember that? Lord, how the men followed you around town."

"They were following you," Casey said kindly.

Shelly laughed out loud at the thought until her mirth was mixed with the wail of a baby.

"Oh, honey, I gotta feed this baby," Shelly said apologetically. "Can I call you back?"

"No, I've got to go anyway," Casey said.

"You come see me," her sister said gently. "I love you, honey."

"I love you, too," Casey said, choking on her words. She hung up the phone and burst into tears.

After a good cry and a deep breath, it was Sales's words that suddenly filled her head. He was right. There was nothing she could do about what already was, only what would be, and her life wasn't going to go on the way it was. She was going to change it. It would take time, but she would change. She would go see her sister. She'd go for a good long visit.

There was a place in life where she knew she belonged. It was somewhere between where she was now and where Shelly was. She could never live on a farm outside Odessa, but maybe she could have a family and children. She knew if nothing else she could do good things with her life instead of striving for empty aspirations of money and fame.

And she was going to start now. She was going to do something that heretofore had been unthinkable, to use privileged information against a client. Strictly speaking, it was wrong. But Casey wasn't going to run her life by strictly interpreted legal codes anymore. She was going to listen to her heart. She was going to find out what was on Lipton's computer disk, and if it could help bring him to justice she would use it. She would somehow get it to the police. She picked up the phone.

Tony was at home.

"I'll meet you at the office," he told her somberly after hearing the bulk of her bizarre story.

As Casey drove to the city, she paid little attention to the traffic around her. She was exhilarated at the thought of turning her life around, of purging everything she'd been and thinking of what she would be. Things weren't all bad. She'd done good work for people, pro bono work, work for free. She could do more. She could stop seeking celebrity and begin to seek justice. She could stop running around the country at the beck and call of the rich and famous and use the gifts she had to protect the innocent. She could represent the unjustly accused who didn't have the money or the power to defend themselves against the awful machine that, once set against you, could grind your life to dust.

Casey realized she was almost there. Remembering Lipton, she looked nervously in her rearview mirror. The traffic of people heading downtown for a night of music and drinking on Sixth Street even on a Sunday night was enough to make it impractical for her to pick out anyone who might be following her.

She certainly wasn't going into the parking garage. It would be dark and abandoned on a Sunday night. Instead, she found a spot on the street. The night was warm, and the damp breeze promised rain. Casey looked up at the churning gray clouds, then cast her eyes suspiciously up and down the street. The only other person in sight was a tall bum whose grocery cart rattled and squeaked stridently as he pushed his way up the street. Casey hurried across the sidewalk and up the steps of the mid-rise office building where she worked.

A night security man was sitting wearily at his desk by the door. With a smile and a nod, Casey stepped into a vacant elevator. Tony was waiting in her office, looking out of place in a triple X pink short-sleeve polo shirt. He was sitting on the small conference table in the corner, and he waved a pudgy hand to her from behind his own portable PC.

"Thanks for coming, Tony," Casey said, sitting down beside him. "Did I keep you waiting?"

"No, just long enough for me to get the layout of Lipton's hard drive." Tony spoke without looking up at her. He didn't want to reveal the range of emotions he was feeling, and he knew better than to try to console her. That would be the last thing she would want. The next-to-last thing would be advice, so he kept to the business at hand.

"The files I've found aren't what we're looking for," he said. "But most likely, anything he didn't want people to find is in some hidden files somewhere. I just need to find them."

"Can you do that?"

"That's what this is for," he said. He held up a gray box with some wires hanging from it. "It's called a Norton Utility."

Tony began connecting the box to the back of his computer. He typed frantically for a minute or two to set the program in motion. When he'd finished, he looked up at Casey and really saw her for the first time.

"You want to talk?" he said.

She looked at him. "No. I'm fine."

"Okay," he said. "I don't know if I totally believe you, but okay."

"Why don't you believe me?"

"You were kidnapped and estranged from your husband all in the same weekend," he said calmly. "Most people wouldn't be completely fine . . ."

With a smile he said, "I don't want to pry and I don't want to drag it out. I wasn't going to say anything, but I just want you to know I care . . ."

"I know you do, Tony," she said with her beautiful smile. "I appreciate it. But I really am fine. What happened with Sales . . . Well, I almost feel like I deserved it," she said. "I know that sounds strange, but that's how I feel. After what I did . . . I don't know. It doesn't bother me. That's all. And what happened with Taylor was a good thing . . . It made me realize what's important and what isn't. What I don't feel good about is Lipton and getting him off."

"There was a jury—" Tony began to protest.

"No," she said, holding up her hand. "Don't, Tony. Don't rationalize it. I know what I did and so do you. I know the line. It was my duty as a lawyer to do everything within the law to protect my client. Yeah, I can justify it to myself and you and every other lawyer in the world, but in the big picture I was still wrong. Now if I can help to make it right, then that's what I'll do."

Before Tony could say anything more, the computer emitted a high-pitched two-toned beep, and he looked automatically at its screen.

"I found them," he said.

Casey leaned toward him. "Can you get in?"

"Let's find out," he said, rapidly pounding away.

Several minutes went by, then Tony said, "Got it! Hang on. Let me transfer them to some regular files . . ."

Casey watched and waited while he hammered away.

Tony said, "Good."

Casey looked with anticipation at the screen. A full-color graphic of some beige fluted columns surrounding the scales of justice filled the screen with a crimson backdrop. The bold title THE LETTER OF THE LAW jumped out at them. Tony moved the mouse down to the menu across the bottom of the screen. Listed was everything from outlines and contacts to schedules and expenses. Apparently, everything to do with Lipton's seminar business was there.

"What's this?" Casey said, pointing to an icon labeled SWANK.

Tony selected the icon, and the computer whirred away until a page came up that was lined with school photos of women from law school yearbooks. Casey's heart raced as Tony scrolled down through page after page. Next to each photo was a vita on the girl that included a physical description, where she lived, and a lewd account of her personality that linked each characteristic to a graphic depiction of a specific sexual act that she was most fond of performing. Much of it was sadomasochistic.

"This stuff can't be true," Casey said, looking at Tony with disbelief.

"I don't know," he said as he typed in a command, "you tell me."

Casey followed his eyes to the screen. There was her picture. At least it was a youthful resemblance of her. There were apparently hundreds of women in the file, but Tony had stopped scrolling and gone right to the letter *W* for Woodgate, her maiden name. Casey read what it said. It disgusted and horrified her at the same time. More than anything, it made her feel terribly unsafe.

"But he never did anything to me," Casey heard herself saying weakly.

Tony searched to the letter *S*. Marcia Sales's picture appeared before them.

"But he did something to her," Tony said solemnly. He went to the menu again and chose to search through the women by location. Atlanta, Georgia, produced four. Casey recognized one of the names as belonging to the girl who had been killed there only a few months before Marcia Sales's death.

"And her," Casey said.

"The question is," Tony added, "how many others?"

"My God," Casey said. The horror of the whole thing was almost too much. "My God."

"He's a sick son of a bitch," Tony said disgustedly. "He's everything the DA said he was, worse even."

"I know that, Tony," Casey snapped. "But it was a big case, remember?"

Tony shot her a nasty look.

"We lost the rock star so we took the law professor," she said in a voice laced with sarcasm. "We were going to get a lot of media coverage for this one, so we jumped all over it."

Tony continued to stare at her.

"Go easy," he said.

"No, Tony," she snapped. "I'm not going easy. It's wrong. The whole thing is wrong."

Calmly he said, "You were a kid out of law school doing minor-league rape cases for the DA before you met me. Now you get six-figure retainers for people in the news, and they call you to do interviews on CNN. That's what you wanted and that's what I got you. So don't get nasty with me. You wanted this kind of practice as much as I did."

"Well, maybe I don't want it anymore."

Tony glared at her, then stood up and started for the door.

Casey sat there alone for a long time. The small noises of the empty building were amplified in the silence of the Sunday night. Her mind spun this way and that like a broken kite in a stiff wind, going back and forth on what she had been and what she would now be. She wondered if Tony would even want to be a part of the new Casey . . . Woodgate. She thought about all the things she could have done differently until she could bear it no longer. She had to do something now. She ejected the disk from the Norton Utility and flicked off the computer before turning for the door.

The code of ethics proscribed disclosing the information she had to the police. The privilege between a client and his attorney prevented that. But what if it was to turn up on Bolinger's doorstep anonymously? It was unethical. Then again, what Lipton had done with her had nothing to do with ethics. The way he had manipulated her to represent him, to help set him free, was a despicable misuse of the law, and she had not only been a party to it, she had been the prime mover. She tucked the disk into the pocket of the light coat she'd taken as a hedge against the coming rain and made for the elevator.

It took several minutes for the car to reach the top floor. Only one elevator was operational after hours, and Casey presumed that one had to come all the way up from the basement, where Tony had taken it to get to his own vehicle. When it finally arrived with the familiar ding, Casey peered warily inside before stepping aboard and pushing the lobby button. She wasn't usually skittish, but after the last few days, she wasn't ashamed of being apprehensive.

Anxious to get off, Casey watched the numbers above the door as they hopscotched their way toward the lobby. But when the car reached the second floor, there was none of the typical slowing that preceded a stop. Casey's heart jumped into her throat and her blood began to race. The *L* button on the panel was no longer lit. She'd pushed it. She was sure she had. She stabbed at it again, but the button only illuminated momentarily before going dark again. She pushed it repeatedly to no avail. The car went right past the lobby. It was as if someone else was in control of the elevator.

P1 was the first level of parking below the street. That floor lighted above the door, but still the elevator continued its descent. It ran past P2 as well, but then began to slow. At P3, the lowest level in the building, the elevator came to a halt. The car was quiet until the doors began to heave themselves open with a mechanical rumble. Casey stabbed at the lobby button once again. The light went on, but as soon as she removed her finger, it went dead dark. She stabbed at it frantically, over and over, while at the same time pounding repeatedly on the Close Door button. Then everything went black.

Casey could hear the dying whine of the elevator motor somewhere below her in the pit of the shaft. Terrified, she pressed herself into the corner of the darkened car and peered out into the yawning gloom of the subterranean garage.

CHAPTER 25

Not far away, in a hip bar on Sixth Street, James Unger was whispering something lewd into a young woman's ear. He took a drink in the face for his efforts. He wasn't angry. He got what he deserved. He was way out of his league, a worn-out government employee, not the slick young law enforcement agent he once was. That was how he'd begun his career, full of hope and grand ideas. Back then he had even fantasized about being the director. But that was then, this was now. He took off his glasses and wiped his face on the sleeve of his golf shirt. After cleaning his glasses, he finished off his vodka tonic. The girl was gone now, and the incredible din of the music made it seem as if the little incident had happened to him in another place and time.

Unger sighed heavily and turned to find his friend. Dean Johnson was standing in front of the band, swaying to the rhythm that wailed from the two massive speakers on either side of the stage. He looked like a fool. A paunch hung down over the front of his belt. The back of his balding head, his thin, sunburned arms, and his big, bulbous nose made Unger look like a catch. In front of the car dealer was the band's lead singer, a raven-headed girl dressed up like a Native American, right down to her beads and moccasins. She had a wicked body that somewhat offset the nastiness of her face, and to the amusement of all the young people watching, she sang her suggestive lyrics right at Dean.

Unger grabbed his friend by the arm and tugged him outside, where the relative quiet of the street rang in their ears.

"What the fuck!" Johnson howled drunkenly. "She wanted me! Did you hear that girl's voice? She wanted me."

Unger only shook his head impatiently. "Let's go home."

His words came out in a long, slow slur.

Johnson looked at his friend in a daze before suddenly grinning and saying, "Not yet. I got a surprise for you."

"What's that?"

"Hookers," Johnson told him, his eyes agleam.

"You're kidding," Unger said. That wasn't his style, but he knew from the last few days that his friend liked to spend every cent of the money he made at his dealership on living well. That meant champagne at dinner, cigars with expensive brandy, and now women. Unger wasn't opposed to it on ethical grounds; it was just something he'd never indulged in before.

"I'm not kidding," Johnson mumbled and began staggering up a side street that intersected Sixth.

"I don't do that stuff," Unger said, trailing him.

"My treat," Johnson muttered. Even though he was from Cleveland, he had adopted a southern drawl, and Unger was suddenly aware of it as acutely as if he were hearing it for the first time. "You ain't gonna go back home without experiencing some of the finest trim Texas has to offer. I'm not talking about a twenty-dollar blow job. I'm talking around the world, my friend. Around the big blue world with a pro in a first-rate establishment."

Unger grabbed his friend gently by the arm and said, "Aw, come on, Dean, you don't really want to go to a whorehouse . . ."

Johnson's face lit up with a smile. He leaned close to his old friend, and with the alcohol riding hard on his breath, he whispered, "This ain't a whorehouse, my friend. This is the Roman Empire . . ."

Unger gave him a puzzled look as his brain did a fast rewind. That was a name that he'd just heard, and it had something to do with something important.

"What did you say?" he said. "What did you call that place?"

"The Roman Empire, my friend," Johnson leered. "There's nothing quite like it."

"The Roman Empire," Unger muttered, and then it hit him. It was the name that Bolinger had mentioned when he filled him in on the Lipton investigation. That was about a dozen martinis ago, but Unger was certain of it now.

"Is this the kind of place where you could have pictures taken and stored on a computer disk, digital pictures?" he asked.

Johnson slapped him roughly on the back and cried out, "That's the spirit!"

"Is it something they do?" he asked impatiently.

"It's a high-tech place," Johnson said. "I never did it, but if any place could do it, this would be the one."

"Take me there," Unger said.

They got into Johnson's red Mercedes coupe and drove uphill toward the downtown area, then down another side street into what looked like a nice neighborhood.

Except for the wind whipping random drops of rain down at them, it was a quiet street on the border of the area where the office buildings began and the hip new urban condos surrounding Sixth Street ended. The few cars parked against the curb were strikingly lavish, and they gleamed like museum pieces under the streetlights. They got out of the candy-apple car and Johnson started up a set of steps, then looked around before backing down and proceeding to the next flight.

"Don't you know where you're going?" Unger asked impatiently.

"I know. I know."

They mounted the next set of steps and Johnson opened the door, gallantly waving his friend into the inconspicuous entryway. A single camera hanging from the corner of the ceiling watched over the doors of a shiny brass elevator. Johnson took a gold card from his wallet and held it up close to the camera.

"You gotta belong to the club," he told Unger happily.

After a minute the elevator doors opened abruptly, and Johnson chuckled.

"After you," he said, motioning Unger inside.

The elevator stopped and deposited them in a large white marble reception area whose chrome fixtures and black leather furniture gave it the look of a funky, well-heeled business office. Johnson introduced Unger to the buxom redheaded woman behind the desk as his old friend from Atlanta. The woman, who wore a low-cut black dress and enough makeup to cover a manhole, showed no interest and only asked them how they would be paying. Johnson dramatically removed the gold card from his wallet again. He shot his friend an accusatory look as the woman ran the card through her machine and asked him to sign off on the one-thousand-dollar charge to Roman Empire Ltd.

With the transaction complete, the woman studied a screen behind the desk in a detached way before showing them down the hall to an empty room. It was a small, private lounge with a black couch, two big, low leather chairs, and silver-framed copies of Paul Klee paintings on the walls that Unger couldn't name but recognized enough to remark that it was certainly a classy joint. On the glass coffee table were two well-worn laptop PCs whose cables trailed off into the wall.

"Can I get you a drink while you make your selections?" the redhead asked. She was polite but distant, and the insect-green contact lenses in her eyes gave her an otherworldly appearance.

Johnson asked for a beer. Unger wanted straight vodka, cold. The woman disappeared for their drinks. Johnson, bubbling with excitement, sat down on the edge of the couch.

"It's all in this computer," he said, going to work with the mouse. "Just like buying a car. Here's all the girls, but look what you can do: options. See? I pick this little number, now I can change what she's wearing. Look, I'll put her in this red lace thing. Look, I can change the color of her hair . . ."

He selected an option, and the girl on the screen, a brunette, disappeared for a second only to come back as a blond.

"Now look at this stuff," Johnson said, his cherry red cheeks and nose shining like a fire truck under their sheen of sweat. "It's like options on a sedan. I can choose the room I want her in, the backdrop, the music, everything!

"You like chains?" he asked with a snicker. "This is what she looks like in chains. You want to see a sample of her getting it on? Look at this! I hit this and I get a video of her on top, or her on the bottom, however I want to see her getting it on. Is this a place or what? It's total high tech."

Unger involuntarily moistened his lips and nodded that it was. He reached for his own mouse on the tabletop as the redhead returned with their drinks.

"You gentlemen need any help?" she asked.

"No, we know what we want," Johnson said, sipping his beer with a knowing grin.

"Uh," Unger began taking a deep breath, "does anyone ever have you take pictures, digital pictures, I mean, the kind you could put on a computer?"

The redhead stared at him imperiously for a moment before saying, "Is that what you want?"

"I . . ." Unger stumbled. "It's not for me. I just wanted to know."

"If it's not for you," she said icily, "then you don't need to know, do you?"

Unger said nothing. He was intimidated by the woman's direct, confident stare. He looked at his friend. Johnson was too elated with his selection of hookers to even notice the interchange. Unger felt totally out of place. He shouldn't have come.

"But you could do it if I wanted you to do it?" he asked weakly.

"If you want pictures," she said, "you let me know."

When she was gone, Johnson told Unger, "When you

decide what you want, you just hit this select button right here in the corner."

"Then what?"

"Then they come get you after a few minutes and voilà! They take you off to your room, and you've got everything you want, just the way you ordered it up. It's living, James. It's living big."

Unger nodded. He was there because he thought it could be something, but his mind was too muddled to know what. He wanted to ask the redhead about Lipton, break her down, interrogate her. But he really had no idea of how to begin. He was out of his league here. Maybe the best thing would be to go along with the whole thing and just see what happened. Maybe one of the girls would know something. Maybe she would be nicer. He really didn't have any intention of doing anything with a hooker, but he had no compunction about spending or even wasting Dean Johnson's money. Easy come, easy go.

He looked at his own computer screen and quickly found a girl who looked like she might talk.

"No, no, take your time," Johnson urged. "Look it over. See how she looks on top. Take a test drive."

"No, this is good," Unger said impatiently. He hit Select, and the computer shut down automatically. "I guess they don't want you changing your mind."

Unger threw down the rest of his drink to preserve his present state of mind. His nerves were starting to wear away at his buzz. He peered casually over his friend's shoulder and looked on as Johnson cried out every other minute for him to "Look at this." Suddenly the redhead appeared in the doorway. She was staring disdainfully at Unger.

"This way," she said, motioning to him with a jagged smile.

Unger was led around the corner and down another hallway. He could tell from the seamless curves in the dress that the hostess wore no underwear. Despite a slight sag she wasn't half bad, an old whore with a knack for business. It was evident that she owned the place. Unger knew enough about prostitution to know that anyone with a joint like this had to be hands-on or else be robbed on a nightly basis.

The hostess showed Unger into a dimly lit bedroom. The walls were faux-painted to look like faded marble. The king-size bed stood in the center of the room, its four bronze posts nearly scraping the ceiling.

"Have fun," the redhead sneered in a husky voice as she shut the door. Seconds later another door opened on the opposite wall and there she was, just the same as she looked on the screen, a tall Barbie doll blond with long, straight hair, a prodigious chest, and thick pink-bubblegum lips. She wore high white pumps and a tight white nurse's uniform, right down to the old-style headpiece.

"Goddamn," Unger uttered, taking a step back.

She smiled at him and stood waiting.

Unger swallowed hard and said tentatively, "Do you mind if I ask you some questions?"

The blond smiled pleasantly back at him. She crossed the room and took his hand in her own, putting the other gently against his cheek.

"You're nervous," she whispered. "Don't be afraid. You can ask me anything. We can talk."

She led him to the bed and they sat down side by side.

"First of all," he began, trying hard to catch his breath and feeling every bit a fool, "do you take pictures? I mean, could someone come in here and do things and have pictures taken and keep them, digital pictures?"

"We can do that," she said, rising from the edge of the bed.

"No," he said, holding her arm. "Not for me. I just wanted to know if someone could do that, and I wanted to know if you've ever seen a man, a professor named Lipton, around here. He might have done some things and had some pictures taken."

The blond glanced quickly at the side door. She gave him a pout and said, "We can't talk about other clients . . ."

"I know," Unger said. "I just figured, you know, between you and me, you might just let me know if it was possible that he was here."

She leaned close to him, and her fingertips gently descended the front of his shirt until they found his crotch. Unger stopped her hand. His heart thumped uncontrollably.

"Anything's possible," she whispered, her lips brushing his own.

He could smell the fresh smell of strawberry shampoo in her silky hair.

"I'm an FBI agent," he blurted out.

The girl froze.

"I just want to get some information. This isn't a bust or anything. I just want to know if you saw this guy I was talking about."

A piercing shriek on the other side of the wall startled Unger so badly that he jumped clear off the bed. A din of crashing and shouting followed the scream, or whatever the initial noise had been. Unger found his Glock, crossed the floor, and yanked open the door. He peered cautiously into the hall. A tall figure backed out of the next room down, shouting unintelligible obscenities back into the room.

"Hey!" Unger shouted, stepping into the hall. "Hold it right there!"

The man, who was fully dressed, turned toward Unger. His face boiled with rage and his bright blue eyes gleamed madly amid the wrinkles of his tan face and wavy blond hair. Unger recognized him instantly as Lipton, the man Bob Bolinger was so desperate to find. It was so bizarre Unger felt he must be in a crazy dream. Lipton marched purposefully toward him, a deranged man with no regard for the agent's gun staring him in the face.

"Stop right there, asshole!" Unger shouted, his voice shaking hysterically. He was acutely aware of the situation. If he pulled the trigger on a weaponless man in a situation like this, his whole career was over.

"Stop!" he shouted fiercely, but Lipton was right next to him now and he shoved Unger aside with disdain, continuing his march down the hall and muttering inaudibly to himself.

In a panic, Unger ran to the door Lipton had come from. The room was nearly empty and more spacious than his had been. It was lit with psychedelic black lights. In the middle was a girl strapped facedown to a kind of gymnastics horse. Her hands and feet were chained to the floor, and Unger dashed in to see if she was still breathing. His heart raced. She looked like she was dead.

Unger grabbed a handful of the girl's hair and lifted her face off the horse. A steady stream of obscenities told him she was fine. He let her head drop back to the padded leather horse and looked around the room. There was a table off to the side that had been dumped over. Scattered across the floor were whips and chains and other instruments, whose purposes were a mystery to Unger.

"What the hell's going on?" the redhead demanded. She stood in the doorway with a small black handgun of her own. "What are you doing?"

"Hey," Unger said, raising his firearm in surrender. "It wasn't me. I just came in here to see what was up. She's okay, though. That was Professor Lipton."

"I know who it was." The redhead glared. "Go back to your room."

She turned and stormed away.

Unger stood frozen for a moment, collecting his thoughts. He passed the lounge where he'd last seen Dean and wondered that he'd seen no sign of him in the hallway. Apparently, his friend was like the rest of the clientele, more concerned with his privacy than with jumping to anyone's rescue. Unger had gone to the scream instinctively, but now his motives were purely selfish.

He'd seen people get lucky, and from a distance he'd studied luck, longing for it his entire career. This was James Unger's chance, and he wasn't about to let it slide. He could pick up Lipton's track here and now and take full credit if it turned out he really was the killer Bolinger claimed. There were no guarantees, but from what he'd heard, Bolinger's theory just might be true. Unger had presumed all along that the case was a dead end because Lipton had most likely fled the country.

Now he knew that wasn't the case. With some careful maneuvering, Unger could turn this whole thing into the chance of a lifetime. Maybe it was his turn now. After all these years, maybe it was just his turn. Unger felt a transformation coming over himself. The old thrill, the moxie, the drive, it all came back to him in seconds and he felt like he was twenty-five again, in his first year with the bureau.

There was no sign whatsoever of Lipton. The old whore was sitting at her desk, smoking hard on a Pall Mall and trying to look as if nothing out of the ordinary had happened. She looked critically at Unger and blew a vicious stream of smoke toward the ceiling.

"It's over," she said dully. "You want your girl back for another go?"

"No," Unger said, nervously at first, then with more authority, "I want to talk with you."

The redhead snorted derisively. "I'm not paid to talk."

Unger's face burned. Then he opened his wallet and slapped his badge down on the desk in front of her. "I am."

The redhead raised her eyebrows in mock concern. "Oh, I've never seen one of those before," she said sarcastically.

"You better look closer, lady," Unger said, feeling the rage of so many years of disappointment building up inside him. "I'm not one of your local dicks."

"No," she said caustically, "you're an out-of-town dick for sure."

Nevertheless she looked more carefully at his badge, and the fact that he was a Fed seemed to make an impression. "So what do you want from me?" she asked, a little more cooperatively.

"I want to know what you know about Lipton."

"He's a client and we don't talk about our clients. Isn't that comforting?" she said, raising an eyebrow.

Up close now, Unger could see the haggard wrinkles beneath the thick coating of makeup. She was a smart-ass old whore, a lowlife, a common criminal, and she was standing in the way of the only chance he'd ever come close to at breaking a big case, at being someone people pointed at and said, "There goes James Unger."

"Let me tell you how this can work," Unger said, looking around apprehensively before he circled the desk. His heart leapt into his throat, and he seemed to be almost outside himself, but he was going to do this. With a sneer of his own, he snatched a handful of her hair, twisted the course red strands in his hand, and slammed her head down against the surface of the desk in one quick move. Then he bent down himself, putting his face inches away from hers and speaking with quiet, trembling malice. "This can work the hard way, or the easy way.

"Here's the hard way," he said. "I call in the locals and have them freeze everybody and everything in this whole fucking building. I then get a search warrant from a federal judge—which is about as hard for me as getting a pack of bubble gum—and I tear this fucking place apart from top to bottom. I arrest your ass for aiding and abetting a criminal suspect, and I call up my friends over at the IRS to lock on to you and every fucking john in your records for the rest of their lives. That's the hard way . . ."

Unger took a gasping breath, afraid of what he was doing, but too committed to his course to go back now.

"You getting the fucking picture?" he asked angrily. "By the way, so you know, I'm here on business.

"I tracked Lipton here," he said, as much to himself as to her, "who is the subject of an FBI investigation, so don't think you've got anything over me, lady.

"Now, the easy way," Unger said, breathing a little easier now. "You take me back into your little office and you give me everything, and I mean every fucking thing you've got on Lipton. You do that for me and I walk out of here a happy man. The next time you hear from me is when I'm giving a press conference on CNN when I nail his ass.

"That sound good?" Unger asked pleasantly. He liked his new role and the power he felt.

She nodded and he let her go. Unger stepped back and the redhead got up. She looked at him fearfully and it made Unger smile. She straightened herself briskly, then led him through a door in the wall behind the desk. They were in a small office with a beat-up metal desk, a computer, a phone, and a large glass ashtray that needed emptying. The redhead looked at her watch and said nervously, "My husband will be back in a half hour, so let's make this fast, okay? It'd be better for everyone if you got what you needed and got out of here before he gets back. I don't want any trouble."

"Fine by me, lady," Unger said imperiously. "You just give me what I want."

She sat down at the computer and brought up Lipton's credit card information.

"This card belongs to a Sarah Lipton," Unger said.

The redhead shrugged. "It works. It's worked for the past three years. As long as I get paid, I don't care whose name is on the card."

"Where's this?" he asked, pointing to the billing address. "Where's Selton?"

"Up I-35 toward Houston," she told him hesitantly. "It's a little town near the Stillhouse Hollow Reservoir. I grew up near there."

Unger allowed himself a beaming smile. This would be news to Bolinger. He'd been frantically trying to find out where Lipton had been hiding and now Unger had it. He tore off a piece of paper from a sheet on the desk and jotted the information down.

"That's all I need," he said, turning to leave.

"You don't need to talk to his girl?"

"No," Unger said dismissively. "I've got everything right here."

"You won't tell him you got it from me," she said, worriedly sucking in her lower lip.

Unger saw Dean appear in the main office looking rumpled and bewildered.

Unger turned from his friend to the whore and said, "Maybe you comp me and my friend for the night and this whole thing never happened. How does that sound?"

The old whore spit out her lip and nodded in assent.

"Good," he said sternly. He ushered his friend into the elevator, and as it went down his spirit soared.

When they hit the street, he turned to his questioning friend and said with a grin, "I can't believe I just did that."

CHAPTER 26

Hey!"

Casey heard the shout from the corner of her dark elevator. There were footsteps running across the concrete, another shout and more footsteps, and the deafening roar of gunfire. The sound of the shots reverberated through the concrete containment. Casey bolted from the back corner of the car to the narrow wall adjacent to the open door. She pressed herself against the elevator's dead panel of buttons, hoping it gave her more protection.

Silence: A dim ghost of fluorescent light spilled into the car. Casey felt her heart thumping at a breakneck pace. Then more footsteps clacking along on concrete, moving more slowly this time, but deliberate and coming her way. Her mind spun. Should she scramble from her hiding place? Whoever had cut the power must know she was there. But there had been a distraction, someone running, someone being shot at. Was it the security guard or Tony? Either way, it might have given her time to flee from her small, dark prison. The steps continued to echo toward her.

She would wait, wait until he came to her, then spring on him with all the fight she had. Casey crouched, trembling, acutely aware of her overwhelming sensation of having to use the bathroom. The footsteps were twenty feet away . . . now ten. They stopped, and Casey thought she would scream. The faint sound of a man's heavy breathing froze her soul. She thought of all the things she had done and all the things she still wanted to do. She was too young to die. She had to wait. If she sprang now, she'd lose her only chance, the only opportunity at surprise, no matter how slight.

"Casey?"

The man's voice was low and rough, but quiet.

"Casey, I know you're there."

Trembling, ready to explode, Casey crouched even lower to the floor.

"Casey, it's me, Don Sales," came the voice. "He's gone. Lipton's gone. He ran. You're safe. Come out, Casey."

Casey felt her limbs go limp. She slumped down to the elevator floor, shaking.

"Casey?"

"I'm here," she said softly.

Donald Sales knelt beside her, pulling her head to his chest. She felt his hand, big and strong, moving in slow, comforting circles on her back.

"It's all right," he told her. "He's gone."

After a minute, Casey regained her composure and rose to her feet, gently separating herself from him. She sniffed and brushed the hair back from her face.

"I'm fine," she said, somewhat embarrassed.

"You have to stay with me," he told her. "He'll get you

if you don't. You've got to help me, Casey. I can stop him, but you've got to tell me everything you know."

"I will," she said. She could see that now, too. As crazy as it might sound, as crazy as it might be, she needed him. Things were out of control, and he seemed to be the only thing solid right now that she could grab on to. "How did you know I was here?"

Sales shrugged. "I followed you. After I left my uncle's, I went right to West Lake Hills to watch the entrance to your development. I knew he would come for you. He's obsessed . . . Shit, I can't believe he got away." Sales slapped the leg of his jeans.

"How did he do that to the elevator?" Casey asked. They were outside the elevator now, and despite Sales's presence, the garage was still eerie.

"Over here," he said, pointing to a utility room whose gray steel door was ajar.

Casey turned to him and asked desperately, "Why do you say he'll come back?"

"Because he will," Sales said unequivocally.

"So what do we do?" Casey asked, trying without success to smooth the anxious edge in her voice.

"Help me find him," Sales urged. "He's got to have a place he's hiding that's nearby. You've got to tell me where."

"I can't," she told him desperately. "I don't know where he is! I have no idea!"

"He was your client!" Sales argued.

"I've got his disk," she said, touching her pocket. "I'll let you see the whole thing, but just get me out of here."

CHAPTER 27

Lipton became suddenly aware of the tension in his face, and he tried consciously to relax each muscle, one at a time. He drove carefully through the streets, checking his rearview mirror for signs of whoever it was who had drawn a gun on him. He doubted a cop would have been in the next room with a hooker and presumed it was just some do-gooder who certainly didn't have the balls to shoot anyone.

A smile crossed his face. Lately, he'd acquired the marvelous sensation that no one could kill him. He felt impervious to the rest of mankind, somehow above them all. He could hunt and kill what he needed and have his whores perform for him. The cycle seemed to be strengthening him.

He felt his face tightening again. It wasn't really the whore he'd been mad at. It was the predicament. He'd used the last remnants of his powder, and as he had feared, it hadn't been enough for him to perform. No, the whore herself was the one he always used, wonderfully docile. She had simpered and begged as submissively as she always did. In fact, since he'd been released after the trial, he'd had an exceptional run of bouts with her to make up for his time in isolation.

But the run was so exceptional that he'd used up every bit of his powerful aphrodisiac. And Casey wasn't going to be an easy victim. The gated community made it difficult to get to her at home. Although he'd scoped it out thoroughly, it would be a risky venture to try to take her from the parking garage; someone could see him and then he'd be trapped. He had abandoned that idea several days ago. He needed to be patient. It would happen in its own time. That much he knew.

He felt her spirit calling to him. All during the trial, her imperious mannerisms had left him dreaming of her at night. She needed him to crush the life from her. She needed him as much as he needed her. She needed to give up her essence to him so he could perform the sexual acts that kept his circle of power intact. It was those acts, he knew after years of experience, that were compounding to generate his invincibility. It was her destiny as much as his.

His own destiny had become clearer and clearer each passing day over the last sixteen years. His first taste of killing hadn't even been something he'd planned. The first had been a student in the audience of his seminar in New York City. She had stared shamelessly at him throughout his talk. Later that night, at the hotel bar in the midst of all his colleagues, she came on to him in a way that no other young woman had before. He'd always heard the stories, and sometimes even seen colleagues who found themselves the amorous objects of nubile young students. And although he suspected there were a number of students who might have given in to his advances, none until then had ever come right out and aggressively pursued him.

Despite his good looks, the girl in New York had been his first experience of a woman actually throwing herself at him. She drank too much, of course, and began to drape herself shamelessly over him, whispering nasty snippets into his ear. Once she'd even brushed her fingertips over his crotch. But back in his hotel room he was unable to perform, despite her unabashed oral attempts at rousing his manhood. And then she mocked him. Her words echoed through the back of his mind to this day. His sexual arousal had always been inconsistent, and his unsatisfying love life had never included a domineering woman. They seemed to affect him more adversely than most. It wasn't just that he'd failed as a lover. It was what she did afterward that put him over the edge. Frustrated and wanting another drink, he decided to go back downstairs. When he arrived, he was acutely aware of the whispering and the smirks on his colleagues' faces. His stomach sank with shame, and he hoped against hope that his fears were unfounded. Then he spotted her, right at the bar where he'd met her.

With a drunken laugh, she pointed at him and shouted for everyone to hear, "Hey, it's Professor Lipton, or I guess I should say professor limp-dick! At least we know there's one lawyer who won't be screwing anyone!"

That night was the most humiliating experience of Lipton's life, and before he'd reached the sanctuary of his room, he knew that he would be back.

Lipton returned to Texas obsessed with revenge. He would show her that he was more of a man than she could ever guess. He painstakingly researched the world's most powerful aphrodisiacs. Most striking to him were the accounts he read about the use of powdered gall bladder taken from the Asian black bear. The sexual essence of that powerful beast, he learned, was contained in the small, bulbous organ. On a subsequent trip to San Francisco, he obtained a small package of the powder. Aphrodisiac in hand, he surreptitiously returned to New York on a plane ticket under a false name that he purchased with cash.

It was a dark, lonely evening in November when he appeared at his first victim's door. She was reluctant to admit him into her small upper-story apartment in SoHo, but he had used all his persuasive powers and finally convinced her. Once inside, he didn't waste any time trying to take her to bed. With disgust, she spurned him, hissing like a cat. It was then that Lipton found his fingers wrapped around her neck, quietly choking the life from her.

When she lost consciousness, he grew afraid. But it wasn't without delight that he stripped her naked, and with a roll of duct tape he'd found in the cupboard above the refrigerator, he bound her tightly. He was in total control. The way her eyes helplessly rolled in panic when she revived stimulated him beyond anything he had ever imagined before. But when he removed his pants and attempted to mount her, she struggled like a roped mustang and the flow of blood to his organ ebbed almost instantly.

In a rage, he yanked a steak knife from the kitchen drawer and split her open from her belt line to her sternum. It was then that he had his epiphany. If the gall bladder from a virile beast could excite sexual prowess, how much more powerful must the effect of that same organ be from a dominant woman? Infinitely so—that was the answer that came to him like a sudden flash of electricity.

So he took it. He took it and he dried it and crushed it into a powder that he could then mix with a drink before performing with a prostitute trained to remain submissive throughout the act. It worked so marvelously that Lipton knew from the very first time that he would do it again and again. And like an addict, his obsession only grew with time and experience. Obtaining his aphrodisiac was only a matter of solving a mental puzzle. Each woman had her own weakness, a time and place that she was isolated, a time and place when he could get to her, subdue her, and take what destiny said belonged to him anyway.

He remembered Casey Jordan from her days as a student. He knew then that she deserved to fill his needs. But back then, he was inexperienced in his method of killing. He went to great lengths to make sure there was never a connection between him and his victims. Now, as he had proved with Marcia Sales, even if he were caught, he would go free. Because the law was his domain, he could commit the perfect crime, making it impossible for a jury to convict him. With his intimate knowledge of the law, he could take the life of another human being without leaving the evidence necessary to prove that he'd done so. More than anything else, almost more than his sexual escapades, Lipton took great delight in his mental brilliance.

There might, however, be one final step before it was Casey's time. Tonight, he believed, was a sign. While his impotence enraged him, he was intelligent enough and calculating enough to realize that he needed to claim one more victim before Casey Jordan got her due. Another easy prey was the next step. Then it would be Casey's turn. The signs were all there. Lipton's manic laughter filled the inside of the van. The thought of Patti Dunleavy delighted him. She was his next victim. He should have known all along that he needed to ingest the essence of the protégé before he devoured the master.

He wouldn't waste any time. He would go to his dead aunt's summerhouse, his perfect haven, and rest for the night. Tomorrow he would have her. He already knew she lived alone. During the long days of preparation leading up to his trial, he had slowly but diligently extricated a tremendous amount of information from her. Everything he needed, anyway, to subdue her with very little effort.

It was clearly her destiny as well. She was a bossy little bitch who, he felt certain, took secret pleasure in emasculating him. Oh, he'd seen her grinning when Casey gave him one of her authoritative instructions on how to conduct himself at the trial. Well, Patti Dunleavy was too damn smart and too damn smug for her own good. He would subdue her and take total control. He would bind and dismember her, saving her sexual essence for himself. He would take her gall bladder and slowly bake it until it was crisp and dry. He would crush it into powder, and by Tuesday night, less than forty-eight hours from now, he would have his little whore and drink the powder and . . .

Lipton felt a remote sensation in his groin. With a smug grin, he turned on the radio and began quietly whistling along with one of his favorite love tunes from the seventies.

CHAPTER 28

After his bout with the hooker and the ensuing commotion, Unger was sober enough to haul Johnson into the car and bully him into helping find the way to the address in Selton. Although Johnson slept on the long, wet drive up the interstate, Unger was able to waken him with a jab in the ribs as he rolled off the exit. With the help of a map, Johnson grumpily assisted in finding their way through the maze of rural roads. After several wrong turns, they found a muddy lane that led them to a long gravel path whose mailbox bore the faded name Lipton. Unger flipped off his headlights and slowly swung the car into the drive. Their way dipped down through the woods and then back up before ending at a tall gray Victorian lake house that rose dripping out of the rainy gloom. Never in his life had Unger felt more alive.

There was a white van parked on the side of the house, and several lights were on. Well short of the house, Unger pulled the car off the drive and killed the engine. He opened his door a crack, illuminating the gloom of the wet woods with the weak light from above the car's rearview mirror.

"What are you doing?" Johnson hissed at the sight of his friend checking the load in his Glock.

Unger gave him a deadpan look and, as if he did it every day, said, "Loading up."

"But what are you going to do?" Johnson asked, his voice slightly strained with panic.

"I'm going to check it out," Unger said coolly, "make sure it's my guy before I call in CNN."

"CNN?"

"Them and whoever," Unger said casually, shutting the door and returning the two of them to nearly pitch darkness while he explained the situation to his friend. "I'm not going to pull off a big arrest like this without some advance publicity. That's how careers are made in law enforcement, my friend. I've seen it happen. It's all about publicity. If this guy is the nut the local police are saying he is, I'll be the one to bring him in. But there's no sense hauling him in unless the media is aware of at least a few of the choicest gory details of the case.

"I've seen it done a hundred times," bragged the emboldened agent. "First, you let the media know that there's this psycho professor out there cutting the guts out of his students all across the land. Then, you have a big outcry to find the guy, and presto! It's James Unger to the rescue. Through my brilliant investigative powers, I apprehend the most diabolical criminal mind since Charles Manson. They'll make a movie out of it.

"But first," Unger said, opening the door again, "I've got to make sure that this is where the guy is hiding out, and not just the home of this Sarah, who for whatever reason is paying this guy's sex bills."

Johnson snickered and asked, "How are you going to explain your little trip with me to the club?"

Unger glared and, pointing a finger at his friend, said, "For the record, the only reason I went in that place was because I deduced that a pervert like Lipton might be getting off on his fantasies with a prostitute. He's got money, so I used my connection with you to find the highest-class place in town and went to investigate. That's how I explain it, and that's how you explain it if anyone asks. This is my chance, Dean . . ."

As he quietly slid out of the car into the downpour, he added, "It was brilliant detective work. That's how you sell it."

"Should I come with you?" Johnson asked eagerly.

"No, you sit tight," Unger told him, and he softly shut the door.

With the light shining brightly from the house and the cloud cover over the moon, Unger didn't bother skulking around in the bushes. He simply walked up the drive and peered in through the lofty kitchen windows. Dressed in a satin smoking jacket and slippers, Lipton was making himself a cup of tea. Unger watched as the tall, elegant professor poured his tea and sat down at the kitchen table with a bag of shortbread cookies.

Unger smiled to himself and returned to the car amid the steady fall of rain. His shirt was soaked and sticking to his skin.

"Is it him?" Johnson asked excitedly.

"It is," Unger said, firing up the car and turning around. "And he's not going anywhere. This place is home sweet home."

"What now?"

"Now," Unger said, casting a sideways look at his friend, "we go get a couple hours of some well-earned sleep. Come morning, I go to work for real."

CHAPTER 29

Casey opened her eyes and smelled coffee. By the time she was out of the shower, there was a bacon smell in the air as well. In the kitchen, Sales met her with a broad if somewhat embarrassed grin. She glanced into the living room to see that the pillows on the couch looked undisturbed. Had she not seen him drop down on his back and fall instantly asleep, she would have doubted that he'd even slept.

"I used the shower down the hall," Sales said, "and I found a razor under the sink. I hope you don't mind."

"No," she said absently. She had insisted that he come inside the house last night rather than sleep in the cab of the pickup truck. The concern she had about Taylor showing up and creating a scene was outweighed by her fear of staying in the big house alone.

"Sit down," he told her. "Do you like to eat?"

"Not usually like this in the morning," she said, adding, "not lately anyway. But when I was a girl, it was an every-morning thing in my family.

"We lived on a farm," she added, unsure of why she was telling him a fact that she normally concealed.

"Good," Sales said, giving her a funny look. In the midst of finishing his preparations, he poured her a hot mug of the strong coffee.

As they began to eat, Casey found that in fact she was quite hungry. When they were finished, she said she would clean up and she liked the way he let her.

"I'm going to give Detective Bolinger that disk," she said as she shut the dishwasher door.

Sales stiffened in his seat. "You're not going to say anything about me?"

"No," she said. "I'm not going to talk to him at all. If I gave it to the police directly, Lipton could have every bit of that information suppressed from a jury, and I want them to see everything that I saw on that disk."

"That's presuming there's a trial."

"I have to presume that," Casey said. "He's not going to stop. But sooner or later, he'll get caught."

"Maybe," Sales said.

"Maybe?"

He looked at her with incandescent eyes. "He's as slippery as anything I've ever seen. He's smart and he's ruthless, but he's also crazy, so he'll do the unexpected . . . that's what's going to make him hard to get."

"Donald, we should be working with Bolinger," Casey urged. "If we turn you in to the police, you could be out on bail and we could help each other. Why should we be trying to find him and they be trying to find him and neither of us sharing the information we have?"

Sales laughed bitterly. Without rancor he said, "For such a smart woman, you make me wonder . . . I told you, I'm not turning myself in. You say I'll get bail. How long could that take? You say a day? What if the day I'm sitting in the public safety building is the day Lipton gets you alone? What if there are complications and I don't get bail? You know about complications, right?"

"I do, but—"

"I'm not doing it, Casey," Sales said sternly. "That's final. Let's just figure out how we can do this my way. You want to give Bolinger the disk? Fine, let him have it. If the police get him before we do, fine. I just want someone to get him. I don't care who."

"What are we going to do?"

"Lipton wants to get you alone. He's been watching you, and even though I chased him off last night, I think he'll pick up the trail again and keep following you. I don't know when, but he will. He thinks he's smarter than you and me and the rest of the world together. He won't be put off by last night. What we have to do is give him the chance to get to you without making it look too easy. It has to be an isolated place and you have to be by yourself, but it has to make sense that you're alone there or else he'll know it's a trap."

"If you're not there?" she asked with alarm.

"I'll be there," he told her. "But it won't look that way. The police staked out my cabin after I ran, but they should be gone by now. I don't think they'll do much more than stop by from time to time to see if I came back. So that's our place."

"But even if he's following me," Casey pointed out, "I don't think he'd follow me to your place, do you?"

Sales shrugged. "He might not, but he wants to get you, and way out there, if he sees you by yourself, well, he just might try it. It's the best place for me to trap him if he does follow you, so I think we should at least try it."

"What if you're wrong about the police and they're still watching your cabin? Lipton won't try anything if they're there, and they'll want to know what I'm doing."

"This is where that disk will come in perfectly," he said. "I was thinking about it. When Bolinger gets his hands on the disk, he's going to take every man he's got and start chasing down leads. I don't think he's going to waste a couple guys out in the hills watching my place. And if they are there, then we'll just have to find some other out-of-the-way places for you to go to that make sense until he makes his move."

"And where will you be? You can't follow me in your truck," Casey said. "He'll see that."

"Don't worry about me. He can't follow us both. When you leave here, I'll follow you to the police station. After that, I'll go out to the hills, park the truck on a back road, and get to the cabin before you do. You just go inside and wait. You can use the phone or whatever and I'll be right outside. If Lipton comes for you, I'll get him."

"When you say 'get him,' you mean you'll capture him?" Casey asked.

"That's my intent," he said. "I told you I would."

"But last night, you shot at him," she reminded him.

Sales flashed an angry look at Casey, but it quickly melted away. "Marcia liked to talk about what she was learning in law school. She used to talk all the time about mens rea . . ."

"A guilty mind," Casey said.

"Yeah, a guilty mind," Sales continued. "She used to say that to be guilty of a crime you have to have intent. I'm not planning on killing Lipton in cold blood. If I have to use this to stop him, I will. Last night, I simply reacted to the situation. I can't guarantee his safety. That's not what you want, is it?"

After a pause, she replied softly, "No. I appreciate what you did for me last night. Thank you. I'm glad you were there, and I certainly understand why you used your gun." She shrugged and said hesitantly, "It's different when you're in it. All the theories go out the window . . . I feel like I'm caught in a spider web or something. I can't see him, but I know that he's out there, hidden away, watching me struggle and just waiting to run out into the open and wrap me up like a fly."

"When you went into the building last night," Sales said, "I stayed in my car out on the street. After I saw your partner's car come out of the garage, I figured you'd be right behind him. When you didn't come out, I decided to go into the building through the garage. It was just chance that I stumbled onto Lipton. He almost had you. When he heard me coming, he didn't stick around. He took off like a flash, and I took some wild shots, hoping to get lucky. But what I'm saying is . . . this time I'll be ready, and he won't get away."

CHAPTER 30

Casey found a meter half a block from the police station. When she stepped out onto the sidewalk, she was momentarily filled with apprehension. Lipton could be lurking anywhere in the busy throng of people. It seemed he was always one step ahead of her despite the fact that there was no way for him to know what moves she was planning to make. Casey searched the street, and when she saw Sales cruising slowly along, slumped down in the front seat of his uncle's blue pickup, she felt suddenly reassured.

With the large manila envelope clamped in both hands, Casey hurried up the steps of police headquarters. Inside, the shift change had left the lobby busy enough for her to simply set her thin package down on the floor and walk quickly away without exciting notice. When she got to the door, Casey paused long enough to see a uniformed patrolwoman stop, bend down, and pick up the envelope, which bore Bolinger's name in bold black letters. The female officer looked around, apparently for the detective who had dropped his package. Casey turned and left, again scanning the crowded sidewalk as well as the busy street for any sign of Lipton.

Bolinger was on the phone and into his fourth cup of coffee by the time the envelope found its way through the department up onto his desk. He waved his thanks to the detective who'd dropped it off and eyed it suspiciously while he finished the call. After hanging up, he examined it. He could feel the disk through the paper. Not knowing if it was a CD for a stereo or a computer or something else entirely, he opened it with caution. The silver disk still didn't tell him anything, so he took it to Farnhorst, who was more in tune with the digital age.

"Computer disk," Farnhorst stated authoritatively. "A blank you use to copy stuff onto. Whose is it?"

"I don't know," Bolinger said, squinting his eyes. "Izenberg dropped it off on my desk and said something about someone finding it on the floor in the lobby. It's got my name on it, but I have no idea where it came from."

"Maybe it's an anonymous tip," Farnhorst joked.

"Can you tell me what's on it?"

Farnhorst raised his eyebrows and said loudly, "You kidding me? You really don't know how to use one of these?"

Bolinger was suddenly aware of all the younger, computer-literate detectives who were sitting around the large room trying their best not to notice his predicament.

"Come on, man," Farnhorst said in a tone that only an old friend could use with the sergeant. "Give me that."

Farnhorst swiped the disk out of Bolinger's hand and rose from his chair with a grumble. Bolinger followed him penitently over to the computers, neither of which was being used at the moment. Bolinger pulled up a chair and watched over Farnhorst's shoulder as he inserted the disk into the D drive and it whirred to life. As Farnhorst accessed the disk, the Microsoft licensing box appeared and he emitted a low whistle.

Bolinger, who had no idea what his friend was seeing, said, "What?"

"Whatever's on here belongs to the professor," Farnhorst said as he began to analyze the directory.

"You mean Lipton?"

"The one and only," Farnhorst told him. "All kinds of shit on here, Bob. It's gonna take me some time to sift through it . . ."

"I don't give a shit if it takes us three months," Bolinger said, grabbing a chair and scooting it right up next to his friend's. "Neither of us is going anywhere until we turn this thing inside out."

"Who would—" Bolinger began the question out loud and then cut himself short. He was pretty sure he knew exactly who would leave something like this in the lobby, and he was better off not saying it out loud.

By lunchtime, they were into the good stuff. When Bolinger saw the bio on Casey Jordan, it made him more certain than ever where the disk had come from. Of course, he appreciated her discretion. As far as he knew, as far as a judge would know, the information had just appeared. If Lipton couldn't prove the violation of an attorney-client privilege, then a jury would see this information. Bolinger felt the excitement of a big case breaking wide open boiling up inside him. This disk would shortcut his efforts by months or even years. Who could say if he ever could have accumulated such information? Even with the FBI's subpoena power, he would have had to enlist the cooperation of random law enforcement people from all over the country to track down stale cases when they all had fresh ones to worry about.

Now, though, Bolinger could check specific names and places and identify victims. With this disk, he could build a case so foolproof all the Casey Jordans in the world couldn't get Lipton off.

"Bob," Farnhorst said, breaking into his reverie, "I gotta get some lunch."

"I'll order some sandwiches. You sit right here."

Bolinger turned to the small crowd of detectives who were watching them from across the room. Every so often, one of them would amble over and catch a bit of what was going on, but for the most part, they kept the respectful distance of spectators at a monumental event.

"Hanson," Bolinger said, "will you get a couple of roast beef sandwiches and some sodas sent up?"

Hanson nodded and scrambled to a phone, glad to help out in any way.

"Hey," Bolinger continued, "don't the rest of you guys have work to do?"

As the group dispersed, another detective said, "Sarge, there's a call for you in your office."

Bolinger gave Farnhorst a look of warning not to abandon his post and got up from his seat. It felt good to stand. The two of them had been sitting for more than two hours.

"Tell you what," he said to Farnhorst, "take five, but don't make me go chasing you down. I got sandwiches coming."

Bolinger picked up the phone in his office. It was Unger.

"How's it going?" the agent asked.

"Fine," Bolinger said impatiently. "I've got a potential breakthrough, so I can't talk."

"A breakthrough?" Unger asked.

Bolinger sensed a hint of alarm in the agent's voice. "Yeah," he said warily.

"You . . . did you find Lipton?" Unger said, unable to disguise the concern in his voice.

"No," Bolinger replied suspiciously. "But I may have some information that will get a lot more people than you and me looking for him. But you don't have to worry about it. I've got the whole thing under control."

Bolinger was about to hang up when Unger shot back, "I want to come down and see what you've got, Bob. I . . . I really want to get going on this case. I've got some things of my own that I can't talk about over the phone, but I may have a breakthrough, too."

"Fine," Bolinger said, feigning as much interest as he could. "Come on down."

Bolinger could and would mobilize his people under the auspices of the Frank Castle investigation. He had that authority and he would use it. He wanted to be the one to bring Lipton down. But on a grander scale, this was an FBI case, and once they found out that murders as spectacular as the ones Lipton had committed had occurred across state lines, they would step in and grab the whole deal. A special task force would be assigned, and a Fed would run it. Bolinger could only imagine the publicity over a murderer set free with the woman who helped him sitting on his hit list. He made a mental note to contact Casey Jordan. Maybe it wouldn't be such a bad idea to keep someone with her in the event that she really had seen Lipton following her. Meanwhile, every Fed in the country would be clamoring for a piece of this case.

It would certainly be enough to make Dean Wentworth forget about his string of bank robberies.

But if it had to be a Fed running the show, it might as well be his Fed. He'd seen Unger's type before. He was burned out before his time, lackadaisical and ineffective. Bolinger could control him. But at the same time, in the interest of staying as close to the case as he could, Bolinger would do his best to make it look as though Unger had outdone himself. He wanted the FBI to think that Unger was not only capable but the best choice of agent to see the investigation to its finish.

CHAPTER 31

James Unger arrived in his charcoal suit, freshly pressed, and an electric blue Italian tie. His hair was slicked back off his big, high forehead and glistening with gel. Bolinger and Farnhorst looked at the agent and then at each other. Unger was a caricature of himself, a trumped-up nerd. The detectives probably would have burst out laughing if it weren't for the unusual emotion burning in the agent's eyes.

Unger had a hard time controlling those emotions as he sat through his computer session with Bolinger and Farnhorst. Things were even better than he'd imagined. The timing of the disk was perfect. They now had spectacular evidence that Lipton was a homicidal maniac of epic proportions. Unger's mind was racing with the kudos he could win if he played this right. This case would change his entire career. But he had to play it right, and part of that meant not saying a thing to anyone about knowing Lipton's whereabouts until he had the media in place.

So it was with great self-control that he listened to Bolinger's exposition about where they were in the investigation and what direction the disk would now take them. The air in the room grew stale, and the early afternoon sun glared down through the windows of the squad room. Unger had shed his jacket and an anxious sweat stained the armpits of his shirt, but still he managed to remain calm, with his tie snugly knotted at his throat. Finally, Bolinger drew to a close.

"So what I'm proposing, James," he said, "is that you call your office in Atlanta and set up a conference call with your boss and whoever is directly above him. I'll be the one to suggest that you head up the investigation because of your familiarity with the case and how far you've taken it to that point. The important thing is that we don't lose the case."

Farnhorst looked on with open amazement. Bolinger shamefully averted his gaze. It was uncharacteristic of him to conspire with someone he didn't know or like, but this was a once-in-a-lifetime case for Bolinger as well.

Unger was unfazed by the local detective's obvious embarrassment at the ruse. He grinned knowingly at the seasoned cop, and it was the closest he had come thus far to divulging the ace he held so closely.

"I'll set up the call," he agreed. "But let's wait until tomorrow."

"Shouldn't you . . ." Bolinger began.

"No, I know how to handle this, Bob," Unger said with a casual familiarity that made Bolinger bite the inside of his cheek. Unger stood to go. "You get this stuff together. I've got some calls I need to make and I'll meet you back here around five. I've got some ideas and I think you'll be able to help me execute them, but I have some work to do first."

With a nod, Unger left the detectives staring after him.

"What an asshole," Farnhorst muttered. "Geez, Bob, if that's not enough to make you puke, I don't know what is."

Bolinger took a deep breath and sighed. "Well, there's not much we can do about it. We can step up our search for Lipton on the premise of the Castle investigation, but we sure as hell can't start calling around the country asking after the women on this list without the Feds. I can only imagine the shit we'd catch if we got out in front of them and trampled on their case."

"Their case?" Farnhorst said disdainfully.

"Yeah," Bolinger said, turning somberly toward his burly friend. "It belongs to them now no matter how hard either you or I wish it wasn't so . . ."

CHAPTER 32

Lipton pitched his voice into a low, gruff mumble, identified himself as Kurt Lamb, and asked for Casey Jordan. The receptionist funneled him to Gina, who began a series of questions that bordered on belligerence.

"I gotta speak to her," Lipton persisted in his disguised voice. "It's an emergency. I'm a client. At least she told me I was. I just met her through her husband. She'll know me."

At the words "client" and "emergency," Gina's protective toughness melted away. She became conciliatory and even apologetic when, after several minutes on hold, she got back on the line and explained that she had tried every means she knew of getting hold of Casey.

"I've left messages everywhere, Mr. Lamb," Gina said. "I'm sure she'll be checking in, and I'll make sure she gets right back to you. Where can you be reached?"

"No," Lipton said with an evil grin. "I can't do that. I'll have to get back in touch with her myself. When do you think would be a good time to call? Do you have any idea when I can reach her?"

"I'm sorry, Mr. Lamb," Gina said. "The office is closing now, but I've left word at her home as well to call me. I wish you'd give me a number."

"No," Lipton said. "I'll just call her at home tonight. Don't worry about it."

"All right," Gina said with concern. It wasn't like Casey to just disappear during the day without even checking in. "If you don't get her for any reason, she usually gets in around eight in the morning and you can reach her first thing."

"Fine," Lipton said, punctuating the end of the call by snapping the phone shut. He sat in the front seat of his van with the air-conditioning blasting. A double layer of clothes, while essential to a perfectly clean crime scene, was an inconvenience in the heat. The fact that someone might see him going into Patti Dunleavy's apartment was of no consequence. The police were looking for him anyway. The thought of being so bold actually pleased him.

It wasn't long before the girl arrived home at the upscale apartment complex. Lipton knew her car, and when she pulled into a shady spot only a stone's throw from his own van, he slid out of his seat and slithered into the bowels of the van, where he could watch her safely from the shadows. Around him were the tools of his trade: roles of tape, a ladder, coils of rope, sharp knives, and tools ranging from James bars that could open back doors to fine wire cutters and soldering irons that enabled him to tamper with phone and electric systems. A metal desk was built into one wall. The same van had served him well over the years and had seen a lot of miles. Even when his aunt was alive, Lipton had kept it at her lake house, out of the way, unnoticed by anyone.

When Patti had disappeared up the decorative white

stairway, he sat down on the swivel chair that was bolted to the floor in front of the desk and flipped on his computer. With glee, he pulled up his special files and went directly to Patti Dunleavy. He had only recently composed her story, and now he reread it with satisfaction, taking the time to add a few particularly titillating lines to her imagined sexual proclivities. Twice again, he read her story, immersing himself in a trancelike state in which his whole universe stopped and focused its entire energy on the destiny that awaited the haughty young girl who begged to be subjugated.

If she knew, if any of them really knew the way in which their sexual essence was contributing to the enhancement of his genius and the virility of his power, he believed they might willingly go to their death. But that wasn't their nature. He shook his head no. It wasn't their nature. They were too stubborn and self-consumed to stop and think. So he had to take it from them. It was his due.

Stirred from within, Lipton picked up his phone off the front seat and dialed Patti's private number.

"Hello?" she said. She sounded fresh to Lipton, as if she'd just come out of a long, cool shower. He imagined her wrapped in a towel, her hair draped about her shoulders in dark, wet strands.

"Patti," he said urgently, "this is Professor Lipton. I'm in serious trouble. Everything's all right, but Casey told me I should call you. She said she'd meet me at your apartment."

"My . . . she didn't say anything to me," Patti said. She was flustered and uncomfortable. "I haven't heard from her. What's wrong?"

"I'm on a cell phone right now," he told her. "Casey told me not to talk on the phone. She just said to meet her at your place. I'm on my way. I just wanted to let you know. I didn't want to shock you."

"You . . . I . . ."

"Don't worry," he said hurriedly. "Casey said to tell you that everything will be fine. I'm sure she's going to call you any minute."

He didn't want her to panic, to bolt from her apartment or make any rash calls. If she believed him, she would wait by the phone.

"Okay," she said tentatively.

"I'll be right there," he said, then hung up.

Lipton took a small, dark duffel bag and began to carefully load it with the supplies he needed. He was in no great hurry. He knew Casey was unavailable and she was the only person Patti would call. After all, he was a client, and confidentiality was sacrosanct. He liked the idea of taking his time, of savoring every moment in anticipation of what he was about to do. He fussed over each item that went into the bag and dwelled affectionately on the role each would play in his scheme. The last thing to go in was a Tech-9, the ultimate handheld firepower. It was for the emergency he'd never had, but to Lipton, thoroughness was its own reward.

Fully prepared, he shouldered the small bag and slipped back into the front seat to look around the complex. There was a young man in a short-sleeve white shirt and tie getting out of an aqua green Mustang. Lipton followed his progress across the lot and into his apartment. When the door closed, he got out of his van and crossed the steaming blacktop. After one final glance around, he slowly began to scale the outside staircase two steps at a time toward the young lawyer's apartment on the third floor.

CHAPTER 33

Casey sat at Sales's kitchen table, unable to focus on the work in front of her. Papers spilled importantly from her briefcase, but she found herself rereading the same passages of a brief Patti had prepared for an upcoming hearing. It was much easier for her mind to wander over the mounted animal head trophies staring down at her from the high log walls, or to consider the rich history behind the different Native American artifacts. There was something strangely familiar about the rustic austerity of Sales's cabin that made Casey uneasy. This was the setting, after all, in which she'd been raised. Her father and older brother had been hunters and she'd grown up on venison.

She had time to be introspective now because her concern over Lipton's appearance had waned nearly an hour ago. Each minute that ticked off the clock seemed to mock their plan. Would Lipton really try to abduct her again after what had happened last night? And, if he did, was he desperate enough to strike at the first possible opportunity? Apparently not.

Casey got up and searched the refrigerator for a diet soda. All she found was orange juice and beer, so she went to the tap and filled a glass, holding it up against the light from the window and looking at the cloudy well water with disgust. It wasn't unlike what she'd had to drink as a girl in Odessa, the same rural setting, the same brackish water. The sight of it was repulsive. She longed for a cold bottle of crystal-clear Evian.

Casey was suddenly and clearly gripped by panic. What if she was kidding herself? Did she really think she could just unravel the life it had taken her so long to weave? Wasn't she actually part of the upper crust now? Wasn't it possible that she needed Taylor as much or more than he needed her? Could she really do without his money, his manners, his good looks, and his connections? Could she really just leave him? Casey felt panic tighten its grip, as if she had suddenly found herself in a hopeless dream. She had never been confused before. All her life she had known exactly what she'd wanted.

Now she felt that she knew nothing. Her heart told her a better life was out there for her. But her mind was spinning, all because of a cloudy glass of water and the familiar feel of a spartan cabin in the sticks. She didn't know if she had the courage to really change her life. Her confidence had been shaken. Her brazen certainty that every move she made in life was the right one had been crippled by the Lipton case. She had been hunted and terrorized. Her husband had betrayed her. All those things, things she never imagined could happen to her, had happened within a few short days.

She held her nose and gulped down a few mouthfuls of the water. It tasted as bad to her as she remembered. Scared and confused, she sat back down and exhaled a long, trembling breath. Then she heard something at the back of the cabin that brought her back to the immediate present, a door slowly opening. She jumped to her feet and tiptoed across the wood-planked floor. The hall leading to the back of the cabin was dark. At the sight of a figure moving toward her, Casey's chest tightened.

"It's me," Sales said quietly. He moved down the hall, gimping slightly from sitting for so long in the same position. "He's not coming."

"I know," she said in an unnecessary whisper. "If he was going to, he would have by now. There's no way he'd think I'd have any reason to stay here this long. I figured after the first half hour that he wasn't coming."

Sales moved through the kitchen and pushed aside a dusty curtain to peer out at the dirt road that led to his place. He let the curtain drop and then went into the great room to his gun cabinet. From the bottom drawer he withdrew a nickel-plated snub-nose .38 along with a calf holster, then returned to the kitchen.

Casey tried to bury her inner doubts for the time being. She watched Sales critically from across the breakfast bar and asked, "What's that for? You already have a gun."

"It's always good to have backup," Sales said. His boot was up on a chair now and his loose pant leg was pulled up to his knee as he strapped the holster to his leg.

"So . . ." Casey said as he spun the cylinder, snapped it shut, and placed it in the holster, "what's next?"

"We just keep setting you up," he said, turning his attention back to her. "Sooner or later, he's going to make a move."

"Sooner or later, as in two weeks from now? Two months?" Casey said incredulously. "I can't live like this. I've got a life . . ."

"Look, I don't know how long," Sales said patiently. "I don't know what to tell you. I'm as frustrated as you are. At least you had the chance to get something done in here."

Casey followed his eyes to the table where her papers were splayed and said morosely, "I wish I could say it did me some good."

Recalled to her duty, she took her cell phone from the briefcase and looked at it for the first time. It was unusual for her not to have gotten any calls.

"You'll have to use my phone," Sales told her, pointing to the countertop, where an old chocolate brown phone sat on top of the yellow pages. "Cell phones don't work out here . . . there's no towers."

"I was just wondering why I didn't get any calls," she said, picking up his phone. She dialed the office, looking at her watch. It was just after five, but sometimes Gina stayed late. She hung up on the answering service and dialed her voice mail. Crossing the kitchen with the phone in hand, she sat down with a pen and her yellow legal pad. The dejection of their failed attempt at trapping Lipton left her feeling foolish and slightly guilty for neglecting the clients who were counting on her. With them, at least, she knew just what to do.

Sales took out a bottle of beer from the fridge and sat down at the table to think while Casey patiently listened to and transcribed nearly two dozen messages.

"Bob Bolinger called," she said, looking up. "He says he needs to talk."

She wrote down his cell phone number but continued to listen. There were only two more messages on the machine, and she wanted to get through them before she rang up the detective. The next message was a strangely urgent plea from Gina to call someone called Kurt Lamb, who claimed to be a client but whom Casey had never heard of. When the next message came, she forgot everything that she'd heard before.

"Casey, this is Patti," came the sound of the young woman's voice over the phone. "I . . . I need to know what's going on. It's Professor Lipton. He's . . . he just called, and he's on his way over. He said you wanted him to come. I . . . I don't know. I'm sorry. I don't mean to overreact, but I wanted to make sure you really talked to him. Can you call me? He's coming and I don't know what to do . . ."

"Oh my God!" Casey exclaimed. Instantly she hung up and dialed Patti's home number. After twelve hopeless rings, she began stuffing her papers haphazardly into the briefcase.

"What happened?" Sales asked with concern. He had risen from his seat and set the beer down half empty on the table.

"We've got to go," she said in a panic. "We've got to stop him."

"Stop who?" Sales asked, grasping Casey firmly by the shoulders. "What are you talking about?"

"Lipton!" she screamed at him. "It's not me he's going after, it's Patti!"

"Your assistant?" Sales said, hurrying now with her toward the front door.

"Yes," Casey said, leaping from the porch and sprinting for her Mercedes.

Sales got in beside her and braced himself as she spun up a cloud of dust and stones backing around in the driveway. "How do you know?" he asked. "What happened?"

"She left me a message," Casey told him, her hands on

the wheel in a death grip. "She said Lipton called her—
that I told him to—that I'd meet him there. I called her
back, but I didn't get an answer."

Sales didn't say a word. He stared grimly at the road.
Casey pointed at her briefcase and instructed him to take
out her cell phone.

"Bolinger left me his cell phone number and I wrote it
down on that legal pad. Get it and call him."

"I can't," Sales said, "remember? There's no towers."

"When will we be in range, do you know?" she demanded.

"About five more miles, I think," he said. "When we
get to the bridge."

Casey stepped on the gas even harder.

"Easy," he said. "It won't do anyone any good if you
kill us."

Casey didn't hear. "He's going to kill her," she heard
herself saying.

"Maybe not," he said. "Maybe we can get there, or the
police, maybe Bolinger can get there."

When they got to the bridge, Sales dialed the detective's number and handed the phone to Casey. They came
to the top of a hill and the Mercedes lifted nearly off the
ground. Bolinger answered tiredly on the third ring. In a
panicked voice, Casey explained the situation. It took
several minutes to communicate through the static of the
bad connection, but finally Bolinger understood. He said
he'd get there as fast as he could.

"I'll get a patrol car there, too. If anyone's close, they
may get there sooner than either of us," the detective said
before hanging up.

Casey clapped the phone shut and tossed it over to
Sales. A salty drop tickled her upper lip and she realized

that tears were streaming down her face. The image of being helpless and abducted herself was fresh in her own mind. While part of her was grateful to have Sales beside her, at the same time another part of her was filled with loathing and fear that anyone could do that to another person. But more than anything, the image of Patti being harmed by Lipton at that very moment pushed her to the edge of sanity.

"How far away are we?" Sales said. He had no idea where Patti lived.

"Not far from here. She's on this side of town in Sunset Valley. Fifteen minutes, maybe ten," Casey said grimly. "We should have known . . ."

"How could we know?" Sales argued. Inside, he was awash with his own guilt. Lipton hadn't really been in the garage the night before. Sales had commandeered the elevator himself to scare Casey into helping him. The shots he'd fired were wasted rounds that he knew no one else would hear three levels below the ground in a garage abandoned for the weekend. While he'd never tell Casey, it was he who should have at least suspected that Lipton might be up to something else. He hadn't seen a sign of him in two days.

"But how could we have known he was going to go after Patti?" he said aloud. "She wasn't on the disk."

"But she fit his profile perfectly," Casey said bitterly. "I should have suspected it . . . The way he, the way he turned it on whenever he was around her at the trial, stroking her for the littlest insight. Even the tone of his voice when he spoke to her was . . ."

She shook her head and said, "I should have seen it. But I was too worried about myself and I never even thought about her."

Sales took the pistol from his belt and carefully examined it, unloading it, sliding the action smoothly back and forth, and reloading it with a metallic snap.

"We'll make it," he said.

Casey unclamped her teeth only long enough to say, "We have to make it. My God, we have to."

CHAPTER 34

Patti was startled by the loud knock. It had come so much sooner than she'd expected. Besides the professor, she couldn't think of anyone else it could be. She hurried to the door and peered through the peephole. It was Lipton. Patti felt a strange mixture of dread and excitement. She couldn't imagine why Casey would send him to her apartment. Of course, that same enigma made it exciting.

Patti glanced quickly back into her apartment. It was tastefully decorated with dark green overstuffed furniture and white walls adorned with silver-framed posters of van Gogh's most famous paintings. Still, she felt self-conscious. She knew instinctively that it was inadequate for someone of Professor Lipton's taste and experience. He knocked again and, with a helpless sigh and a painful smile, she opened the door, letting in a hellish wave of heat from the outside.

Lipton greeted her with the same warm, handsome smile that he had when they'd first met. The gleam in his eyes would have made her think he was on drugs if she didn't know better. He also looked somewhat heavier to her, and then she realized that it was because of his clothes. Strange that he should be clad from head to toe in a dark sweat suit that he'd zipped to the top of his throat. Even his short walk from the parking lot had left his bronze forehead bathed in sweat. There was also something on his back, a duffel bag maybe, whose strap was wrapped around one shoulder and across his chest.

"Come in," she said, smiling and flipping her hair nervously behind one ear. "I wasn't expecting you this soon."

"Thank you," he said, stepping across the threshold and closing the door behind him. With a small laugh he added, "I was really just around the corner, you know."

Patti nodded and turned to lead him into the living room without noticing that he paused to throw the bolt on the door.

"Would you like something to drink?" she asked. "A soda?"

"Nothing at all," he told her, assessing the layout as he slowly followed her in. The kitchen was on the left. Beyond it was a combination dining area and living room that ended at a set of sliding glass doors leading out to a covered terrace. There was a door opposite the kitchen that led to a half bathroom. The door to the bedroom itself was toward the back of the living room on the right.

"Please, sit down," Patti said, positioning herself in front of the bedroom door with a coffee table between them. There was something unnerving about the professor, the way he was dressed and the way he looked at her. Patti knew something was wrong, but she didn't want to admit to herself that she'd done a foolish thing by letting him in. She told herself over and over that everything was fine.

"Do you mind if I use the bathroom?" he asked suddenly.

"No, please," Patti said, pointing, glad to have him out of her presence even for a moment. "It's right there behind you."

"Thank you," he said urbanely. Inside the bathroom, Lipton shed his small canvas bag and removed a pair of thick wool dress socks as well as some black leather driving gloves and a small cloth object. The other things could wait. He set the bag on the floor in the corner.

After pulling the socks over his shoes and the gloves over his hands, he looked at himself in the mirror. He, too, saw the glaze in his eyes. He was beaming, strong and virile. Nothing could stop him. It was the flush of destiny. With great satisfaction he took the cloth object and stretched it over his head. Besides the two holes for his eyes, there was only one other opening in the black mask, a small slit he could breathe through. He was death.

"Patti?" he said softly with his gloved hand on the doorknob. "Patti?"

He heard her crossing the room.

"Is everything all right?" she said, standing back from the door, still insisting to herself that everything was perfectly fine.

Lipton emitted a nervous chuckle and said, "The door, it's stuck. I can't get out. Is there a trick to this?"

Patti stood where she was.

"Patti?" he said. "Help me, will you?"

"All right."

Lipton held the doorknob tight until he could sense her pressing against the door, putting all her strength into it.

With one swift motion, he twisted the knob, yanked it open, and caught her by the throat as she fell toward him.

For almost two seconds, the shock was too much for Patti to overcome. In that time he'd thrown her down to the floor and mounted her with all his weight bearing down on her chest. Then she began to fight, and in that area she didn't disappoint him. Wildly she clawed and kicked, her nails falling harmlessly on his nylon suit and her feet striking nothing but air. Then she began to punch, tight little fists thrown with remarkable ferocity, but waning by the second.

Lipton bore down with all his strength, cutting off the blood to her brain, but at the same time keeping his thumbs on either side of her larynx to maximize the pressure on her carotid arteries. Soon her limbs did nothing more than twitch, and he felt a thrill run through him as her eyes rolled back in her head. Immediately, he let go of her neck and scrambled into the bathroom for his kit. Within seconds, he had stripped her naked and bound her wrists, ankles, and mouth tightly with his tape. Once she was secured, he took the time to neatly fold her clothes and set them on the back of the couch, saving the underwear for himself. Those he would use to clean his knife and save as a trophy of his conquest.

After all, she was his now. Her essence belonged to him. It was waiting there for him. But he wanted her awake. He wanted her to know just how much power he had. All the whispering between her and Casey during the trial, he'd seen that. He knew they talked about him. He knew they made jokes between themselves about his impotence. Strong women loved to emasculate a man, especially a man of his great intellect. They paled next to his mental brilliance and they were bitter about it. Now she would know. She would know that he was a sexual beast and that he would use her own sexual essence as a fuel for his latent passions.

Lipton whipped off his mask and stuffed it into the bag with his other things. He stood over her, waiting and staring hungrily at her naked figure until he felt a remote stirring within his groin. Part of him wanted her badly, but he would not risk that. He needed his powder, and he needed a woman who would not only succumb to him, but beg him for it. He conjured up the image of his little whore downtown and turned that over in his mind until Patti began to stir. Soon her eyelids would flutter to life and she would see him there, standing over her in complete control.

Lipton bent down and took the long, cruel-looking knife from his bag. Lovingly, he unsheathed it. When her eyes finally opened, they were wide with horror. Lipton began to talk and as he explained to her what he was going to do and why, he also chortled quietly but uncontrollably at the pitifully smothered shrieks and moans that escaped her injured throat.

"Are you crying now?" he asked, mimicking concern. Then with venom he added, "You should have thought of that when you were mocking me! When you were laughing at me and looking like a little slut and thinking that there was nothing I could do about it. But there is something I can do! I can do this!"

Lipton bent down over her thrashing body and pinned her with his knees. Expertly, he inserted the point of his knife just below her rib cage and slipped it down toward her belly, opening a hideous bloody gash in her torso. Her terrified strangled screams mingled with Lipton's laughter, filling the room with inhuman noise.

CHAPTER 35

Casey raced into the parking lot. Over the scream of tires, Sales asked her which unit belonged to Patti.

"Three-C," Casey said, remembering the first week Patti moved in and proudly invited her for a spaghetti dinner. "The top corner at the far end of the building!"

Sales pointed toward a white van at the other end of the lot and said, "He's here!"

Casey slammed on her brakes, sending the car in a sideways skid. Sales leapt from the vehicle before it had even stopped. Casey slammed the car into park and chased Sales up the stairs as fast as she could. When Sales got to 3-C, he tried the door's handle once before kicking it. The door shuddered from the blow but stood strong. Spinning around, Sales leaned forward and kicked back like a mule, bursting the door from its frame in a cascade of splintered wood.

With Casey now just behind him, Sales sprang into the hallway in a crouched position. Lipton, warned by the first kick at the door, welcomed him with a deafening hail of bullets from his Tech-9, sending Sales back out the doorway as quickly as he'd come. When the gunfire stopped, Sales waved a hand up high and came in low again. This time there was no gunfire. He edged into the apartment, knees bent, his Glock extended with both hands in a shooting position.

After a moment of silence, Casey peeked in after Sales. He had reached the living room now, and as he ducked into the bedroom gun first, Casey rushed toward Patti's inert body. A dreadful shriek escaped her lips at the sight of the gore. Blood was everywhere. She rushed for the phone and dialed 911. Her mind barely registered Sales as he burst from the bedroom and out onto the terrace. Gunfire cut through her shock, and she realized that Sales was firing over the edge of the railing.

Lipton had climbed down the outside of the building, hanging and jumping from terrace to terrace until he reached the ground. Sales caught only a glimpse of him as he raced across the grass and rounded the corner of the building. After two wild shots, he dashed back into the apartment and past Casey to the outside stairway without a glance. From there, he couldn't see Lipton's van. He took the steps three at a time, cursing loudly when he saw the van shoot across the lot and out into the street. Seconds later, Sales was at the wheel of the Mercedes and, with tires shrieking, fast on Lipton's trail.

A squad car was next to arrive. Having come from the opposite direction, the patrolmen had no idea that they'd missed Sales's wild chase of Lipton by thirty seconds. Bolinger wasn't far behind the cruiser. He knew from his radio that a 911 call had been made from the girl's apartment and that an ambulance was on its way. When he and Unger pushed through the crowd of onlookers and walked through the apartment's shattered doorway, they were struck by the scene of Casey, bloody to the elbows, bent over Patti's body. She was sobbing hysterically, with the two officers on either side of her not knowing what to do.

"Seal this place off," Bolinger told them. "Get all those people the hell out of here."

Relieved to have some direction, the patrolmen exited the apartment. As Bolinger got closer, he gasped at what he saw. The girl had been opened in exactly the same manner as Frank Castle and Marcia Sales before him.

"My God," he said. "Lipton."

Unger saw it, too, and suddenly bolted for the kitchen sink, where he began to vomit what was left of his lunch.

Bolinger knelt down next to Casey, but like her, he had no idea what to do. The grisly wound was so extensive that he couldn't imagine how he could stop the bleeding. With Patti's insides exposed, he was afraid to apply pressure to anything. With the tips of his fingers, he felt for a pulse in her neck.

"She's alive," he said in wonderment.

Casey looked down at him in disbelief.

"Get some towels," he told her. "Look in the bathroom."

The towels were clean and white and Bolinger laid them gently over the girl's gaping wound and pressed gently down on them to try to stem the flow of blood as much as possible without damaging her internal organs.

"Get a knife in here, James," he said over his shoulder. "Come cut this tape off."

Unger did as he was told, also glad for something more to do than rinse out the inside of his mouth at the kitchen faucet.

"What happened?" Bolinger asked Casey. "Can you tell me?"

Casey shook her head. "When we got here, Donald kicked in the door and Lipton started shooting. When he stopped, we waited before we went back in. By the time we did, Lipton was gone. Donald went after him . . ."

"Sales?" Bolinger asked incredulously. "Donald Sales?"

"Yes," Casey said blankly.

Bolinger didn't get to ask his next question because the paramedics arrived. Casey tried to go with Patti to the hospital but the paramedics refused to transport a non–family member.

As the ambulance roared away with its sirens blaring, Bolinger, who had supervised the total containment of the area, put his hand on Casey's shoulder. The two of them stood inside the yellow tape under a low-hanging birch tree on the sidewalk that led from the parking lot to the building.

"How did you end up here with Don Sales?" he asked, looking at her over the top of the flame he was using to light up a Winston.

Casey's face went blank with the practiced poker visage of a lawyer who knew better than to give information away. Then, with a sigh, she dropped her facade and simply said, "He saved my life. Lipton was after me, and Donald stopped him. We were trying to draw him out when I got a message from Patti that he was on his way to her place. I called you and we got here as fast as we could. When Lipton took off, Donald went after him. I left my car in the lot out here when we went in, and he must have taken it to follow Lipton. Where they are now, I have no idea . . ."

"But I do."

Both Casey and Bolinger turned their heads. It was James Unger. The frumpy FBI agent stood there in his best suit, his hair slicked back, with a pair of clip-on sunglasses presiding over his crooked grin.

"I wanted to make sure," he lamely explained to Bolinger. "I had to check out a couple of leads I had this afternoon, but it paid off. I know where Lipton is."

"How?" Bolinger said.

"It's a long story. I didn't want to say anything until I was sure, but it's something I've been working on. He's been staying in a lake house up at Stillhouse Hollow Reservoir. The place belongs to a trust in the name of Sarah Lipton," Unger said importantly. "His aunt. Lipton is the trustee. He's using the house and her credit cards and checks, too. They all belong to the trust."

With just a hint of condescension he added, "That's why you haven't been able to track him down. Everything he's done over the last few months, he's done in her name."

"Where's the aunt?" Bolinger asked without acknowledging Unger's slight.

Unger shrugged. "I don't know. She could be anywhere. She could be dead."

"Let's go," Bolinger said.

"You think that's where he's headed?" Casey asked them.

"I don't know," Bolinger told her, tossing his cigarette to the sidewalk and grinding it out with his toe, "but it's the only thing we've got."

Casey rode with them in the back of Bolinger's cruiser. Bolinger drove fast. Unger sat beside him in silent thought.

From time to time, the agent's fingertips would flicker to his glasses, readjusting them nervously on his nose before fading down to his lap, where he would caress the wallet in the front pocket of his pants. In it were all his points of contact written on a carefully folded sheet of paper. He'd spent the afternoon feeling his way through the media, making sure he had access to the right people and titillating them with promises of a diabolical serial killer about to be taken down by the FBI. His diligence had paid off. He now had the home and cell phone numbers for news producers at each of the three major networks as well as the *Today* show, *Nightline,* and *Larry King.* The minute the arrest was made he'd start dialing, and it was him they'd come to interview.

All he needed now was a little more luck. If Sales somehow ran Lipton to ground, much of Unger's thunder would be stolen. If, however, Lipton managed to escape, sooner or later he'd return to the lake house, and when he did . . .

CHAPTER 36

Sales jammed on his brakes and dipped back inside the double yellow line. A tractor-trailer hummed past with his sonorous air horn blaring. The next instant, Sales crossed over the line again, this time accelerating past a Volkswagen bug just as it topped a rise in the road. The scream of the little car's horn and its driver's middle finger never registered with Sales. His focus was on the white van that was up ahead weaving smoothly through four lanes of traffic. When the road widened to four lanes at the bottom of the hill, Sales, too, was able to move much faster.

The height of the van had made it possible for Sales to draw a bead on the professor from the moment he pulled out of the apartment complex. Compared with his own pickup truck, the maneuverability of the Mercedes and the power of its large engine gave him a superhuman feeling. Exhilaration and the car's true capabilities had enabled him to steadily close the gap. But after Sales's first wild pass, Lipton began to drive like a maniac. Then it became a game of chance. There were few risks either of them was unwilling to take, and it seemed only a matter of time before one or the other would end in a fiery heap of crushed metal and glass.

Sales careened up behind a delivery truck in the left lane. He flashed his lights and leaned on the horn. For a moment, he lost sight of the van. The instant the ponderous truck began to move into the right lane, Sales floored the accelerator. But in that same second, he realized that Lipton had dipped through a small break in the center guardrail and was now racing full speed in the opposite direction. In the fleck of time it took for the two vehicles to pass each other, Sales could clearly make out the professor's contorted grin.

Sales's mind suddenly slowed and it seemed almost a matter of hours while he considered all the things he could or should have done to stay on the professor's tail. In reality, it was less than twenty seconds before he reached the next intersection, spun in a wild U-turn, and began his chase anew. But those seconds had been too costly. The white van was nowhere to be seen. Sales slowed his progress along the four-lane road, his head on a crazy swivel, scanning the parking lots and driveways of restaurants, strip malls, and gas stations for any sign of the hidden van. It was hopeless. He sped five miles in one direction, nearly halfway back to the apartment complex, before turning around and racing back.

Sales's stomach was in knots and a salty wave of nausea swept over him. The image of Lipton's sneering face as he went the opposite way in the van had burned itself into the forefront of his brain. It was a sight that would haunt him the rest of his living days. He knew that, and his breathing became shallow and strained. A sweat broke out on his upper lip and forehead, despite the cool blast of the big car's air conditioner. It was that same feeling of panic he'd felt when he'd called his daughter's apartment and gotten no answer. It was that sense that everything had gone wrong and nothing would ever be the same again.

Lipton was gone, and every instinct Sales possessed as a hunter told him that he wouldn't get that close again. Lipton had experienced too much pressure. He had already proved that his obsession with Casey wasn't insatiable. He'd moved on to Patti. His next victim would be on the other side of the country, perhaps the other side of the world. Sales's head began to throb. A low, pathetic stuttering noise rumbled in his throat, the sound of panic. The fleeting urge to pull over, put the Glock in his own mouth, and pull the trigger was so palpable he could almost taste the tangy metal barrel.

"Fuck that," Sales said angrily and aloud.

He had to think like a hunter. Right now, he was hunting an animal. That was what Lipton was. Despite his money, his urbane manner, and his dashing good looks, he was an animal, not a human being, an animal. Sales knew how to think like an animal. When stalking an animal, one had to predict its path of escape and head it off. Lipton was hiding somewhere. He was sure the white van was tucked in behind one of the myriad buildings lining the busy road. When he came out, whenever that was, he would head for his warren. He would seek a path to safety using the quickest, easiest route. Sales considered the area he was in. The closest highway was 290. The question was: east or west?

"Play the odds," Sales told himself. It was an unemotional decision determined by pure math. West led to the open country. East led to Austin, the loop around the city, or Interstate 35, which could in turn lead to San Antonio or Dallas. The possibilities were infinite. There was a cloverleaf where 290 met the loop. He had to get there as fast as he possibly could. If his hunch was right, and Lipton was hiding, then he might have a chance to pick up his trail once more. With all the speed traffic would allow, Sales got onto the highway. At the cloverleaf, he did a quick illegal U-turn to get himself up on the overpass. He pulled over on the narrow shoulder where he could see the oncoming traffic entering the loop and follow it in any one of three different directions.

His emotions were in check now. He had chosen the best strategy he could think of, and now he needed to wait. Patience was just as critical to the hunt as accurate anticipation. Ten minutes went by, then fifteen. On its journey westward, the sun had dipped into an oncoming bank of broken gray clouds, giving the day a sudden purplish tint. Sales fiddled with the dial on the face of his watch and strained his eyes as far into the distance as he could for an eastbound white van. Every minute or so he'd see something white and his heart would race. With every false alarm, he grew more and more certain that Lipton had either chosen to stick to the back roads or beaten him to the highway.

Then he saw another white vehicle coming toward him. It was a truck. No . . . it was a van. Sales's heart thumped like a broken machine. He took a deep breath. He had to see Lipton without being seen. He didn't want to get into a crazy game of chase, there was too much chance involved in that. He was better off following from a distance. When the van veered off the exit just short of the bridge, Sales slumped down in the seat. Not that it would make a difference. The car alone would give him away. If Lipton recognized it, the chase would begin anew. Sales wanted Lipton lulled into a sense of security. Only then would he run himself to ground. If that happened, Sales wouldn't make any of the mistakes he had in the past.

The professor exited the loop where it intersected route 35 and went north. Sales whipped his car around and stayed with him, sometimes falling as far back as a half mile where a flat stretch of road allowed. Thankfully, there was still enough traffic for the Mercedes to blend in. The van itself stood out above most cars. Sales's hands remained rigidly fixed on the wheel, and by the time the van exited at Selton they were painfully cramped. Sales took no notice, though. Now was likely to be the most difficult part of following Lipton. Sales wasn't intimately familiar with the reservoir area, but he knew it was rural. If Lipton got too far ahead, he could make a quick turn-off and be gone forever.

Luckily, in less than a mile of twisting road the pavement turned into dusty stones. The van left a trail of brown dust that was as easy to follow as a rabbit in fresh snow. In less than ten minutes, Sales was driving past the faded box that bore Lipton's family name. He continued on, not knowing how well positioned the professor might be to keep an eye on the entrance and not wanting to spook him. Besides, Sales was much more comfortable approaching the house through the woods than he was walking up the drive.

The next closest driveway was nearly a quarter mile away, a little-used track that led to a small cottage. Sales pulled in and got out, checking the load in his Glock out of habit and taking in the rich, cool scent of the towering pines. Suddenly the pungent smell of a wood fire filled his nose. Sales wondered if it had anything to do with Lipton. The wind was certainly coming from that direction. The woods were growing dark with the coming dusk, but Sales's eyes adjusted quickly. Spurred on by the scent of the fire, he moved off in the direction of Lipton's place with the easy stealth of a mountain cat.

CHAPTER 37

There was a large black barrel on the side of the tall Victorian house. A sizable fire had been laid inside it with dry twigs and split logs soaked in starter fluid. Beside the barrel, stacked ten feet high against the side of the old wooden house, was an enormous confusion of sticks and branches. Lipton stuffed a wad of inside-out clothes, the blood-soaked outer layer he'd removed outside Patti's apartment, into the barrel. In the bottom of the barrel a wick of newspaper protruded from a quarter-size hole in the rusty metal. Lipton bent down, struck a match, and ignited the blaze. He watched without emotion as fiery orange sheets of flame engulfed the clothes. Soon it became so hot that Lipton had to step back.

A warm breeze from across the water escorted the black smoke away from the house and into the towering trees. Lipton looked critically at the sky. The sun was down and directly above, a tilted half moon was shot through with the horn of a ragged cloud that portended a dark rain from the north. Everything was a factor, and Lipton considered his prearranged plan of escape as he shifted the Tech-9 in the waist of his pants and mounted the porch steps. For the moment he would leave the snapping blaze to its own designs.

Inside the house, Lipton went directly to the phone. It was an old dusty thing, faded black. He dialed 911.

"Nine-one-one, what's your emergency?"

"Just listen," Lipton said, adding a touch of hysteria to his voice to make the whole thing believable. "This is Professor Eric Lipton. I'm going to kill myself. I can't take it anymore. The police have persecuted me long enough. They've ruined my life! Do you hear me? They've ruined everything! They won't leave me alone! I'm going into my basement and I'm going to end it. My blood is on their hands! I'm an innocent man, but I'm going to kill myself because of them! You tell them that!"

"Sir—"

Lipton slammed down the phone. He knew 911 automatically registered the address of every call. He knew they would send the police and that his voice would be preserved on tape for the media. It was much better than a note. He wasted no time gathering his things. There was no evidence of panic in his movements, just a hasty efficiency. Devising plans for every eventuality was something Lipton delighted in. Although he had never intended to leave his safe house in a rush, he had made provisions in the event something unforeseeable happened. And how could he have foreseen Sales's arrival at Patti's apartment the moment he had cut her open?

While he stuffed the last few items into his backpack, he went back over the day. His only error was in failing to make certain the girl was dead. Had he done that, he wouldn't have to run. But in the confusion of his escape, he'd forgotten all about Patti Dunleavy. She very well might die from the wound he had inflicted, but in hindsight, he should have put a bullet in her head on his way out the back. Without her testimony against him, he could laugh in the face of the police. Sales, the only other person who'd seen him, didn't count, and once again, every shred of physical evidence was in his burning barrel. But the possibility of the girl's survival made it imperative that he not only leave the area, but probably the country as well. A few years in South America with a new identity might be in order. He had several from which to choose.

Because he was so brilliant and so thorough, he would throw the authorities well off his trail and exit the States with the ease of a casual tourist. Lipton delicately placed his computer in the smaller of his two bags and then deposited them both on the back porch.

Down in the cellar was a large horizontal meat freezer. In it was the frozen body of Walt Tanner, the love-stricken traveling salesman who matched Lipton's body type exactly. The body was a useful prop in the drama over which Lipton was master. Lipton undid the padlock and lifted the lid. Tanner's knees were crunched up to his chest and his eyelashes were frosty white like powdered sugar. Slip knots Lipton had tied more than a year ago secured a frozen clothesline around his neck and knees. Hoisting the slack end of the line over his shoulder, Lipton heaved the body up and out of the freezer and dragged it into the middle of the damp concrete floor. That would be the epicenter of the heat, ensuring the survival of nothing more than bones. He reached into the freezer again and extracted the gun used to kill Tanner. He laid that next to the body and mounted the stairs.

Lipton knew all the angles by which the police could

positively identify the bones, and he had done everything possible to thwart that investigation. It began by securing and destroying every X ray ever taken of his own teeth and bones and ended with a thorough cleaning of his home, purging it of hair from the obvious places. Because they had no DNA from Marcia Sales's apartment, the DA had never taken DNA samples for the trial. That would have been counterproductive. So now, the only way it could be conclusively proved that he wasn't the man with an apparently self-inflicted bullet hole in his head would be to exhume Lipton's mother and do a comparison sample. Even if they went to that trouble, it would take the police weeks if not months to work through the red tape, and by then Lipton would be so far gone it wouldn't matter. If nothing else, the bones would buy him time.

On the porch, Lipton hoisted a duffel bag over each shoulder and made his way around to the side of the house. He froze, only for a second, but it was long enough to distinctly hear the crunching of gravel beneath the tires of a car moving slowly up his drive toward the house. It was too soon to be a response to his call and this puzzled him. It really didn't matter, though. He sneered in the direction of the approaching car. Carefully, he placed the bottom of his foot against the side of the burning barrel. With a swift shove, he pushed its burning contents over and into the brush pile. In seconds, the flames began to lick up through the sticks, spreading to the clapboard siding of the house. Lipton did a quick calculation and decided that even if the police in the approaching car did get inside the house, their search would never get as far as the cellar before the whole place was an enormous funeral pyre.

He strode rapidly down the back path toward the

boathouse. Inside was a small skiff. In case one broke down, Lipton had attached two small outboard motors to the transom. On the other side of the reservoir, his dead aunt's Buick Riviera sat waiting at the end of a dusty lane. It was the perfect escape, the perfect execution of a perfect plan. Before going into the boathouse and closing the door behind himself, Lipton glanced up at the sky and chortled quietly to himself. It even looked like the rain would hold off long enough for him to cross the water and disappear for good.

CHAPTER 38

Bolinger drove slowly down the gravel path looking and listening carefully for any sign of the professor. He didn't want to come clattering up the drive and give Lipton any advance warning. Nor did he want to rush into some kind of ambush. The car windows were open, and they all smelled the smoke. Unger sat beside him in the front seat fidgeting like a kid in a barber's chair. He hadn't found the nerve to start making his media calls, partly because of Bolinger and partly because he wasn't certain of success. In the back was Casey, silent but intensely alert.

"Smoke," she said quietly.

Bolinger nodded his head.

"He's here!" Unger burst out excitedly at the sight of the van beside the house.

"I don't see my car anywhere," Casey commented.

Bolinger said flatly, "Sales lost him."

"You want me to go in the front and you go in the back?" Unger said, pulling the gun from his jacket.

Bolinger gave him a somber look before saying, "No, we'll go in the front together and cover each other."

"Sounds good," Unger said. His only experience in this sort of thing had been a two-week seminar nearly fifteen years ago and a hefty dose of *NYPD Blue* on television.

Bolinger brought the car to a stop just shy of the now dusty white van. Cautiously they got out.

Bolinger turned around in his seat and spoke forcefully. "Stay right here," he told Casey. "I mean it, don't move from this car."

Bolinger and Unger got out of the cruiser without closing the doors. Quietly, they approached the front steps. The surrounding trees and the coming night hid the smoke billowing from the back side of the house. The sounds from the snapping fire were cloaked in the wind-blown pines. Upwind from the blaze as they were, the difference between the smell of a campfire and a nascent inferno was negligible.

Just as the two detectives disappeared into the tall gray house, Casey spotted the form of Donald Sales emerging from the woods near the far corner of the house. But instead of moving her way or toward the house, she watched him quickly set off at a right angle, jogging in the direction of the water. It was obvious that he'd seen something the police hadn't.

Casey got out of the car and headed after him. She kept a good distance from the house, avoiding it as if it were something alive lying in wait for her. When she rounded the far corner, not far at all from where Sales had emerged from the trees, she was confronted with the shocking sight of the back half of the house awash in crackling flames. Part of her wanted to cry out to the police inside, but making herself known to Lipton if he was lurking in the vicinity was unthinkable, so she remained silent, crossing the back lawn in cautious pursuit of Sales.

*   *   *

Sales knew before he broke through the smoke-filled trees that everything was amiss. He could see the orange flames and the police cruiser with its doors wide open parked behind the van. But when he broke into the open, he saw the chance he thought had probably gone up in flames with the house. Out of the corner of his trained eye, he just made out a tall shape fading into the trees that climbed halfway up the bank of the reservoir toward the house.

Most people would have stopped to think about what they might or might not have seen, so fleeting was the image. But trained his whole life in the ways of the woods, where small signs were conclusive proof, Sales didn't miss a step but took off across the back lawn. Instinct took over and he crouched warily as he entered the gloomy stand of pines.

Soft needles muffled his footsteps as he hurried along through the trees. Near the end of the path, he could begin to make out the shiny black surface of the water and the dull gray sides of the boathouse, an architectural sister to the main house above. There was no one in sight, but Sales could hear low noises coming from inside the boathouse. A set of mossy wooden steps took him down the bank and onto the dock. The dock itself wrapped around the boathouse, part of it extending well out into the water. There was a door in the nearest corner but it was shut tight.

With the memory of the Tech-9 fresh in his mind, Sales had no intention of barging through a door and drawing its fire. Determined not to give Lipton any warning of his approach, he circled the house to look for an opening through which he could get an idea of what was going on inside and maybe even have the chance at a clean shot. Circling the boathouse, he stepped carefully on the dock to ensure silence. When he reached the far side of the building, he could see that there was a large mullioned window in the center of the wall. He could also see that instead of extending out onto the water, the dock on this side actually wrapped itself around toward the front of the boathouse.

With his heart thumping wildly, Sales drew close enough to the window to peek in. The garage door to the lake was open and the dim remnants of twilight spilled in, allowing him to see Lipton's dark form bent over the small outboard engine of the skiff he'd lowered into the boat slip. The aluminum craft, tossed about by the incoming chop, made the sound of a distant gong as it bumped against the slip's sidewall.

Sales ducked back down and, crouching beneath the window, then scooted along the dock toward the corner of the boathouse. Without tipping off Lipton, he could round the corner and have a clear shot at the professor before he even knew what was happening. Sales's palms broke out in a sweat. His words of promise to Casey rang out strangely from the back of his mind. He'd said he'd bring Lipton to justice. He'd promised that if she helped, then he wouldn't summarily execute the professor. But that was when he was desperate for her help. Now it was just himself and Lipton.

The image of his murdered daughter's face came suddenly into the forefront of his mind as clearly as if he were seeing her in person. He could hear her voice, her laugh, even smell the scent of the shampoo she always used to wash her long dark hair. Tears of anguish rolled hot down his face, and Sales took a deep breath to calm his nerves, determined to shoot straight for the kill.

After three deep breaths, he rose from his crouch, rounded the corner of the boathouse, and leveled his gun. At the same instant, Casey burst into the boathouse through the shrieking wooden door. Lipton sprang from the skiff and was on her like a voracious spider. Sales screamed for him to freeze. Afraid of killing Casey in the process, he eased the pressure from his trigger finger.

Lipton quickly spun Casey in front of him as a shield and shoved her toward the boat. From the waist of his pants he pulled out the Tech-9, and with the short, nasty barrel pointed at Casey's head he shouted, "Drop the gun, Sales! Drop the gun or I'll blow her head off!"

Sales knew instinctively that Lipton would kill Casey either way. She was dead. That was that. He sighted the pistol on the professor's forehead, moving the barrel as his target bobbed from side to side behind Casey's face.

"I'll kill her!" Lipton screamed. "Drop it!"

Sales lowered his stance. He'd get just one shot.

CHAPTER 39

Lipton didn't need Sales to drop the gun. All he needed was a moment's hesitation. He got that, and the inside of the boathouse echoed with the roar of gunfire.

Bullets from the Tech-9 filled the air like a swarm of angry bees. Sales's body jerked crazily. He fired three useless shots into the air as he was pummeled backward and into the water. Lipton continued to spray the spot where Sales had disappeared beneath the surface, leaving only a red foamy swell of bubbles and blood.

"Get in!" Lipton screamed at Casey, shoving her roughly into the skiff. He climbed in behind her and fired a single shot over her head.

"Get down in the bottom of the boat, goddamn it!" he bellowed.

Casey scrunched herself onto the boat's bottom, ducking her head as low as possible behind the metal seat. She was too shocked to do anything, too shocked even to think. She was simply reacting to the immediate threat of Lipton and the machine pistol he wielded in his right hand.

With Casey cowering in the bow of the boat, Lipton turned his attention to the motor. Two more pulls and the outboard clamored to life in a cloud of blue smoke. Lipton unhooked the mooring line from a cleat at the edge of the slip and eased the craft out of the boathouse. Once he was clear of the structure, he opened the throttle and the boat took off like a spurred stallion, raising its front end spiritedly above the waves.

But twelve feet was as far as they went before something heaved the small skiff wildly sideways. Lipton was nearly thrown from the boat. Casey gasped, certain they would capsize. Lipton let up on the throttle at once, and Casey peered up over the seat to see what had happened.

Behind them in the water, thrashing and roiling the water like a harpooned shark, was Sales. As the boat chugged past him, he had come up bleeding from the bottom and gotten hold of the line trailing from its stern. It was the same line that had been used to secure the boat to the side of the slip. In his haste, Lipton had simply tossed it into the water.

When the professor realized what had happened, he reached into the bottom of the boat and stood, ready to empty the rest of the magazine into Sales at nearly point-blank range. From his spot in the water, Sales saw what was coming. Gagging already, his lungs half filled with a mixture of blood and water, he made a fruitless attempt to suck in a huge breath so that he might submerge himself beneath the reservoir's protective surface. But Lipton had him this time, and there was no boathouse foundation to absorb most of the gunfire. Sales knew in that split second that he was going to die.

At the same time, Casey sprang from her spot in the bow of the boat. She shoved Lipton squarely in the back, knocking him headfirst into the dark water. Sales was on him like a snake, and together the two men went down. Casey looked over the edge of the boat at the place where the two of them had gone under. She yanked an oar from the bottom of the boat and stood poised to smash Lipton's skull if he should surface within striking distance.

Bloody bubbles burst through the surface, and then there was a series of bright flashes and small explosions that lit the murky depths like a handful of underwater cherry bombs. After a moment of eerie silence, the surface of the water exploded as both men broke into the air for a desperate breath, each with his hands locked on to the other's neck. Then they went down again, and it was quiet except for the hiss of broken bubbles.

Every muscle in Casey's body went tight. Noiselessly, she urged Sales on in his pitch-black battle. Suddenly, he burst through the surface, alone. The desperate sound of his lungs sucking in oxygen rang out across the water. Casey held her oar out to him and he grabbed it, allowing her to pull him to the boat and help him up over the gunwale, dripping blood and water into the skiff until her feet were sloshing in the crimson brew. Casey sat on the bow seat and allowed herself to shake uncontrollably. Sales lay sprawled in the mess, his chest heaving like a dying fish, one leg dangling over the side of the boat.

The unexpected horrible gasping wail from the stern of the boat made them both jump. Sales spun around crab-like, still lying in the skiff's bottom but with his head propped up against Casey's leg. From behind the boat's motor, Lipton's haggard face appeared. His hair was plastered to his head, and blood rushed from his mouth and nose. His mangled hands, with three fingers shooting off at odd angles, were clamped tightly to the gunwale. After two more pitiful gasps for air, he directed his attention toward the two of them, his nemesis and his lawyer.

In the fading light, Casey could hear the shouts of the police as they came down through the trees. Lipton's damaged face twisted itself into a devilish smirk, and he began to giggle maniacally. He tilted his head back now and laughed even harder. He was laughing at them. Sales knew it. Casey knew it.

"Donald," she shouted suddenly, "no!"

Sales's pant leg was rolled up to his knee. From beneath it he had removed the little snub-nose .38 and was now pointing it at Lipton's head.

"Lipton," Sales hissed venomously.

Lipton heard his call in the midst of his amusement and his face suddenly went blank, then froze in an instant of terror.

"This is for my little girl," Sales said, spitting his words and then pulling the trigger. A small orange flame lit the gloom, illuminating for a brief second the dime-size hole the slug punched into Lipton's forehead before expanding around its hollow point and blasting through the back of his skull in a spray of brains and blood.

"Freeze!"

It was Bolinger and James Unger. They had rounded the corner of the boathouse, and they stood there on the edge of the dock with their guns pointed in the direction of the boat. Sales held up his hands and dropped the gun.

"Where's the professor?" Bolinger shouted. The tempest was rising now, and only a stout call could be heard above the sound of the wind as it washed through the trees.

"Where is he?" Unger demanded loudly, his voice breaking with hysteria.

"He's dead," Casey heard herself say tiredly.

"Dead? Come in here," Bolinger instructed. "Can you row in?"

Sales lay gasping for air in the bottom of the boat. Casey climbed over him and fitted her oar back into its oarlock. With a dozen hard strokes they were bumping back up against the dock.

"What happened?" Bolinger demanded of Casey. "I heard the shot. What happened?"

Casey looked up at him and then at Sales, whose pale, wet face plastered with long strands of his black hair showed no emotion whatsoever.

"I can't talk to you about it, Detective," she said reflexively, then added, "and neither can he."

"What? Why the hell not?" Unger snapped, stepping forward, his body posture brazenly challenging her.

"Because," she said, looking from the two irritated police to Sales, "this man is invoking his Fifth Amendment rights and I can't say anything to you at this time . . . I'm his lawyer."

EPILOGUE

Casey stood before the jury with the power and majesty of a Celtic princess, her deep red hair twisted high up on her head like a crown, her eyes afire with conviction. Her forest green closely tailored suit showed off the strength of her body as well. For the final time, she had presented her argument and it was a good one. Now, all she needed was to close the deal, lock them in.

"To convict my client of murder, I want you to remember this: The law requires that such a crime be an intentional act, proved by the prosecution beyond a reasonable doubt. Furthermore, and just as important, is the fact that any of us has the right, the *right,* to use deadly force if we feel our own lives are in jeopardy . . ."

Casey let her gaze pass over them all, individually, so they could each get the full sense of her conviction.

"A long time ago," she said quietly, "when I was being introduced to the law and its intricacies, I, like many of us, felt the need to punish someone, anyone, for a criminal act. It's an innate reaction. We see someone hurt, we want someone to be punished. But I was told back then to think about this, and these words changed my life: What if it were you . . .

"What if it were you, or you, or you, or me?" she said, letting her open hand pass over them all before coming to rest on her own breast. "What if it were you, and what if it were true?

"Think about that, ladies and gentlemen," she said, raising her voice gradually as she spoke. "Think about what I've told you here over these past few days. Think about what my client, a fellow human being, has been through. Now, imagine it was you, you were in that very same situation . . . and imagine everything I've told you was true . . .

"My client is not guilty," Casey said, quietly again, "not of a crime. My client is innocent . . . Please, I ask you, let justice be served."

Casey looked at them long and hard, reading their faces. Inwardly she smiled. She had them. They belonged to her the way a great stage actor could own an audience on the Friday night opening of a celebrated play. She stayed there, letting the energy flow between them until she felt it begin to ebb. At that perfect moment, she turned and sat down. Only then was there a whisper, only then did anyone in the entire courtroom dare to move.

Tony leaned her way and whispered, "Should I have someone get us some sandwiches while we wait?"

"No," she told him, smiling gently. "I've got plans for lunch already. Besides, there won't be time for sandwiches."

"What do you mean?" he asked.

"This won't take more than twenty minutes."

Casey was wrong.

It took twenty-four. The jury foreman stood and

handed the verdict to the bailiff, who handed it to the judge. She read it, handed it back, and told the foreman to please read the verdict.

The foreman, a lineman for the telephone company, was nervous and unused to speaking in public. Forgetting most of the formalities, he simply blurted out, "We're the jury and we find the defendant not guilty."

Emotion washed through the courtroom like the crest of a flood. While Tony patted her on the back, Catalina Enos buried her head in Casey's chest, sobbing hysterically and begging her in broken English to accept her heartfelt thanks. The husband's family burst out into angry shouts and had to be forcibly removed from the courtroom.

After accepting the district attorney's perfunctory congratulations, Casey put her arm around the young girl and ushered her out of the courtroom and down the steps without bothering to stop for the shrieking mob of reporters hungry for sound bites. She'd let Tony handle that part of it. It wouldn't do her any good anyway.

When she'd finally fought their way through, Casey tucked the still sobbing girl into the front seat of her Mercedes and got in beside her. They'd optimistically gone over their plan during the past several weeks. Casey had located a halfway house for women in the Houston area that had agreed to take Catalina and help her through a job-training program until she became self-sufficient. The home provided counseling for women who lived in fear like Catalina, and Casey assured her that she would be quite safe from her husband's family since no one but she and a trusted friend would know where she was.

Casey drove through the downtown area to an IHOP resting in the shadow of the highway overhead. Donald

Sales sat in a vinyl booth by the window drinking coffee and reading the paper. He looked up in surprise when they walked in.

"I thought I'd be here all day," he said.

"You know I work fast," Casey said with a smile.

"This is true," he replied, signaling for them to sit down.

"Sit and eat, Catalina," Casey told the girl. "You've got a long drive. This is the friend I told you about. I trust him with my life, Catalina, and so can you."

The girl smiled bashfully at Sales and scooted into the booth. Casey slipped Sales an envelope.

"What's this?" he asked, his eyes sharpening.

"For expenses," she told him.

Sales snorted and handed it back. She took it, knowing better than to argue.

"Sit down," he told her.

"I'd love to, but I can't," she said. "I've got a meeting."

Casey held out her hand. Sales took it and she bent over and kissed him on the cheek.

"Thank you, Donald," she said.

"What for?" he said brusquely. "Kidnapping you, or being a stellar client?"

It had taken several weeks for the media storm surrounding Lipton's death to subside. But during that time many months ago, Casey had worked assiduously to convince the district attorney that he would be best served by dropping any and all charges against Donald Sales. Bob Bolinger had been instrumental in her efforts. And although it was certainly unorthodox for a cop to help prove someone innocent, Bolinger privately told his friends that it was no more unorthodox than letting James Unger take all the credit for bringing down Lipton.

After she'd secured Sales's freedom, Casey had turned all her energies toward getting a mistrial declared for Catalina. Using every contact she'd ever made, she accelerated the appeal, got the new trial, and even succeeded in sullying Van Rawlins's reputation by having him removed from the case.

"Both," Casey replied now, backing away. "You changed my life."

"For the better?"

"I think so," she told him. "I don't know . . . I hope so."

Casey got back into her car and went to the better side of town. A valet parked her car for her, and she walked in through the etched glass doors, searching for the best table in the house. He would be waiting for her there. She saw his familiar smile and waved cheerily herself as she glided through the busy place, drawing the attention of every man who was unaccompanied by a woman and even some who were. Out of the corner of her eye, she saw a friend at the bar to whom she gave a discreet little nod.

Sitting gracefully, she met Taylor's smile by flashing her own perfect teeth. He rose from the table, took her hand, and kissed it gently.

"You look radiant," he told her. "You look absolutely stunning."

"I feel good," she told him, sitting down across from him and picking up the wine list. Taylor, dressed to perfection himself in a navy blue windowpane suit, gazed appreciatively at her while she perused the selection. A tall, trim waiter appeared in a bone jacket and black bow tie.

"A bottle of the Iron Horse brut," she told him.

"Very good," he said, taking the list with a questioning look at Taylor.

"How about some Dom?" her husband suggested.

"No," she said with a close-lipped smile. "Iron Horse is every bit as good, just a little less expensive."

Taylor chuckled at the thought and asked, "Why the champagne?"

"Oh, two things," she said perkily. "First, I won a huge case . . ."

"Excellent!" he said enthusiastically.

The waiter arrived with the wine and opened the bottle, which she told him to simply pour.

"Second," she said, raising her glass, "because today is a new beginning."

They touched glasses softly, and each of them sipped their wine delicately.

"It is good," he said. "And I'm glad you feel like today is a new beginning. I think that's what it should be. I think that's how we should approach things, Casey. We need to forget the past and move forward like we were meeting almost for the first time."

"Like strangers?" she asked inquisitively.

He gave her a strange look and said uncertainly, "I guess that's right."

"Well, you're right about forgetting the past. And I'd like to make it a clean break, through and through. That way we can both begin again."

Casey removed a document from her purse and unfolded it. She handed it across the table to him along with a gold pen.

"What?" he said.

"It's our divorce," she told him pleasantly. "That way we can really start over."

"You mean get divorced and get remarried?" he said with a confused grimace.

"No," she said. "I mean get divorced and start over, like strangers."

"You want me to court you?" he said, annoyed.

"No," she told him with a straight face. "I don't want you to court me. I don't want anything from you. This document gives you everything but my personal bank account and my car. I don't want anything from you, Taylor . . ."

"I'm not signing any goddamned divorce!" he said, raising his voice and drawing stares from the surrounding tables. "It's not going to be that easy for you, little miss lawyer. You don't just lead me on and—"

"I never led you on," she said forcefully.

"You asked me here!" he shouted. "You said you had a proposal to make!"

"Of course I did," she said, seething. "And I do. This is my proposal. You sign this paper here and now or I'll dig in and fight you for every penny, every piece of art, and every stick of furniture I ever laid my eyes on. My deal is a clean break and you keep your money and everything else. All I want is my life. I want my life to start over . . . This is your last chance at a deal like this, and you know me well enough to know that I'm not bluffing."

Taylor's face twisted with rage. He snatched the document and looked it over before violently scratching his name on it and throwing it down on the table in front of him. He stood then and grabbed his glass of champagne, raising it to douse her.

"You see that man at the bar?" Casey said firmly before

he could do it. "He's a police detective, and if you so much as spill a drop of that wine on me, he'll throw you down on the floor, handcuff you, and drag you out of here like the punk you are . . .

"So go ahead, Taylor Jordan," she said defiantly. "Make a move . . ."

Bolinger saw his cue and stood, pulling back his coat to reveal his badge, his gun, and a gleaming set of handcuffs.

Taylor fought for composure, and actually managed to drink the wine with trembling lips before setting it down and striding indignantly out of the restaurant without another word.

"Would you please ask that gentleman at the bar with the gun and the badge if he'd like to join me for some champagne?" Casey said to the gaping waiter.

Bolinger sat down and everyone else returned to their lunches.

"Classic," he said to her, holding up a freshly filled glass. "I wish you were on the right side of the law."

"Meaning?" she said archly.

"Meaning I wish you were helping put people away rather than keeping them out," he told her gruffly.

"What about people like Donald Sales?" she said, adding, "and Catalina Enos?"

"No, I know about them," he said, "I'm not talking about them. They were innocent. I'm talking about the bad guys."

Casey laughed at him, her mirth filling the space between them like a brilliant bouquet.

"So what next?" he asked.

"I'm off to Dallas," she said. "Everything's packed and on its way. Patti is already there."

"How is Patti?" he asked. He knew that after Lipton's attack she'd only been in the hospital for a short while, but it had always seemed strange to him that after what he saw there were no complications.

"She's fine," Casey said. "There never was any critical damage to her internal organs. She's got an ugly scar, but the doctor's told her that was all."

"So she's in Dallas?" Bolinger repeated.

"Yes, hopefully with my office all set up. All that's missing is me. I figure a new life needs a new place to begin."

"More lawyering?"

"Of course," she told him. "There's a regional branch of the LDFU in Dallas and they've offered me a very prestigious position."

"LDFU?" he asked. "Never heard of that."

"It's the Legal Defense Fund for the Underprivileged," she told him. "Trust me, it's prestigious. A lot of people just don't know about it."

"How can it be prestigious if a lot of people don't know about it?" Bolinger asked dubiously.

Casey smiled for a long while, thinking. Then she said, "Because I know."

More
Tim Green!

Please turn this page
for a
bonus excerpt
from
his new novel,

*THE FOURTH
PERIMETER,*

available in hardcover
February 2002.

It was the taste of metal wiped clean with gun oil. It was the taste of horror, of death. Collin's teeth bit instinctively into the gun's barrel, and he closed his eyes against the coming blast. In the brief instant before it came, his mind replayed the events leading up to this crisis. In vivid slow motion he was afforded the opportunity to regret a million moments that he could have rewritten to prevent what was about to happen.

Pernicious fog, heavy with the moisture from the warm river, shrouded the old brick buildings, casting gloom on their normally cheerful wooden signs. The cold spring's last dying gasp had rushed down the Eastern seaboard from Canada and so, everything was obscure and ill defined. Collin Ford rolled slowly down King Street under the hazy yellow light of ancient lampposts in his pewter Toyota 4 Runner. He might have been any young man in any American city. Most had renovated areas of bygone commerce that hugged some once-vital body of water, and most were teeming with young professionals at night. But he wasn't any young professional, and the capital of the United States wasn't just any city. Collin was an agent in the Secret Service.

Unlike many of his young counterparts, money was of little concern. He had a substantial trust fund. But that was something he neither relied upon nor talked about. His concern, rather, was one of distinction. Collin had no desire to outdo his father in business even if he could. As well-off as they were, Collin's father taught him from an early age that while wealth could be beneficial for certain things, it wasn't something to strive for. So instead, Collin had set his sights on rising in the ranks of the Service and surpassing what even his ambitious father had accomplished before he had left the Service to develop a high-tech business.

Collin found a spot for his truck on a side street and hunched over, pulling his blazer close before slouching up the brick sidewalk to a place called Harpoon Alley. A pleasant amber glow spilled out of the large mullioned windows. Inside, he spotted his friends in the midst of the crowd hunkered down at the bar. He slipped through the door, into where it was warm and dry, and dodged his way through the throng. He ordered a Coke from the bartender and greeted his friends with a timid smile.

"You're late," his friend Lou said, looking pointedly at

his Rolex. Lou was tall, handsome, and blond, a former college swimmer. Collin was his opposite in looks as well as demeanor. Lou was the kind of guy who introduced himself to strangers with total ease. Collin, while singularly intelligent, was reserved, average in height and build, and dark-haired, with hazel eyes.

"One of my kids needed a ride home," he said with a shrug.

"Your kids?" asked Allen, a preppy-looking lawyer with stylish glasses who was more acquainted with Lou than he was Collin.

"This guy is like the original saint," Lou replied, taking a swig of beer. "Instead of using his trust fund to travel Europe in style, he buys uniforms for a kid's basketball league. Instead of working for his old man in a Manhattan high-rise, he hoofs it all over the country sleeping in Motel 6es waiting to take a bullet for the president."

"It's a good thing," Lou exclaimed with his hands in the air. "Don't get me wrong. But I'm just not prone to a guilty conscience or else I wouldn't be able to stand hanging around with you."

"Like, handicapped kids or something?" Allen inquired, blinking behind his glasses.

Collin looked at Allen out of the corner of his eye and took a drink of the Coke that had just arrived in a pint glass.

"They're at-risk kids," he explained, satisfied that Allen wasn't trying to poke fun at his kids. "And we just won the City League Championship for ten- and eleven-year olds . . ."

Collin was beaming now, and he looked at Lou expectantly. Lou knew better than anyone that Collin had gone into this not knowing the first thing about basketball. A couple months back when the two of them were on their way to a party, Lou had asked for a breath mint. Collin carelessly told him to check in his briefcase, and that's when Lou discovered the book on basic strategies of the sport that he'd borrowed from the library.

"Hey," Lou said now with genuine admiration, "that's great Collin."

"I know it," Collin said with a self-deprecating grin. "But these kids worked so hard. You should have seen their faces when I handed out the trophies. The trophies were as big as the kids."

"Now that calls for a real drink, by God," Lou said, signaling the bartender for another round. He pointed to Collin, and told the bartender, "And make his a pint of Foster's."

"You can certainly have one or two to celebrate," Lou said brightly, as the glasses arrived. "I mean, that's really great."

Effusive over his victory, Collin gave in and raised his glass. It wasn't long before he had two pints under his belt and was working on his third. He was rehashing his zone strategy for his friends on the bar using balled-up cocktail napkins when Collin caught sight of a familiar face from across the bar. He stopped what he was saying in mid-sentence.

Lou followed his gaze and emitted a low whistle.

"Wow," he said.

"That's her," Collin heard himself say. He was suddenly and acutely aware that he was wearing his old blazer rather than the new double-breasted Italian one his father had given to him at Christmas and that he'd forgotten to brush his teeth before he came out.

"Who?" Lou asked.

"Her," Collin said, buttoning and then unbuttoning his jacket, "the girl I told you about. The one I see in my coffee shop. She's . . ."

"Incredible," Lou said. Allen nodded appreciatively and uttered his concurrence.

Her hair was black and straight and her eyes a striking green. They were almost feline and hinted of the Orient. But her high cheeks, thick red lips, and long straight nose were more reminiscent of the Mediterranean. Her skin was bronze and her tall, striking figure was snugly ensconced in a cashmere turtleneck and pleated black slacks.

She had taken the one empty stool on the opposite side of the bar and ordered a drink. She was alone and while nearly all eyes were on her, she seemed unaware. There was something delicately innocent about her, and Lou knew in an instant why she had been the first woman in over a year to distract Collin from the girl-friend that had dumped him for an NHL hockey player.

"Go talk to her," Lou urged.

"No," Collin said, "I can't. Look what I look like."

"What are you talking about? You look fine," Lou said.

"I don't even know her name," Collin said weakly.

"I thought you said you've talked to her," Lou protested.

"I've said 'hello' and things like that," Collin replied, taking a nervous swig from his glass. "But I haven't *really* talked to her, and I don't know her name."

"Dude, she's looking right at you," Allen said, nudging Collin in the ribs.

Collin looked up and smiled foolishly. The girl smiled back and gave an embarrassed little wave.

"Go!" Lou hissed, surreptitiously grabbing Collin by the back of his blazer and urging him away from them.

Before he knew it, Collin was standing there in an empty space, his friends jerking their heads at him like idiots and the girl smiling patiently from the other side of the bar. Collin took a deep breath and worked his way through the crowd.

By the time he got to the other side, it was too late. A big guy with a gold watch wearing a dark Armani suit had wedged himself right up alongside her and was already making his pitch. Collin dipped his head and slipped past as if he were really on his way to the rest room after all. He was struck by the strong smell of the man's cologne and further reminded him of his own tousled appearance. But as he passed, the girl reached out and tugged him toward her. Collin stumbled and bumped into the guy sitting on the next stool.

"Excuse me," the girl said abruptly to the interloper, "this is my husband."

Collin met the other man's hostile glare with a confused look. Then, without thinking, he bent down and kissed the girl on her cheek.

"Hi," he said, then straightened up and gave the other guy his best forbidding Secret Service look. The man opened his mouth as if to speak, but his resolve visibly wavered and he quickly melted away. Collin turned to the girl with a grin.

"I never saw that before," he said.

"It worked," she told him. "I'm Leena."

"I'm Collin," he said, taking her hand. "Collin Ford. I'm the guy from—"

"The coffee shop," she said with a suppressed smile, "I know. I was wondering if you were ever going to talk to me."

"You were?" he asked.

Leena nodded and said, "I'm not very good at meeting people. I'm new here. I guess you've been here for a while. I saw your friends . . ."

"About three years," he told her. "Originally from New York."

"The city?"

"Close by," he said. "Now I'm with the Secret Service."

"Not very secretive, are you?" she said archly.

Collin blushed despite himself.

"Your friends are staring at us," she added with a smile.

He gave them a dirty look, but all that did was incite them. "They're morons," he said.

"Want to go someplace that isn't so . . . crowded?" she suggested.

"Sure."

Collin led her out into the fog. She had a dark full-length coat over her arm and stopped outside the door to put it on. Collin helped. The shapeless coat hid her spectacular form and left Collin eager to get to someplace warm, where she would take it off again.

"Thank you," she said in a soft tone that thrilled him. She was almost too sweet.

He started down toward the water, and she said, "No, let's go this way. I know a good place."

He shrugged and walked along with her in the mist past storefronts, restaurants, and bars.

"How about here?" she said, pointing around the corner to an out-of-the-way place. They went down a small set of stairs into what was once a cellar. It was darker than Harpoon Alley, darker and dingier, and Collin felt remarkably at ease. They found a pair of empty stools at the long bar in the back corner.

"Can I take your coat?" Collin asked.

Leena pulled the garment tight to her shoulders, and

with a feigned shiver said, "No thanks, maybe after a drink."

A lanky bartender who wore two silver hoop earrings as well as a thick dark beard ambled over and asked what they wanted.

"How about a vodka?" Leena said, looking at Collin expectantly. "I'm not much of a drinker, but sometimes I think it's the best thing in the world to take away a chill."

Collin hesitated, but only for a moment. "Sure."

"Two doubles," she told the bartender, "straight up."

Collin fished out his wallet and slapped a fifty-dollar bill down on the bar without comment. He never noticed that while the bartender filled his glass with vodka he gave the girl nothing but water.

When the drinks came, Leena held hers in the air and touched Collin's glass.

"To new places, new friends," she said, and with a mischievous smile added, "and secret agents . . ."

"I said Secret Service," he told her with a smile. He liked her sense of humor. And in fact, as they talked, he found he liked everything about her. Leena was remarkably similar to his ex-girlfriend. They both had fathers who were bankers. They both studied fine arts, rode horses, and loved the symphony. The similarities didn't even bother him. For nearly a year now, anything that reminded him of Amanda had caused a pang of regret. But Leena was like an improved version of his old girlfriend. She had none of Amanda's haughty and sometimes frigid nature. Leena was warm and open, and before Collin knew it, he was dead drunk.

He was buzzing comfortably when she finally said in a bashful whisper, "I'd like to go home with you."

Collin looked at her, stunned. Tears were welling up in her eyes, and he asked, "What's wrong?"

Leena blinked and looked up at him through her long lashes. "I'm just so lonely. I haven't been with anyone in so long. I'm sorry, I know it's not right, but I can't help it. I've seen you now for weeks, and I think about you all the time. I can't help wanting to be with you . . ."

Collin almost choked.

"No, no, no," he slurred. "Don't you worry. I don't mind. I'd love to have you come home with me. Please, come . . ."

She smiled tentatively and stood up. Her coat fell open, and the sight of her perfect body thrilled him. But when he rose, Collin staggered half a step backwards. Leena helped him into his windbreaker like a mother sending her son off to school. She pulled her own coat close around her shoulders and tied it tightly at the waist. Then she hooked her arm through his and led him through the bar with her head slightly inclined so that the curtain of dark hair hid her face until they walked up the dirty stone steps and out into the cool damp night.

"Where's your car?" she asked.

"This way," he slurred and walked unevenly around

the block, relying heavily on her much steadier gate. When they arrived at his truck, she asked him if he was all right to drive.

"It's not far," he said.

Collin could drive better than he could walk. Without a word, Leena let her hand drift to his thigh. His blood raced, and in less than ten minutes they were in front of an expensive row of town houses right next to the water. He led her up the brick walk. Inside, he flipped on a couple of lights and his sound system before directing her to the couch. He found a couple bottles of Bud Light in the back of his refrigerator left there by Lou months ago when they had a small Super Bowl party.

He sat down on the couch next to Leena and offered her the beer. She sipped it, then put it down on the coffee table. They continued to talk, and Collin continued to marvel at how similar, but better this girl was than the one to whom he swore everlasting love, the one who had deserted him. And as the minutes passed and Collin finished not only his own beer but hers, it seemed to him that he was immersed in some blissful dream.

"Do you want to go upstairs?" he asked her, his head starting to nod.

"Yes," she said quietly. "I'd like that."

Collin led her up the stairs to his bedroom, a spartan place with a large bed on a bronze frame resting in the middle of the hardwood floor and a view that normally let him gaze across the river at the lights of the capital.

With maternal tenderness, Leena helped him out of his clothes and pushed him gently back onto the bed.

"I have to get something from my purse," she said. "I'll be right back."

Collin frowned as he watched her disappear back down the stairs. If he weren't completely drunk, it would have seemed ludicrous to lie there like that, stripped naked with his clothes in a pile on the floor. On the night table lay his gun. Drunk as he was, his training didn't allow him to do anything careless with his gun. It was the first thing he'd removed. He recalled a joke from his past, something about a gun in bed, but the punch line escaped him. Collin chuckled drunkenly and sighed.

Downstairs, Leena took the beer bottle she'd touched and put it into her purse. She turned off all the lights. Then from the same purse she removed a handkerchief. She draped it over the lock and the handle of the front door and opened it into the misty night. After waving the handkerchief back and forth several times, she pulled the door shut without latching it. Quietly, she climbed the stairs. Collin was still there, lying where he should be. She crossed the room and smiled at him as she picked up his clothes.

"Let me fold these for you," she said.

"No, no, don't worry about that," he slurred. "You're too sweet. Forget my clothes."

Behind her, Leena could hear the stealthy footsteps of two men ascending the stairs.

"I'm going to turn out the light before I undress," she said calmly, "then I'll be there."

What happened next happened fast. The light went out, and two dark figures entered the room and pinned Collin to the bed. Leena crossed the room quickly. From its holster on the nightstand, Leena extracted the big standard-issue Secret Service Glock 9mm, jammed the gun into Collin's screaming mouth, and pulled the trigger. The men stepped back from the bed, and she calmly handed one of them the gun before hurrying out of the bedroom and down the stairs, leaving them alone with the choking, gurgling sounds of death. In the front room, she pulled back the curtain and scanned the walk up and down as far as the fog would let her see. There was no one and nothing to be seen or heard. She left the house without any apparent urgency, walked around the corner, got into a black Jeep, and drove away into the murky night.